MW01147392

BUNKER®

Lock and Load

Book 4

Mission Critical Series

Written by Jay J. Falconer

www.JayFalconer.com

Published September 14, 2017

by BookBreeze.com LLC

ISBN-13: 978-1976412806

ASIN: B072J9NWJG

CHAPTER 1

The heat from Stephanie King's beating chest soaked into Jack Bunker's skin as the reunion hug continued in front of Tuttle's place. He was happy to see her, too, and the rest of the gang who hailed from Clearwater, Colorado. Her son's ten-year-old arms couldn't reach all the way around Stephanie's legs, let alone Bunker's, but it didn't stop Jeffrey from trying.

Everyone else had tears in their eyes, including the Sheriff and his deputy, Daisy—the same woman who'd pulled a gun on Bunker after learning his darkest secret at the miner's camp.

Bunker thought they'd patched things up after the incident, but was still worried she might turn on him now that she knew he used to ride with the infamous Kindred biker gang.

Or at the least, share his background with the town's chief law enforcement officer, Gus Apollo. Keeping one law enforcement officer on your side is hard enough. Trying to manipulate two would be impossible. Something would go wrong. It always does when you're lying about your past.

Until a second ago, Bunker thought the emotions pouring out of those in attendance were a result of the near-fatal execution he'd just stopped with his long-range sniper shot. It was a work of perfection. Part shooter, part weapon, especially when that weapon was a TrackingPoint Precision Guided Rifle.

When you take down three masked men with a single long-range shot, a sense of relief should have been permeating the atmosphere. Yet it wasn't. The air felt stale and heavy. Almost putrid.

Stephanie pulled back from the tender embrace, her eyes filled with tears. Her tone turned somber when she spoke. "We needed you here ten minutes ago."

"Why? What happened?" he asked, his gut tightening after hearing the words.

Stephanie didn't answer. She turned her gaze to the women in attendance. Daisy and a gray-haired woman he'd seen in town were on their knees, consoling Megan and a mysterious brunette he didn't know.

Sheriff Apollo aimed a firm eye at Stephanie, lifting an eyebrow. "Where are Franklin and Cowie? Are they okay?"

Stephanie shook her head. Her eyes indicated she wanted to speak, but something was holding her back. Something painful.

Bunker pushed past Stephanie with his focus on the tiny black girl, Megan, and her innocent face.

Stephanie let go of his hand as Bunker continued, moving closer to the precious soul he'd saved from certain death on the bus. He stood motionless behind the old woman hugging Megan.

Every tear that rolled down Megan's cheek impaled his heart with the savagery of a red-hot dagger. Normally the ten-year-old was a beacon of joy, filling the air with her exuberance. But that wasn't the case at the moment.

Megan was absent, both mentally and spiritually, her eyes locked in an empty stare, focused on something over the shoulder of the woman cradling her in her arms. It was clear the entirety of Megan's being was under siege, suffocating the poor girl.

Apollo asked again, "Where's Franklin? Cowie?"

More seconds ticked by without a response from Stephanie. Everyone else seemed to be avoiding the question, too, not wanting to speak or make eye contact with Apollo.

Bunker knew the situation meant only one thing—bad news. Terribly so. The kind of bad news that squeezes your chest a few seconds before you hear the actual words.

He knew from his days in the military that the all-consuming feeling of dread had a habit of transcending time and space, breaking the laws of physics to arrive early. The earlier it arrived, the worse the news, giving everyone in attendance a sensation of impending doom.

Someone must have died.

It was the only conclusion that made sense. Otherwise, there would've been a response to Apollo's question by now. From someone: the kids, the women, the men.

A group of this size would never remain silent, not after what had just happened with the bloody, last-second deaths of the attackers.

"They're inside," a long-haired boy said in a slow and deliberate tone, breaking the quiet. A tall blonde woman stood behind him, her hands resting on the tops of his shoulders, squeezing at random.

Bunker recognized the young lad from the bus crash. He was the kid who tossed his backpack out of the broken window and took off in a flash, before Bunker could stop him.

The boy pointed at the old woman consoling Megan. "My grandma was there when it happened. Franklin is d—"

"That's enough, Victor. You don't need explain," the woman standing with the boy said. "He knows what happened."

"Both of them?" Apollo asked Dicky, the large man standing next to him. Apollo's expression indicated he wanted to ask a different question, but settled on this one.

Bunker figured the Sheriff had tailored his words to protect the children from having to endure any more drama than was necessary. Especially with all that had happened recently. These kids always seemed to be in the center of everything, taking the brunt of death head-on.

Dicky's head slumped before he finally spoke to Apollo. "Sorry boss. They came out of nowhere."

Bunker knelt next to the old woman and Megan, avoiding the girl's injured leg and its heavy knee brace. His mind searched for the proper words, but all that came back was a cloud of dust.

His tongue was empty, but not his heart, feeling compelled to comfort the child in some way. Yet he wasn't sure how. Former hardcore, white-supremacist bikers with no kids and a bloody stain on their military record usually don't have a deep connection with children they just met. Or adults, for that matter. But Megan Atwater was different, and it wasn't solely due to her rescue from the bus.

The old bag let go of Megan and stood up, as if she did so specifically to give Bunker access. He raised his hands a few inches, then pulled them back, not sure if the emotional girl wanted a hug from him.

Stephanie and her motherly instincts would know exactly what to do for a child in need, but he had no clue. Before he could make a decision, Deputy Daisy appeared next to him, throwing her arms around the other woman sitting next to Megan. A brunette. Distraught. About thirty. Someone he didn't know.

"I'm so sorry, Misty," Daisy said, the two of them starting a symbiotic cry inside an arm-filled hug. She pulled away for a second, then shot Bunker a nod before she spoke again. "Bunker and I tried to save your father, but we got here a second too late."

The woman's familiar name and Daisy's words came together in Bunker's mind. He knew who the girl was: Misty Tuttle. Frank Tuttle's daughter. The woman who threw away her lifelong friendship with Daisy when she ran off with a foreigner shortly after high school.

"Was it these same men?" Misty asked the deputy, pushing the words through her trembling lips.

"No, it was someone else. Earlier."

Misty turned her eyes to the old woman who'd been comforting Megan. "Angus *and* my dad? Both of them?"

The lady shook her head, the skin on her cheeks sagging.

"Please Martha, tell me it's not true. Please."

Martha's face flushed a deep red color. "I can't. I'm so sorry."

Misty's cries shot up a level, her hands shaking against Daisy's shoulder blades. "Oh God! No! Please no!"

"It'll be okay," Daisy said, her voice cracking through her tears. "I'm right here. Just let it out."

"This is all my fault. We never should've come back."

"It's not your fault, Misty. It was these men," Apollo said, standing with Dicky, Dallas, and the Mayor's grandson Rusty, who Bunker had met a few days earlier in town. "They did this and now they got what was coming to them."

"But I never got a chance to tell my dad . . ."

"I'm sure he knows how much you loved him," Daisy said, her tone confident.

"It's just not fair."

"No, it's not. But you'll get through this. I promise. Look around. You have a lot of friends who will be here for you, every step of the way."

Misty cried for another minute before she spoke again. "But you don't understand. We just got engaged. That's part of why we came back. I wanted Dad to know. From me. About the engagement and everything else."

Stephanie broke her silence, her tone soft yet to the point as she addressed the long-haired kid from the bus. "Victor, maybe you and your mom should take Megan to your grandmother's house. Where it's quiet. She needs to lie down and rest for a bit. She's been through a lot today."

"I'm sure we can make room for both of them," Martha said, looking at Daisy, then motioning to Misty. "Everyone should eat something, too."

Daisy nodded.

"Can I help, Mommy?" Jeffrey asked, his nose sniffing as he wrapped his hand around his mother's.

Even though Stephanie's son had just been through yet another traumatic, death-defying incident, the boy didn't seem scared or withdrawn. Bunker wasn't sure if Jeffrey had become immune to the nonstop evil or not, but the boy was showing incredible strength. Far more than he was at the moment.

Kids are much stronger than adults think, he decided. Most adults, that is. Bunker's dad never cut him any slack, about anything. Everyone else in the neighborhood back then seemed to shield their kids from the harder aspects of life. And death. In the long run, he didn't think that approach prepared young people for the harshness of humanity. A harshness that would continue to escalate after the apparent cyber-attack and EMP that had taken down society.

Before Stephanie could answer Jeffrey's lingering question, Megan brought her pear-shaped eyes to Bunker with a crane of her neck. A second later, the girl's emotions came to a boil and let go all at once.

Megan's mouth shot open in a silent, sick-like grimace as her eyes ran thin. Then the waterworks exploded, sending streams of tears down her cheeks, more than double the amount before.

She leaned forward and wrapped her rail-thin arms around Bunker's neck, then bawled into the soft of his shoulder, the volume intensifying by the second.

Bunker held her tight, her chest heaving in concert with the uncontrollable waves of misery flooding out. His chest, arms, and hands could feel the pain escaping from every pore in her body. Her emotions bled into him, racing past his defenses and taking residence deep inside his heart.

When the tears came to Bunker's eyes, he knew he wasn't going to be able to hold them back. Her pain was now his pain, even though he hadn't known her long. All he could do was hold this child and wait for the turmoil to pass. It might take minutes or hours, but he wasn't going to let go of this precious girl.

Sure, if he had a choice, he wished he was somewhere else, but Megan needed him. So did the others, their lives inexplicably commingled with his, well past the point of no return.

CHAPTER 2

Megan slowed her crying and leaned back from the hug she was in. She looked at the towering white man who'd saved her from the bus, Jack Bunker. He was almost as tall as her father, but his muscles were bigger.

Despite his scary tattoos, she could tell he was a nice man, not a mean one like the others who had hurt her and her dad.

When Jack was around, she felt safe. Not just because he'd saved her and her friends more than once. It was more than that.

She wasn't sure what it was called, but when she was in his arms, it felt like home. A home that was now missing her mom and her dad. She couldn't believe it. Both of them were dead. Even her favorite horse, Star, was missing. All she had left was Jack and her dad's favorite horse, Tango.

Megan wanted to go inside Tuttle's trailer to see her father, but she was scared to look at his body.

Or his face. The bad men had shot him. There'd be blood everywhere and a big hole from the bullet. It would be too gross. She didn't think she could do it. She wanted to, but she didn't know how.

"Jack?" she asked in a weak voice, her lips shaking.

His tone was gentle and fatherly. "Do you need something, sweetheart?"

The tightness in her chest wouldn't stop growing, making it hard to breathe. It hurt. A lot. Her lips were trembling even more now as the words arrived, air shooting in and out of her mouth in bursts. "I, uh, think I want to go see my papa. But I'm not sure I can do it. Will you come with me? I don't want to go alone."

"Sure, Megan. Anything you need. I'm not going anywhere."

"Ah, no. That's not a good idea," Stephanie King told Jack in a firm voice, her hand still latched onto Jeffrey's. "Little girls shouldn't see those kinds of things."

"No offense, Steph, but I think you might be overreacting a bit," Jack said.

"How do you figure that?"

"Kids are stronger than you think."

"Really, now. And I guess that observation is based on all your years of experience? Being a parent, I mean."

Jack shrugged, his eyes drifting into a long stare. "It's what my father would have done. He believed in facing everything head-on. Especially tragedy. Regardless of age. You can't outrun death."

"Well, then. That explains it," she said with attitude.

"Explains what?"

Stephanie opened her mouth to say something, then closed it as if she'd just had a change of heart. After a couple more seconds went by, she shook her head and said, "Never mind. It's not important."

Jack looked confused, his eyes squinting. "Not important, huh?"

"No, it's not. Let's move on. Okay?"

"Look, my old man might have been more than a little tough on me, but facing things is what makes you stronger. Sure, most people didn't understand him and more than a few hated his guts, but he was always fair. No matter what the situation."

"Sure, whatever," Stephanie said after a long exhale, rolling her eyes. "They're both in the master. Down the hall on the right."

Jack nodded, flaring his eyebrows before he spoke again. "Megan, sweetheart, are you positive you want to go inside? It might be pretty hard to see."

She wanted to be strong for herself, but more so for Jack. He was brave and she wanted to be like him. "Yeah, I think so. As long as you come with me."

"Well, you need to be sure because I don't want you to be scared. We don't know what the bad men did, exactly. Maybe I should go inside first and check it out?"

When Jack let go of her and tried to stand up, Megan grabbed his hand and wouldn't let him leave. He just couldn't leave. *Bad things always happen when Jack leaves*, she thought. *He's got to stay.*

"Please, don't go, Jack. Don't leave me here. Take me with you."

"It'll be hard, darling."

"I know, but papa needs a goodnight kiss, like we did every night before I went to sleep. Otherwise, he'll have bad dreams. Forever."

Jack sucked in a sudden breath, then turned to Stephanie, his voice different than before. He sounded sad, like she'd hurt his feelings. "Sorry, Steph, but I'm doing this. I'm taking her inside."

"That's a mistake."

"Maybe, but she needs to say goodbye to Franklin. You heard her. He needs a goodbye kiss. We can't deny her this one chance, no matter how hard it is."

"I don't think you're hearing me. She'll be traumatized."

"I hear you, trust me. I just went through this with Dallas after what happened to his father. But in the end, we all have to face this—eventually. Even little girls. More so now than ever before with everything that's happening out there. We can't shield them forever."

Stephanie dropped her head and shook it. When she brought her eyes back up, she looked tired and maybe a little upset. "Don't say I didn't warn you."

Jack bent down and slid his arms under Megan before picking her up. Her bad knee was sore, but he was being gentle.

Megan wrapped her arms around his neck, avoiding the scars on each side. They looked like they still hurt, the skin rough and ugly. She wanted to ask about them, but didn't want him to get mad or be embarrassed.

Like her papa always told her, it wasn't really any of her business. "Some people are just different, that's all," he'd say. "Don't stare. It's impolite."

Sheriff Apollo came forward and stepped in front of Jack, his hands adjusting the waistband of his pants. "Do you need some help?"

"Nah, I got this, Sheriff."

"Are you sure?"

"Yeah. A little privacy is probably a good thing."

Sheriff Apollo nodded, his eyes looking away as if he was thinking about something else. "You're probably right."

"Though you might want to get some ice on your forehead. Looking pretty swollen, Sheriff."

Apollo rubbed his hand across the raised area above his eye. "Yeah, they got me good, that's for sure."

"Let me take a look at it," Martha Rainey said without hesitation.

Jack flashed a strange look at Apollo. Megan thought he looked confused. Probably wondering why the old woman would get involved like that.

"She's a trauma nurse," Apollo said, sounding like he was proud of her.

Martha put her hand on the side of the Sheriff's face, not letting him move. "Former trauma nurse, though nowadays they'd call what we did back then a Physician's Assistant, just without all the extra pay. I was born a generation too early, I'm afraid."

Apollo pulled away from her as if her hand was bothering him. "I appreciate the help, but the gash on Dicky's cheek takes priority. Gonna need a lot of stitches."

Martha swung her head and glanced at Dicky, craning her neck in the process. She was going to need a stepladder to reach the big man's face, his head way above everyone else, including Jack's.

Megan's mind filled with a flash of memories, each one showing Martha stopping by the supply store on her father's ranch for a can of saddle soap. The last time she came by, her grandson Victor was with her, but he didn't look happy about it.

Megan didn't think the Raineys had horses, so they wouldn't have saddles, but every month the old lady would buy some, regardless. Always on a Wednesday for some reason. And always the same brand: Kiwi. Martha would step up to the counter with her purchase, while whistling a pretty, soft tune. She'd stop the melody long enough to smile before taking out a bag of homemade taffy and offering a piece to Megan. It was sticky and gooey, but yummy.

Jack tapped the Sheriff on the shoulder. "You guys might also want to think about setting up a perimeter. We need to start focusing on a defensible position with access to town cut off. This is about the only choice to make camp."

"Or make a stand," Apollo agreed with sharpness to his words.

"Exactly. We both know this is going to get a lot worse before it gets better, so it's up to us to provide a safe place for these kids."

"I agree. Tuttle was well prepared," the Sheriff said, stepping aside. "Let us know if you need anything."

"Will do."

"Jack?" Megan asked, after the Sheriff disappeared.

"What's up?" he answered on the way to the front door of Tuttle's house.

Megan wasn't sure if she should ask, but decided to anyway. It was important. "What about Misty? She lost somebody, too. Doesn't she need to come inside with us? You know, to say goodbye."

"I don't think she wants to, honey."

"But she needs to, like you said. We all have to be strong and face stuff like this."

"Deep down she probably does want to say goodbye, but sometimes people just can't bring themselves to do it. That's her choice, Megan, and we have to respect it. Everyone's different when it comes to bad things that happen. Some people are extra brave like you and want to go inside, while others need to stay outside. Not everyone is the same and we have to let her deal with this in her own way. Does that make sense?"

"Yeah, well, sort of. I just hope she's okay. It's not good to be alone when you're sad."

"She's not. Daisy is with her. They're BFFs from a long time ago."

"I wish I had a best friend, but there aren't many kids out where we live."

He grinned. It was a little smile, but she liked it. She thought he should do it more often so he wouldn't look so scary to people who just met him.

Jack's smile grew bigger when he said, "Isn't your horse your best friend? What's his name again?"

"Star. Yes, he is. I just hope he's okay."

"Maybe when this is over, you and I can take Tango for a ride and go find Star. Would you like that?"

She couldn't hold back a grin, though her heart was still hurting. "You'd do that for me?"

"Of course I would. We just have to make sure it's safe first."

"You promise?"

"Yes, I promise."

She hugged him as they continued through the front door and went inside.

The house had a strange smell to it. It was gross, but she'd smelled worse. Usually in the stables when she was cleaning out the stalls.

She figured most people didn't know that horses are super messy and they poop a lot. Tons of it and it really stinks. There was so much when she did her chores that it would fill the wheelbarrow all the way to the top. It was really heavy, but she was able to take it out back and dump it all by herself.

It was hard work, but her father said she had to do it. Even when she was tired. He wanted her to grow up big and strong and be able to handle stuff on her own. Sort of like now. She didn't want to go inside, but she needed to. It's what big girls do.

At least Jack was here, so she didn't have to go alone. He was strong and would protect her, like her papa would have done.

CHAPTER 3

Bunker turned his body at an angle to make room for the cargo he was carrying down the hallway of Tuttle's place. The girl in his arms was dead quiet, lying on her back with her head to the right, keeping an eye on where they were going.

For some reason, his heartbeat was out of control, thumping as if he'd just run a thousand-meter dash. But not just any dash. A dash through the hostile streets of Afghanistan with a loaded rucksack on his back.

Normally he was in control of both his pulse and his breathing, but right now, right here, he was struggling, even though he'd been in far more precarious situations than this.

Before his next breath, a scene from his past rose up and landed in his thoughts. When his eyes blinked, the entire incident played out in an instant, filling his mind's eye with a rush of vivid imagery.

White trails of smoke following a fresh salvo of RPGs.

Explosive impacts shaking the air as the rocket-propelled grenades destroyed the foundation of a building not far from his squad.

The bitter smell of propulsion that followed, hanging above the combat zone like some kind of pestilence.

The horrendous claps of .50 caliber machine guns sending round after round downrange, each bullet creating pressure waves that traveled faster than sound.

Headset squawking in his ears.

Commands arriving across the airwaves and men responding.

The clatter of equipment and boots scrambling for cover.

Flashbangs going off in the distance as another entrenched terrorist got what was coming to him.

The rattle of M16s.

Pops of pistol fire.

The stench of burning tires and rotting garbage in the street. Strong enough to make a billy goat gag.

Bloodcurdling screams coming at him from every direction. Some in English. Others not.

All of it intense.

For some men, the sensory overload during combat was more than they could bear. A few froze in the heat of a battle. Others would break down. Some got tunnel vision, focusing only on their primary target and forgetting to listen to commands or pay attention to changes in their surroundings.

Falling victim to any one of those symptoms meant you were probably going home in a body bag, or hauled to medical on a stretcher covered in blood.

If someone asked, Bunker would tell them he didn't believe in *Fog of War*, as most would call it. To him and his fire team, it was more along the lines of *Mutually Assured Chaos*. Or Big MAC Attack for short. Sure, it was a private term his team tossed around, but it fit.

Despite the intensity, Bunker never had an issue staying focused and advancing to do what was needed, regardless of the indescribable bedlam surrounding him.

He assumed his battle hardness was due to his father's relentless preaching, training, and of course, pop inspections. He'd come to learn over the years that everything his father had put him through was done for a reason—to prepare him for what would come next, in all walks of life.

Bunker was born to fight.

He knew it.

His old man knew it.

Yet here he was, in a singlewide trailer with a fragile girl in his arms, carrying her to a rendezvous with the body of her dead father. A man Bunker knew and respected. A man who'd just been executed without a second thought by a band of thugs in the mountains of Colorado.

Bunker had seen his share of corpses, most riddled with holes and body parts askew. But this face-off with death was different. Something inside him had set his adrenaline on fire. He wasn't sure he could keep it under control.

When he looked down at the injured girl, his eyes met hers. He wondered if she was staring back at him in order to draw strength in some fashion, like some kind of emotional conduit.

"You okay?" he asked her, faking a steady voice. Her tears were gone, but the wetness down her cheeks remained.

She nodded with her upper lip tucked under, but said nothing. He understood what she was feeling. She didn't have to say it.

"It'll be okay. I promise," Bunker told her as they arrived at the open door to Tuttle's master bedroom. He didn't enter. Not yet. He wanted to take a quick survey while she couldn't see inside.

Like Megan, this room had seen its share of turmoil in the past few days, first with Tuttle's ambush by the man in black, and now Franklin Atwater's murder. So much blood and violence in close proximity to kids. Innocent kids who were forced to grow up all at once with an invasion looming and countless other threats waiting in the shadows beyond Tuttle's property.

Sure, there were other actionable items and several friends needing his attention, but none of them were more critical than this mission.

It's the little things that count, he told himself quietly. Important things. Things that keep your sanity in check, and your humanity. Not just

Megan's, but his. The others would have to wait a few minutes, especially the adults.

Two bodies lay lifelessly in the bed. The closest was Franklin. He was in the prone position and shirtless, with his muscular shoulder covered in a wide bandage.

The wrap was bloody, but not nearly as red as the discards stuffed in a wastebasket sitting a foot from the bed. The wire-mesh receptacle was half-full of red and white cloths. Martha must have been busy trying to stop the bleeding before the hillbillies showed up, tossing the old rags away like unwanted bills.

He smirked. Some good it did for the proud Army vet lying dead in the room occupied by a former recluse—a country hermit who was obsessed with all things conspiracy related. If the swatch of newspapers on the walls could talk, they'd tell a tale few would believe.

The other body was on the far side of the bed, twisted over in an awkward position with its right side facing up. Bunker had never met the man known as Angus Cowie, but given what he'd learned, the corpse belonged to Misty Tuttle's boyfriend from overseas.

The blood splatter on the wall behind Cowie indicated he'd been shot sitting up. It meant the man must have regained consciousness and probably saw the gunman coming for him. The hole in his right palm supported that theory, most likely caught in the bullet's damage path while trying to protect his face.

It was a gruesome scene to be sure, but what he worried most about was the gaping hole in Franklin's head. It was visible from the doorway. So was the blood on the cowboy's face, his head propped up by a pillow. His eyes were still open, but looking in two different directions after his ocular control had let go upon his death.

Stephanie was right. The girl shouldn't see this.

"Megan, I don't know about this. It's pretty awful, honey. I think we should go back outside."

"No, Jack. I need to do this. Take me in, please. I have to say goodbye."

Bunker held back a response. He didn't have the words, her voice cutting through his armor and squeezing his vocal cords.

"Please, Jack. Please," she said, tears taking over her eyes once again. She continued her appeals, her voice like acid, eating away at the petals of his heart.

He wanted to deny her request, but couldn't find the strength, his insides a swampy mush. "Okay. But if we do this, I need you to close your eyes for a minute. There are a couple of things I need to do before you open them. Can you do that for me?"

"Uh-huh," she said, her eyelids slamming shut.

"All right, keep them closed until I tell you to open them."

"I will. I promise."

He walked through the door and put her on the floor at the foot of the bed. Her eyes were still closed, so Bunker went to Franklin's body as planned.

First up, he needed to cover the hole in the man's forehead. After a quick scan of the room, he realized the items he could use were limited.

Martha had left a pair of scissors on the headboard and some used bandages in the waste bin, but little else. He had hoped to find medical tape— the preferred item—but he didn't see any rolls.

A pile of pushpins, a magnifying glass, and a yellow marker were in the room, sitting on a stack of unread newspapers by the broken window on the far wall. They'd been moved since his initial visit with Daisy. However, unless he was going to complete Tuttle's article review, they weren't going to be of much help.

The blood around the entry wound was still fresh and glistening, giving him an idea. He tore off a six-inch strip of newspaper from one of the nearby articles on the wall and folded it over several times, until it was slightly larger than the wound.

He tucked the edges under so they locked together in a fold, then put the wad of paper on the wound. The blood worked like glue, adhering the makeshift bandage to the man's skin.

Not bad, he decided. It reminded him of the mornings when he decided to shave. Inevitably, he'd have to use tissue to cover the cuts from the perpetually dull razor. Otherwise, the bleeding would run down his chin.

Unfortunately, the cover-up wasn't perfect, blood seeping into the newsprint along the edges. Yet it was better than letting Megan catch a visual of the gunshot hole in her old man's face.

A traumatic image like that would stick with her until the end of time. This was going to be hard enough as it was. Bunker didn't want the memories of her father jaded any more than they had to be. Not if he could lessen her pain in some way.

He ran his finger over Franklin's eyes to close the lids, then grabbed a handful of used bandages from the trashcan. He lifted Franklin's head and wiped up most of the blood and tissue, then tossed the rags back where he'd found them. He turned the pillow over to the cleaner side, then repositioned the dead man's head so it looked natural.

Bunker had done all he could for his Army pal. Now it was time to fix the deadly scene on the other side of the mattress. He walked past Megan and headed to the far side of the bed.

"Can I open my eyes now?" Megan asked.

Bunker figured the sound of his footsteps and the rush of air past her cued her question. "Not yet. Hang on. Almost done."

"What's taking so long?"

"Just another minute or so, sweetheart. Don't open your eyes yet." Bunker rolled Angus onto his back, then positioned the man's hands across his chest, like a mortician would do. Then, as he did for Franklin, Bunker covered the forehead wound with folded newspaper.

Next up, he needed to devise a quick solution for the blood splatter on the wall. Some of it had landed on the nearby paper, but the rest had stuck to the naked drywall.

He tore down the newsprint that had red on it, then turned his attention to the area of drywall covered in blood and tissue. The gruesome mess covered about six square feet and had spread out in all directions.

If he had a sponge and a mop bucket, this would have been an easy fix. Cleaning supplies were probably stored in the mobile home somewhere, but Bunker didn't think he had the time, nor did he want to leave Megan in here alone. She was already running out of patience. If he left the room now, she'd almost certainly open her eyes too soon.

He had a better idea. One involving the eleven pushpins remaining in the clear plastic tray that sat on top of the stack of papers behind him.

Bunker grabbed eight of the pins, along with three full-sized sheets of newspaper, then put them on the wall to cover the splatter in large, overlapping squares. The sheets were from a section of the paper that featured dark-colored ads, obscuring the red splotches behind them. The pins slipped into the drywall without much pressure, making quick work of the evidence.

After a final survey of the room, he believed he'd done all he could in the time allotted. He returned to Megan's side of the bed and took a knee next to her, his heart still running in overdrive. "Okay, I'm finished. You ready?"

Her eyes remained closed when she said, "Uh-huh."

When Megan's hands came up for him, he obliged, slipping his arms under hers to pick her up.

Bunker wondered if she was actually going to see this through. It wasn't going to be easy, but not just for her. In truth, a big part of him hoped she'd ask him to turn around and haul her outside before she opened her eyes. "Last chance to change your mind."

"I'm okay," she answered in a timid voice.

He exhaled, letting the anxiety ease a bit before he stood her next to the bed, just beyond Franklin's right side. "Open your eyes when you're ready. But remember, we can leave anytime. Just let me know. I'm right here."

Her weight leaned into his as Megan took control of her balance. When her eyes opened,

Bunker expected her to break down instantly, but she didn't. Instead, the ebony skin across her cheeks held its solemn look as the tears came.

Megan reached out for her father's hand, her fingers shaking with tremors of grief. Unlike Cowie, Franklin's arms were down along his sides, lying in wait next to his hips.

Her grip looked soft when she made contact, almost as if she was afraid she might hurt Franklin in some way.

"Papa? It's me, Megan. I'm here now so you're not alone anymore." After a two-count, she twisted forward and took a seat on the edge of the bed, her injured leg angled away from the mattress.

Bunker took a step back to avoid her knee brace and give the girl some privacy. It felt wrong to stand there and watch her torment, but he wasn't sure what else to do. He hoped she'd give him a sign if she needed him.

When she spoke again, the words were chaotic and uneven, gasps of air breaking up the delivery. "I'm sorry it took me so long to come in and say goodbye, Papa," she said in a trembling voice, sniffing twice before she continued. "But I was really scared at first."

Megan picked up his hand and held the back of it to her cheek. "I know I'm supposed to be brave, but it's so hard. I don't know what I'm supposed to say."

Bunker sucked in a breath and held it, his gut twisting into a knot. He wanted to speak up and guide her along, but the words failed him. Nothing sounded right in his head.

Her tears intensified, streaming down her cheeks and landing on Franklin's hand. "I'm sorry I made you mad before we went to church last Sunday. I was gonna pick up my room, but I forgot. I didn't do it on purpose, Papa, so please don't be mad at me. I'll do better. I promise."

Bunker turned his head away for a moment, hoping some newfound strength would find him. Megan's words were killing him, even after surviving the bloody sands of Afghanistan and years of knock-down, drag-you-away-on-a-stretcher street brawls with The Kindred.

He couldn't believe it. This was who he had become—a giant, tattooed marshmallow, eaten alive by the words of a tiny young girl saying goodbye to her father.

When he brought his eyes forward again, he saw her kiss the back of Franklin's hand gently, holding her lips against his dark skin. A few seconds went by before she adjusted her grip, opening his fingers and putting his palm against the curve of her cheek.

Her voice trembled, matching the shake in her hands. "It's time to sleep now, Papa. Don't be afraid. The angels are coming for you."

Bunker fought back the tears welling in his eyes, using a quick wipe of his fingers to usher them away. He was thankful nobody else was in the room.

"When you see Mommy in heaven, tell her I miss her every day. I'm gonna miss you, too, Papa. You've been the best daddy in the whole world."

Just when Bunker thought Megan was going to get through this goodbye without a breakdown, it came. Not all at once, but in waves. Her stomach started to convulse and so did her sobs, the tears gushing out from somewhere profound.

She looked up at Bunker, her face twisted in a full-on grimace. Her cries were silent at first, waiting for air from her lungs as her chest began to heave. When the sound arrived, it came with the volume of a wolf howl, her cries uncontrolled.

When she reached out for him, Bunker flew to her side in a flash. He wrapped her in a hug and held her tight. "It'll be okay, sweetheart."

"I'm sorry. I tried to be strong, Jack, but I can't."

"No, honey, you're being super brave. Just let it out until there are no more tears left. We have all the time in the world."

CHAPTER 4

"That poor girl," Stephanie said after hearing the wail from inside Tuttle's place. Megan's cries were not only deafening but heartbreaking, consuming every molecule of air in front of the trailer. "I tried to warn him."

"Bunker was just doing what he thought was right," Sheriff Apollo said. "It's all any of us can do at the moment."

"Maybe one of us should go in there?" Rusty asked.

"I'll go," Dicky said, taking a step forward with his back straight and chin stiff.

"Not until I'm done," Martha said, straining to draw another suture through his check as he moved.

"I'm sure that's good enough," Dicky answered, his hand stopping hers.

"You need a couple more stitches."

"Nah, just cover it and I'll be good."

"That'll leave a nasty scar."

He lifted up his shirt, giving everyone in the yard a prime view of his six-pack abdomen and impressive chest. He pointed at a ten-inch scar along his torso, running vertically across his slender ribcage. "You mean like this?"

"Yeah, like that. What happened?" Martha asked, her wrinkled hands cutting the suture with a pair of scissors.

"ATV accident. It's what happens when you're not paying attention to the sand dune in front of you."

"What did we miss?" a new voice said from behind the group, its tone loud and laced with sarcasm.

When Stephanie whirled around, she saw Albert Mortenson, the heavyset deputy she knew from high school. He was puffing noticeably. "Albert? What are you doing here?"

"Trying to stay alive," he said, pointing at the burly man walking next to him. "Not an easy feat when you're walking with a guy whose sole purpose in life is to piss off the Russians."

Stephanie recognized the stocky man. It was Burt Lowenstein, the town mechanic.

The third member of the new arrivals was the skinny deputy she'd met earlier when Albert and he broke up the argument with her ex in front of Doc Marino's clinic. She thought his name was Dustin, but wasn't sure. His hands were fiddling with a knapsack strapped to his back.

"I take it you ran into them," Apollo said.

"Yeah, you could say that," Burt answered, his grin looking forced.

"Anyone hurt?"

"Just their pride after we gave them the slip."

"Are they close?" Rusty asked, his eyes pinched and head turned slightly.

"Doubt it. We took the long way around. Made sure they weren't following us. I know a few shortcuts."

Albert rolled his eyes. "Well, I don't know about that. They're not shortcuts if we took the long way around."

"They got you here in one piece, didn't they?" Burt snapped.

"Barely," Albert said, his lungs still working to catch up. He pointed at the skinny deputy. "Am I right, Dustin?"

Stick boy didn't answer.

Before another word was uttered, Misty stood up in a flash of movement and pushed away from Daisy's embrace. Daisy got to her feet as well, then the two of them took off in a rush, entering the front door to Tuttle's place.

"Was it something I said?" Albert said in a smartass tone, throwing up his hands.

"I'm afraid a lot has happened," Apollo said, his tone firm.

"Obviously. Was it the Russians?"

"No. Somebody else. We got ambushed by some lowlifes," Victor added with a flip of his hair, his mom shooting him a piercing look after he spoke.

"Misty's boyfriend was the first to be shot," Stephanie said.

"Misty? As in Misty Tuttle?" Albert asked. "That was her?"

"Yep. Back from her trip overseas apparently," Stephanie said. "I feel for her. First her father and now her fiancée."

"Frank's dead, too?" Burt asked, his face twisted.

Stephanie nodded. "I'm afraid so. But he's not the only one."

"Who else?" Dustin asked, his voice as thin as his shirt.

"Franklin Atwater," Apollo answered. "Bunker's in there with Megan right now."

"Poor bastard," Burt said.

"The guy with all the horses, right?" Dustin asked Albert.

Albert sent him a nod, then turned his focus to Apollo. "So, Bunker's here? Cool. I've been wondering when I might meet the man with all the tattoos. And a big pair of balls, apparently."

Apollo didn't react to Albert's attempt at humor. "Well then, I guess today is your lucky day. But I'd suggest checking the attitude a bit. He's been through hell, too."

Stephanie walked to Martha and Allison Rainey. "What about that food you mentioned earlier? We should all eat something, and I'm sure these kids need to rest. I'd suggest your place. You know, until we get things arranged over here."

"You mean more digging," Martha said in a matter-of-fact way.

Stephanie nodded. "Something tells me we're going to be doing a lot of that around here."

Martha put a hand on her daughter's arm, just below the elbow. "Allison, why don't you bring Megan over when she's done inside?"

"Okay," Allison said before turning her head and looking at her son.

"I'll watch Victor," Martha said. "You go. Take care of the girl. I'm sure Bunker could use a break."

Allison turned her shoes and headed for the entrance to the trailer.

"Jeffrey, come here," Stephanie said, waving her hand three times until he responded.

"You too, Victor," Martha said.

The other kid, Dallas, stood with feet frozen, looking as if he was waiting for his name to be called.

Stephanie made eye contract with the quiet boy, then asked, "Are you hungry?"

"Yeah. Starving."

"Then why don't all you kids head over to Mrs. Rainey's place? She'll fix you something to eat."

Apollo pointed at Dicky. "You go with them and keep an eye on things."

"You got it, chief."

"If   anyone   approaches,   notify   me immediately."

Stephanie held Jeffrey's hand as Martha led the group to her place across the road. Victor and the new kid, Dallas, were right behind Martha, chatting about something like old friends. Their voices were low so she couldn't make out the words, but they were definitely excited.

Dicky followed beside her, his hands holding a rifle flat against his bulging chest. He kept watch on the area ahead, scanning to the left first, then the right. He repeated the same process a few more times before she decided it was time to say something.

Stephanie looked up at her escort, marveling at his sheer size. She knew Dicky from town, but had never been this close to him. Nor had she relied on him for anything before. Certainly not her life and that of her son.

The threat of death changes a person's perspective. And their awareness of anything new, she decided, noticing her view was about a foot shorter than his. Bunker's stature was intimidating, but nothing like this guy.

She motioned at the rifle in his hands. "Tell me you know how to use that thing?"

"Yeah. Been hunting all my life. Shouldn't be a problem."

She wasn't as confident, but didn't want to upset the man by questioning his skills. A different approach was needed to drive home her point.

"I hope you're right, because these particular animals can shoot back."

CHAPTER 5

Mayor Buckley stood in the trampled grass of the town square, wondering how much worse this day would become. Bill King was on his left and Doc Marino on his right, both having a hard time standing still, as were the rest of the residents of Clearwater.

Everyone was packed in tight, including Stan Fielding and his twin girls, who were huddled only a few inches in front of the Mayor.

"Seriously?" Buckley mumbled, as another set of unmarked trucks pulled up, this time arriving from a side street that dumped into the center of town, directly adjacent to the Catholic Church and its soaring bell tower.

Now that the Russians had taken over, he wondered if Pastor Green would ring the bronze-colored bell before service this coming Sunday. Then again, maybe Sunday Mass would be suspended altogether. He wasn't sure. The Pastor might cancel.

As expected, a flood of Russian troops scampered out of the arriving trucks, adding to the imposing force already occupying town. The additional military presence made the side of his neck itch, the sensation centered on the same spot where FEMA had injected him with their MH2 treatment. He scratched with vigor, digging his fingernails into the skin around the bandage, but not enough to draw blood.

When Buckley turned his head to Doc Marino, he found the physician's dark, inset eyes trained on him. It felt as though the healer was monitoring his actions for signs of derangement.

Or maybe Marino was gathering vitals with his eyes. Hard to tell when you're standing next to an ancient doctor who was content with small town medicine, despite his Harvard education. The man was an enigma and always on duty, even while stuffing his face at the annual Forth of July picnic.

"It's not your fault," Doc said in a whisper, his Italian accent evident. Even after all his years as a naturalized citizen, he still sounded like a foreigner—an overly slender, mild-mannered Italian who stood only 5' 5" tall. His one vice: homemade brew—the kind with double the alcohol content and a sugar level sure to give steady drinkers chronic liver disease.

"Yes. It *is* his fault," Bill King added, looking at Doc. "Buckley screwed the pooch, big time."

"You don't have to remind me, Bill. Nobody feels worse about this than me. Though I do remember you being there with me. I know you won't admit it, but it wasn't just me who got fooled by the FEMA rollout."

"Hey, I raised concerns—a couple of times. Especially after the Wal-Mart trucks showed up. But no . . . as usual, nobody listens to me."

"At this point, it doesn't matter, gentlemen," Doc said, the words heavy in his accent. "We need to stay focused and work together. All these people will need leadership."

"Let's just hope this doesn't get any worse," Buckley said.

"Any worse? How is that even possible?"

"That's how," Doc Marino said, pointing to an eight-wheeled transport pulling up, its diesel engine grinding to a stop in front of the crowd. The camo-green vehicle featured a massive gun with a cannon that seemed to stick out a mile. A squad of men shot out of the transport and scampered to the raised platform that had been erected at the head of the square.

Most of the new arrivals were outfitted like the others already in town, heavily armed and wearing tactical gear. All except one. The lone exception carried only a sidearm and was smoking a cigar with vigor. He had the forearms of a bodybuilder, though the rest of him looked slender.

"Must be their leader," King said after a twitch of his eyes. "Looks like a real asshole."

Another soldier moved across the stage and gave the Commander a megaphone, his steps measured. The cigar man turned the unit on and held it up to his mouth, while a brigade of Russian flags doubled as a backdrop behind him.

After a momentary squeal from the speaker, the man's voice rang out in English, though the words carried a heavy Russian accent that obscured the crispness of the syllables.

"Citizens, my name General Yuri Zhukov. This town under Russian control. Follow orders and you not be harmed. Food, water, supplies are here. More coming. You are safe, but must follow orders."

Buckley's shoulders relaxed a bit. "Okay, at least they're not here to harm anyone."

King shook his head before he spoke in a whisper. "Yeah, until we hear his demands. You heard him. We have to follow orders. God knows what those are going to be."

"Quiet!" Doc said in a sharp whisper.

Zhukov continued, the device amplifying his voice louder than before. "I repeat. This is Russian territory. Disobey and we shoot you."

The crowd buzzed after the last statement, mumbles and whispers erupting in every direction. The tension in the square rose, everyone moving closer to each other, as if huddling provided some form of sanctuary against the great red menace.

Buckley's mind turned to a conversation he'd had earlier with Bunker about the coordinated, high-tech attack. Bunker used his theory to explain why US troops hadn't made an appearance, or the National Guard, and now it appeared he was right.

Under other circumstances, Buckley would have expected the military to be involved by now. Somewhere along the way, someone would have noticed the Russians rolling across the countryside. Hell, even the State Troopers would have intervened.

He didn't want to believe it, but Bunker's theory seemed to fit—a cyber-attack was unleashed before the EMP to take down the eyes and ears of everyone who could pose a threat to the invasion force.

Then again, there was a chance the US Army had engaged the invasion force somewhere along the way, possibly even local law enforcement, but lost badly.

Sure, he conceded that his idea might be nothing more than wishful thinking, but the hypothesis wasn't a total stretch. Not if he factored in the size of the incursion needed to pull off something like this—assuming of course, this rollout was happening across the country.

The obvious problem in defending the continental USA stems from the fact that American forces are spread out across the states, usually involved in some kind of on-base training exercise. It wouldn't take much for domestic forces to become complacent, not expecting a localized attack. All eyes would be on the borders and in the sky, not focused on the streets beyond the security fence.

With a good portion of our active forces deployed overseas, and busy hunting the latest terrorist to take up residence on the high priority target list, domestic security might have suffered. If so, it would be easy to be compromised by an enemy with the will, the might, and the balls to green-light their plan.

Zhukov stood silent for a minute as another soldier wheeled a two-shelf cart across the stage. It was about ten feet long, with a set of batteries occupying the lower shelf. The second shelf contained a bank of electronic gear, though its power must have been off since none of its lights were illuminated.

The General ambled to the cart and flipped a switch, bringing a bank of lights to life across the front of the equipment. He turned to the crowd and spoke through the loudspeaker once again, skipping certain connector words in his version of broken English.

"Compliance agent injected," he said, pointing to the left side of his neck. "We track you. You leave without permission, explosive detonates. Try to disable, also detonates."

Buckley stopped scratching his neck when he heard those words, yanking his hand away.

"So much for those thirty days of injections. I guess that was all bullshit," King said. "I knew something wasn't right with that whole thing."

Stan Fielding turned around and stared with intense eyes, his face flushing red. He pointed at the circular bandages on his girls' necks. "You let them do this. How could you, Mayor?"

Buckley didn't have an answer for the single father. The man was right. He'd let this happen. Just another failure on his already full resume.

At this point, his seat in the Governor's office was nothing more than a pipedream. Not that his future political aspirations mattered in the grand scheme of things. Lives were at stake. So was everyone's freedom. The Russians were here for a reason and *this* was just getting started. Whatever *this* was.

There was one consolation, though. At least now he knew why he'd heard a metal click when the FEMA injections were administered. They were implanting the tracker and explosive.

"Remember when FEMA mentioned they had a list?" King asked, his question coming out of nowhere.

Buckley took a few seconds to locate the memory. "Yeah. It was after we asked about treating the residents out of town."

"How could they have that information?"

"Not sure. But this was obviously well planned."

"No shit, Sherlock. But not only that, they must've had help from someone. You know, on the inside. Otherwise, how could they get their hands on a detailed list like that? I'm pretty sure our government doesn't track that type of stuff. Not real-time info about who's in or out of town. So the Russians couldn't have stolen it from some computer hack."

"Or maybe they do track us," Doc said without hesitation. "The skies are covered with satellites. Who knows what they are really watching? They've admitted to spying on everyone. Nothing is sacred. Every phone call. Every Internet post. Every email."

"Or they could've had spies in town. For a while now, setting this up," King said.

Buckley agreed with King, but he wasn't about to cave to the man's pressure. "Okay, I see your point, but what do you expect me to do about it?"

"I don't know, show a little concern maybe?"

"Trust me, every cell in my body is concerned right now. For everyone. Including you."

"I'll bet the new guy, Bunker, is part of all this. I mean, come on. He just shows up out of the blue and bingo, we're invaded. Sounds a little suspicious to me. Plus, now we have this General trying to bribe everyone with truckloads of free food and supplies like he's our best buddy. Then he tells us we'll explode if we don't follow along like sheep. Seems damn clear to me. None of this is by accident. They've been planning this for a while and must have had inside help to pull it off."

"Trust me, Bunker is not part of this," Buckley said.

"Yeah, you say that now, but how do you really know? This was all orchestrated with precision. They could've easily placed sleeper agents in town just waiting for the go-ahead to take action."

King had a point. Buckley shrugged.

"What if our government is in on it somehow?" Stan Fielding asked, his tone serious.

Fielding's theory had merit. "It would explain a few things," Buckley answered.

Stan nodded. "And you have to ask yourself, why send a General? This town can't be that important."

"Unless it is," King added.

Zhukov aimed the megaphone to the side, pointing it at another truck pulling up. This vehicle was a long flatbed, loaded with a stack of poles that stretched from one end of the rig to the other.

Buckley figured they were at least fifty feet long since they hung over the rear of the trailer by a couple of feet. They could have been made of steel or plastic; he couldn't be sure.

Behind the flatbed was a ten-wheeled mobile crane, its hook swaying in front of the windshield as it crawled along under its own power. The lowercase letters "anipsotiki" were stenciled on both the front of the cab and the side of the crane's main boom.

Following the crane was yet another flatbed, this one transporting two rectangular pieces of cargo that filled the trailer from front to back. Each section was wrapped with a red tarp and strapped down in multiple directions.

Buckley watched a team of men remove the straps, then pull the tarps away with a theatrical flair.

King didn't hesitate. "Generators. Big suckers."

"At least we'll have power again," Fielding said.

"Looks like they're gonna be here a while," Buckley said, thinking of the residents who were out of town. The Russians had sent out patrols in their ATVs looking for them. He hoped that God had stepped up to keep them safe. Or Bunker had, assuming the man was still alive and in the area. Nobody had seen him since the Sheriff sent him with Daisy to Tuttle's place.

King lowered his eyes and stared at the ground for a few seconds. Then he shook his head before aiming his focus at Buckley. "Jesus Christ. We are so fucked. So is my son, wherever he is. We're gonna have to do something, and fast."

CHAPTER 6

Daisy Clark found the light switch at the bottom of the ladder and turned it on when her feet found the loose dirt at the bottom of Tuttle's hidden bunker in the barn.

Everywhere she looked, the room was brimming with treasure—not just any treasure; this was the type of stash that could inflict endless amounts of damage and death.

"Jackpot!" she announced, hoping Sheriff Apollo could hear her from his position above the trap door in the barn.

"What did you find?"

"Everything! You need to get down here."

"On my way," he said, his feet appearing on the top rung of the ladder a few seconds later.

Daisy waited for his arrival, then held out her hand to lead his eyes to the inventory. "Look at all this."

Apollo didn't answer right away, his mouth agape. He walked to the wooden rack of weapons installed on the wall, then ran his fingers over two of the rifles stored vertically on the left, their barrels pointing up. They were both pump action shotguns, their distinctive slide-action fore-end evident.

The next three guns were assault rifles, 5.56 caliber, if Daisy had to guess, bringing Apollo's hands to them quickly. She estimated their barrels were only sixteen inches long, perfect for gunfights in tight spaces.

"M4 Carbines," he said, snatching one in his hands. "Colts." He played with the folding stock, then held it up to his shoulder. His eye went behind the sights as he pretended to search for targets in the room.

He brought the weapon down, with his attention lingering on the twelve-inch secondary attachment hanging under the front of the barrel. It had its own trigger and the word "Havoc" stenciled on the side.

"A flare launcher, sir," Daisy said in case her newly-appointed boss had questions.

Apollo nodded, then studied the hundred-round drum installed in front of the trigger guard. He ejected the firepower upgrade and inspected its contents for a three-count. After a flash of his eyebrows, he mounted the magazine back to the weapon with a firm hand. "He spent a bundle on this stuff."

"Must have thought World War III was coming," she quipped, pointing to the pile of the banana-shaped magazines sitting on the shelf below the rack. They looked to be of the thirty-round capacity, but there were at least five more hundred-round drums as well.

"Bunker's gonna love this," Apollo said, putting the rifle back in the rack. "And the communications gear we found upstairs."

Daisy agreed, thinking about the radio sets and the working batteries they'd discovered. She nodded slowly. "Thank God Tuttle was a paranoid nut. Those homemade Faraday cages really did the trick. I didn't know you could turn a storage cabinet into one of those."

"Then again, was Tuttle really so paranoid? After all, what he feared would happen, did."

"True. It's like they say, it's not paranoia if you are actually being followed. He looks like a genius now."

"I don't know if I'd go that far. There's a fine line between insanity and genius," the Sheriff said, walking to the far end of the rack, bypassing at least a dozen rifles.

The longest of the barrels belonged to hunting rifles, Daisy decided as she followed her boss. Each had a high-powered scope and a sling for carrying.

The second cabinet was smaller than the first and built differently. It was more of a display case and angled for presentation, featuring a line of semi-auto handguns. Glocks mostly, though there were a few Rugers and Colts mixed in.

There weren't any revolvers and that surprised her. Tuttle obviously liked them, having a cowboy gun at his bedside before he died—a .357 magnum revolver, maximum firepower for a man of his size. Perhaps Tuttle only kept the semi-autos down in this bunker. His revolver stash may have been somewhere else.

On the floor beyond the weapons cache were at least fifty cardboard boxes of ammo, still sealed in their bulk shipping cartons. Some were critical defense loads with hollow point rounds to inflict maximum damage once they entered the body cavity.

JAY J. FALCONER 64

Others were standard-tipped. All of them were lethal if the shooter's aim was accurate.

Apollo knelt down and inspected the first column of containers, his eyes taking in the black lettering that indicated the manufacturer, caliber, grain, and quantity of rounds. He seemed most interested in the .223 caliber ammo, his fingers ripping open the top seal on the 1000-round container. His hand went in and pulled out one of the rifle rounds. He held it up in front of his eyes. "Full metal jacket. Green tip. That'll do some damage."

Daisy wasn't shocked by the amount of ammo on hand. Nor was she surprised by the illogical order of the stockpile, the boxes mixed and stacked haphazardly. She would've arranged them by caliber to allow for quicker restock.

At least the waist-high collection of green-colored ammo cans was organized, their grab handles facing up. She snatched the top one. It was heavy. She opened it. Inside were 30-06 rounds. Mostly for hunting. Another ammo can held .223 rounds. The third one she checked had the larger .308 rounds, yet she didn't remember seeing a rifle chambered for that ammo.

Must be around here somewhere, she thought to herself as she continued walking behind her boss. She figured all the ammo cans were full and ready to go, which would explain why the 1000-round boxes of bullets hadn't been opened yet. They were being held in reserve, for when Tuttle's version of World War III started.

A clothing rack with four caster wheels stood in the adjacent corner, its line of garments hanging from the central aluminum bar. However, this wasn't your typical lineup of clothing. It was tactical apparel, at least two dozen forest-green camo shirts of various sizes to the left, with just as many pairs of pants to the right.

An unmarked container the size of a dishwasher sat just beyond the end of the rack. Its top lid was open, giving Daisy an angled view of the tactical vests sitting loosely on the box.

Tuttle must have inspected the delivery, but never bothered to stuff the items back inside. Again, not surprising given the disheveled state of the man's home.

Apollo picked up the first vest and inspected it, testing the Velcro seals on the magazine pouches.

He then turned his attention to the cross-draw holster along the front.

"Are any bulletproof?" she asked, wondering if Tuttle had finished his purchase with some body armor. Since the Russians had cut off access to town with roadblocks, they wouldn't be able to get to their gear room inside the Sheriff's office.

Apollo dug through the rest of the box of vests, then reported, "Not that I can see."

Gas masks, hiking boots, gloves, safety glasses, and scores of earplugs rounded out the garb, all of it sitting in clumps nearby. The man even had a few thousand feet of paracord bundled and ready to go. It was sitting on a thick, folded stack of cargo netting—camo-colored, of course.

Apollo went to the backpacks leaning against the third wall and picked up one of the six. The pull of gravity on the straps told Daisy they were full, much like the two hiking packs in Tuttle's middle bedroom. However, these were camo-colored and about half the size.

The Sheriff opened the top zipper to inspect its contents. "The man has been busy. I'll give him that," he said, angling the open pouch toward Daisy.

Her eyes ran a quick check as Apollo pulled items out one at a time, her mind making a detailed list of the inventory.

Magnesium fire starter kit.

Quart-sized plastic drinking bottle.

Smaller metal water bottle with a strap and twist cap.

Mobile water filtration system and pump.

Three feet of rubber tubing.

Three green bandanas.

Pack of water purification tablets.

Container of waterproof matches.

Chainsaw in a can.

Mini-fishing kit.

Three military ready to eat meals.

Two energy bars.

Three granola bars.

Handful of beef jerky.

Advil to go pack.

Metal cup.

Small cooking pot.

Magnifying glass.

Folding knife with a belt clip.

Heavy-mil garbage bag.

Blue 10x10 tarp.

Two pairs of wool socks and gloves.

Orange beanie.

Pack of steel wool.

Mobile first aid kit.

Reflective survival blanket.

Dog tag reflector with a compass.

Spool of twine.

Fixed blade survival knife and sheath.

Head lamp and strap.

Extra batteries.

Glow sticks.

Pouch with twenty $5 bills.

Folded area map.

Notepad and pencil.

Can of bear spray.

Small measuring tape.

Can opener.

Toothpaste and brush.

And finally, a bar of soap.

"That's one hell of a bugout bag," Apollo said, standing with his hands on his hips, admiring the inventory.

"Yeah, good luck getting all of that back inside," she said with a smile, her boss rolling his eyes.

"He obviously spent a lot of time putting this together. I'm guessing the other packs have the same items."

The last of the unexplored walls grabbed Apollo's eyes next, specifically the six-foot banquet table. Its foldout legs appeared weak and its wood veneer top had several deep scratches. On it were a stack of bundled white paper, each three feet long and rolled lengthwise, with a rubber band around their middle.

The Sheriff took one of the rolls and slid off the binder. The paper unspooled as he pushed the other rolls to the side, then laid the paper out on the table.

Daisy stood next to him, her eyes drawn to the same discovery. It was an area map of Clearwater County showing the rivers, lakes, mountains, forest, roads, bridges, and the mines in the area. But someone had drawn on it in red ink, creating a loose collection of shapes resembling circles and ovals. Eleven of them, to be exact.

Apollo pointed to the farthest one on the right. "Silver King Mine."

Daisy nodded, then pointed to the ink in the middle. "Mason's Bridge. Where Stan's wife died."

The Sheriff continued with the next one, moving left. "Patterson's Meadow."

"As in Jim Patterson?"

"Yep. The one and only," he answered.

"Isn't he dead?"

Apollo nodded. "Eight years ago, if I remember right."

She tapped her finger on the meadow. "Why do you think he circled it so many times?"

"Not sure."

"I guess it would make a nice spot for a hunting cabin. The mountains around it would protect it from the winds," she said, checking the other circles. All but one of them was indicating another bridge in the area. The last circle was for the abandoned Haskins Mine, an old phosphate pit that had long been extinct. "What does all this mean?"

"Not sure," he said, unspooling another map. It also showed Clearwater County, only it was a topographical map, defining the contours of the terrain, including elevation.

The third map contained climate information for the entire state. Apollo tossed it away, moving on to the fourth, which was a detailed road map. It showed the roads, highways, and railways in the area, each in a different color.

There was more ink on this map, too, only Tuttle hadn't drawn circles. Instead, he drew long, squiggly red lines that seemed to run from point to point, many of them connecting at common locations.

Daisy pointed at one of them. "What do you think these are?"

"My guess . . . Frank was marking the old logging roads."

"Why?"

Apollo shrugged. "The only reason I can think of is to move his supplies without anyone noticing."

"Or as escape routes," she added.

* * *

Victor Rainey waved at his new friend Dallas to keep up as he turned a corner around another stack of pallets in the rear half of Tuttle's barn. He could hardly contain himself. "The best stuff is back here."

"How do you know all this?" Dallas asked, his legs working double-time to catch up.

"When Tuttle was done working outside, he'd sit in his old truck and drink a bunch of beer. I could see him from my grandmother's porch with a pair of binoculars. All I had to do was wait until he went inside to tap a nap, then I'd sneak in here. Tuttle would be out for hours."

"Old people tap a lot of naps."

"Yeah, my grandma, too," Victor said, nodding. "If my mom was in town working, I usually had plenty of time to explore before she got home."

"Didn't the old guy keep the doors locked?"

"Yep, but picking a lock is easy. My dad showed me how before he died. Tuttle was so clueless, it wasn't funny. As long as I put everything back the way he had it, he never noticed."

"Can you show me how?"

"It takes a lot of practice."

"I don't mind. I wanna learn."

"Maybe later. There's something really cool I want to show you by the workbench."

They ran by a dozen more pallets of shrink-wrapped boxes, taking two more turns on their way to the workshop. The last set of items they passed was a wall of stackable water containers. Victor didn't know if the five-gallon jugs were full or not, but there were a lot of them. Enough that he couldn't see over the top.

Tuttle had built his workbench out of 2x4 lumber, with a vise on each end. The workspace stretched from one end of the wall to the other and had to be thirty feet long. All kinds of stuff cluttered the top, thrown into piles on the surface.

Tuttle had a ton of hand tools, plus heavy spools of electrical wire and several rolls of electrical tape. A box of screwdrivers sat by the rolls of duct tape, and next to them, three hammers, a mound of wrenches, and at least twenty boxes of nails and screws.

To the right was a hacksaw, pair of vise grips, a box full of measuring tapes, six box cutters, a pack of magic markers, red shop towels, three cans of motor oil, and a bunch of other crap.

The Husqvarna chainsaws at the far end must have been in for repair, one of the three missing the chain. Victor had seen them elsewhere in the barn before today, but never back here. At the time, he thought about starting one of the heavy, tree-eating machines, but never did. The noise would have woken Tuttle up from his afternoon nap.

A coffee maker and pot sat on a rolling cart in front of the bench, complete with two cans of coffee and a stack of filters on the shelf below. The coffee in the pot looked like it had dried onto the glass.

Above the bench were open storage cabinets crammed full of junk. Everything was a mess. The man must have been collecting for years, especially the batteries, steel wool, and axle grease. He had gobs of it, just thrown in the cabinets like a madman.

"Is this what you wanted to show me?" Dallas said, standing in front of the workbench. He looked confused, his eyebrows pinched as he stared at the endless clutter.

"No, it's over here," Victor said, turning left and walking to a bunch of items covered up with faded yellow sheets. He pulled the cover off the first to reveal a four-foot-long piece of equipment. It looked like an ancient sewing machine with a few parts missing along the top.

It was made of cast iron and sat on its own integrated pedestal, with a pair of foot pedals installed below and a metal seat out front. Victor had played with its various handles and wheels before, so he knew they worked and hadn't rusted shut.

"What is that?" Dallas asked.

"A foot-powered lathe."

"For what?"

"Turning metal and wood. They make bowls and junk with it."

"Really?"

Victor nodded. "Saw it on YouTube before the Internet went down. I think this one can make stuff out of metal, too."

"Looks old."

"Yeah, I'm thinking from the 1800s, just like old man Tuttle himself."

Dallas laughed. "No doubt."

"Tuttle was just like my grandma. Old people never throw anything away and need projects to keep themselves busy. Otherwise, they fall sleep in front of the TV. Grandma's into jigsaw puzzles."

"I hate those. They're so boring."

"No lie. I like to take one of the pieces when she's not looking, just to mess with her. That way, when she's almost done, I get to finish it with the missing piece."

Victor worked his way around to the far side of the lathe. "Help me push," he told Dallas, peering down at the caster wheels mounted to a sheet of plywood holding the lathe.

The two of them moved the machine about fifteen feet, leaving it a foot away from the welding equipment on the other side of the shop. Tuttle had several torches of different sizes. Some had tanks, while others had a long electrical cord. He wasn't sure why the man needed so many.

Victor returned to the next covered item. He knew it to be a ten-inch wood joiner made of cast iron steel. It was old, like the lathe, but it was electric and not foot-powered. He pulled its protective sheet. "Tuttle has them all on wheels so he can move them. Let's get this one out of the way, too."

It took some effort, but the boys got the heavy joiner rolling. They wheeled it across the workshop and parked it next to the lathe. Had they chosen a spot farther to the left, they would have run into the man's blacksmithing equipment. Tuttle's anvil was pitted and a little rusty. So was the pounding hammer. Like the other equipment in the room, the forge was also on wheels and looked ancient.

Victor pointed at the base cabinet exposed after the equipment move. It featured two plywood doors with a latching mechanism made out of a bent nails and hooks. "Check out what's in the bottom."

Dallas went to the door on the right and opened it.

"What do you think?" Victor asked.

"What is that?" Dallas asked, his tone energized.

"Samurai sword."

Dallas put his hand in and pulled at the weapon, but it was stuck. He angled his arm sideways to work the item through the door of the cabinet. He spun around and held it up, still in its protective sheath.

Victor smiled. "Go ahead. Pull it out."

Dallas didn't hesitate, sliding the blade free. He put the sheath down on the workbench and wrapped both hands around the grip.

Victor remembered the first time he held the sword. "Pretty, cool, huh?"

"For sure," Dallas answered, slashing the blade back and forth before pretending to stab someone with it. "I'll bet this thing is worth a fortune."

"That's what I was thinking. Now that Tuttle's dead, someone needs to take good care of it. I was thinking maybe you should."

"Really? Me?"

"Yep."

"Awesome," Dallas said, putting the blade back into its protective carrier. The kid brought his eyes to Victor. "I'll bet Tuttle has a lot of other cool stuff. Maybe even some guns."

"So far, I've only found the sword. But I do know where there are lots of guns and ammo. Explosives, too."

"Where?"

"At Franklin Atwater's store."

"The horse stables?"

Victor nodded. "My grandma took me there a bunch of times."

"You still think it's all there? You know, after what happened to him."

"It was a few days ago when I was there. I found a pistol hidden under his desk."

"Can I see it?"

"I wish. It fell out of my pants when a bunch of men in black showed up and started chasing me."

"We should go look for it. Must be around there somewhere."

"If those men didn't take it."

CHAPTER 7

"We're gonna need more men if they're serious about staying here," Albert said to Dustin as the two of them leaned against the front of the fertilizer stacks, watching the activity in Tuttle's barn.

"Yeah, seems like a long shot. I know this Bunker guy is one serious badass, but how in the world are we going to stop a convoy like the one we saw back on the road?"

"We won't. They're nuts."

"As nuts as Burt wanting to head back to town?"

"So you finally agree with me?" Albert asked.

"Of course I do. We're partners."

"That's not how it came across before."

"I know, but that was different."

"How's that?"

"We're not stuck in the woods."

"Oh, I see. Your loyalty shifts depending on which way the wind is blowing. That's pretty weak."

"Dude, you really need to chill. I'm on your side."

"Only until something else pops up. Then you'll bail again," Albert said, unable to stop his disdain from fueling the words.

Dustin didn't say anything, his lips running quiet as his eyes dropped to the ground. After a long pause, he looked up and pointed at the mammoth of a man, Dicky, who was busy directing a forklift out of the barn. "Maybe we should think about lending a hand. You know, do something constructive."

"Nah, looks like they got it handled."

The new guy, Bunker, was behind the wheel of the machine, its engine churning under the strain of a massive spool of barbed wire hanging from the forks. It was clear Bunker was running the show with his endless barking of orders.

Albert motioned at Bunker, waiting for Dustin to catch up with his eyes. "I don't like that guy."

"Who? Bunker?"

"Yeah. Something seems off to me. I get that everyone is in love with the guy, but he rubs me the wrong way. I mean, who is he really, other than some overgrown testosterone sack?"

"He seems okay to me."

"Of course you'd say that. The wind just shifted."

"Maybe if you got to know him better, you'd feel the same way."

"I doubt it. He just runs around giving orders and telling everyone what to do. Like he owns the place. It's really starting to piss me off."

"I don't know; he looks like the kind of guy you wanna have on your side, not the other way around."

"Why? Because he's tall and slicks his hair back?"

"Well that, and he's pretty big. Those tattoos are kinda intimidating, too."

"Dude, just because you look tough does not mean you are tough. Trust me. Some of the guys I used to work with were half his size and they were some of most feared badasses in Southern California. I know. My crew used to have to deal with them all the time. Like I've said before, looks can be deceiving."

"Yeah, maybe you're right."

"Of course I'm right. You just need to listen to me once in a while."

Dustin shrugged, his tone changing to one of guilt. "I still feel like we should be doing something."

"Don't worry about it. They'll ask if they need something, especially the new guy, Mr. All Bark and No Bite," Albert said in a flippant tone, his eyes locked on the tattooed man with scars on his neck. He watched Bunker work the controls of the forklift with precision. Right then, an intense sense of déjà vu washed over him. "Damn, he looks familiar."

"Bunker?"

"Yeah, can't seem to place him though." Albert wasn't sure if he'd seen the black-haired man in one of the many warehouses or back alleys he'd been in during an exchange, or in some other capacity. But the man was familiar in some way. No doubt about it.

"Hey Sheriff, check it out," Daisy shouted from somewhere in the barn behind Albert. Apollo and the hot deputy had had been in the back for the last half hour, searching for something.

"Good work," Apollo told her, his voice wandering through the stacks of pallets. "Looks like the inventory map was out of date."

"Probably hasn't been updated since Helen died," she answered.

"Then we need to keep looking. No telling what else is in here. See if you can find some rechargeables."

Albert pulled his feet in as the Mayor's grandson Rusty walked past with a red, heavy-duty toolbox in his right hand, grunting and leaning hard to the left with every step he took. The kid had tree trunks for legs, but they weren't helping with the weight of the metal box. Rusty followed the forklift, heading for the entrance to the barn.

"That kid's gonna wreck his back walking like that," Dustin said.

"If someone asked me, I'd have Dicky carry it. That brute wouldn't break a sweat," Albert said, turning his eyes to Dustin. "Now, let me tell you, that guy is *tough*."

"How do you know?"

"Used to watch him mow down opposing teams back in high school. He has this switch inside of him, that once it goes off, watch out. He sent more than one defensive lineman to the hospital back in those days."

"You went to the football games?"

"Sure. Wasn't much else to do on Friday nights. Though I usually had to sit by myself. But of course, that shouldn't surprise you, right?"

"Nope. Had the same problem, which is why I skipped the ten-year reunion. Figured what was the point? I couldn't stand most of those assholes anyway."

"What high school again?" Albert asked, realizing he didn't know where Dustin was from. He knew the stickman had moved to Clearwater recently, but that was the extent of the guy's background.

"Arcadia High School. Phoenix."

"Hot down there."

"You got that right. You never stop sweating from March to November. But everyone has a pool, so that doesn't suck."

"Really? A pool, huh? I can't picture you lounging by a pool."

"That's because I never did. Not a big fan of the whole swim trunk thing."

"Yeah, me either," Albert said as Bunker parked the forklift just beyond the door.

The man jumped off the vehicle, laughed, and then slapped Rusty on the back after the kid delivered the toolbox with a grunt.

"That'll put some hair on your chest," Bunker joked.

"What's in this thing?" Rusty asked.

"Hopefully not rocks," Bunker said, taking a knee. He opened the box and dug around inside, pulling out a pair of hand tools and giving them to Dicky. He stood up. "Why don't you get started? I've got a couple of things to take care of inside. I'll be right back."

Bunker walked through the door and made his way toward the fertilizer stacks. Along the way, he snatched two shovels that were leaning against a crate of bleach, ammonia, Tide detergent, and other cleaning supplies wrapped in clear plastic.

Dustin stopped slouching against the fertilizer bags and stood upright when Bunker arrived.

Albert remained in a causal slump.

"Looks like you two need something to do," Bunker said, his tone deep. He forced a shovel into Dustin's hands and tried to do the same with Albert.

Albert pushed the handle away. "Sorry, dude. Diggin' ain't my thing."

The shovel came at him again. "Well, today it is. Everyone has to chip in if we're gonna get this place ready."

Albert refused to grab it, even though Bunker was pushing it with force against his chest. "You do know that this is all just a humungous waste of time, right? Only a complete moron would think any of this will accomplish a damn thing. Especially with what's out there right now. Ever heard of the term *Force Multiplier?*"

Bunker's chin tightened as he spoke through clenched teeth. "Yes. As a matter of fact, I've lived it. On both sides, my friend."

"Well, first of all, I'm not your friend. And second, if you lived it, it means you served, so you know I'm right. We don't stand a chance against the Russians and all their firepower. It doesn't matter what we do, we'll be slaughtered like mindless sheep."

"Look, I don't have time to explain it all. But trust me, I've got it covered. Right now, we have a few dead to bury and you two just volunteered. I need five graves out back. On the double."

Albert couldn't believe the audacity of this man. He tapped the tip of his index finger against the star on his chest, then pointed at Dustin's badge as well. "In case you haven't noticed, we're both

JAY J. FALCONER   88

Deputy Sheriffs. So tell me again, who put you in charge?"

"It just so happens, your boss did."

Albert smirked, unable to hold back his attitude. "In charge of what? Landscaping?"

"Of all things tactical and practical. So I'd suggest you two get digging."

"Graves are not tactical," Albert answered, swinging his eyes to Dustin for a few seconds. "Can you believe this guy? Talk about dense."

Bunker's eyes twitched, reminiscent of a cowboy preparing to draw down in a Wild West gunfight. "They are, if the right bodies are being dumped into them. As it stands now, we only need five, but I could easily make it seven."

Dustin's voice cracked when he spoke. "Albert, maybe we should do what the man says."

Albert held up a hand to shut Dustin up, never taking his eyes from Bunker. "Why don't you get Dicky and that Buckley kid to do it? They look like a couple of eager beavers. Dustin and I are taking a break. Been a long day, if you know what I mean."

Bunker looked at Dustin, then back at Albert. "Now, I've asked you nicely. More than once."

Albert wasn't worried. "Like I care. You really need to get over yourself, dude."

"Albert? Come on. Let's just do this," Dustin said.

Albert grinned, feeling emboldened. He wasn't sure why, but something inside was driving him to confront this man. It felt primal, almost as if he was being compelled to expose the man's temper.

"At this point, Bunker, it's all about mind over matter. Right now, I don't mind and you don't matter. So run along now and go impose your will on someone else. Dustin and I are busy."

Bunker flew forward, grabbing Albert by the shirt collar. His powerful arms swung Albert around and pushed him back a good ten feet, until something hard smacked into his back.

Albert put his hands up. "So now what? You gonna hit me?"

"Thinking about it."

"Well then, take your best shot. But I should warn you, you might just regret it."

Dustin voice was more agitated now. "Albert, please. Let's just go outside. It's not a big deal, really."

Bunker shook his head in disgust, his deadpan eyes burning a hole into Albert's face. "You know what, Albert? I've decided that I don't like you. Or your attitude."

"The feeling's mutual, bub. Now let go of me and back the fuck up."

Burt walked into the barn with a partially eaten apple in his hand, his teeth in chew mode. "Well, well. What do we have here?"

Dustin ran to Burt. "You gotta do something. Bunker's gonna kill him."

Burt chuckled. "Let me guess, jumbo opened his big mouth again."

"You could say that," Bunker answered, his eyes still locked on Albert. His grip tightened, lifting Albert to his toes.

Burt stopped his approach, then leaned against a crate with his elbow on top. He crossed his feet, his teeth tearing into the fruit for another crisp bite. "Go on boys, don't let me interrupt," he said with his mouth full.

"So what's it gonna be?" Bunker said, his words warming Albert's cheeks.

Dustin ran back to Bunker. "I'll dig the graves," he said, his tone frantic. "Just let Albert go. We're all friends here."

Albert took a deep breath, keeping his fear in check. Something in Bunker's eyes wasn't legit. He could sense it. The man wasn't going to turn physical. "See there, now we have a real solution. One that didn't involve me bowing to your one-sided demands."

Bunker paused for a few moments, then let go of Albert's shirt. He backed away a second before Rusty and Dicky came into the barn.

"Seriously? That's it? Well, that wasn't worth the price of admission," Burt said, turning and walking toward the exit.

Sheriff Apollo appeared at the door, meeting Burt just beyond the doorway. "What's going on?"

"Nothing, unfortunately," Burt said, stopping for a moment to relay the answer as the Sheriff cruised past him.

Albert waited for the Sheriff to arrive, then motioned at Bunker. "Your guard dog here just physically assaulted me."

"Why?"

Albert huffed, making sure his tone drove the point home. "Because I told him no and he didn't like it."

"Maybe you should do what Jack says. I did put him charge for a reason."

Albert turned to Apollo, eyes squinting. "So you're going to go with him over your own deputy?"

"Thanks for reminding me," Apollo said, his hand snatching the star from Albert's chest. He did the same with Dustin's badge. "Been meaning to repo these for a while now."

"So that's it? We're fired?" Albert snapped.

"I warned you up front. This duty was only temporary."

"See, I told you this would happen, Albert," Dustin said after the Sheriff walked away.

"Yeah, it sucks. So what?" Albert said, flipping his head to the side when he spoke.

An instant later, Bunker took a step forward. He leaned in close, his heated breath filling Albert's nostrils. "Like I said before, we all need to pull together. No exceptions. So I'd suggest that both of you *embrace the suck* and get those graves done before you and I have another problem. Am I clear?"

"Crystal," Dustin said, tugging at Albert's arm. "We'll get it done."

Albert didn't respond. Nor did he move, tearing Dustin's fingers from his arm.

Bunker turned and followed the Sheriff's path out of the barn. Rusty and Dicky followed him.

Bunker's odd choice of words about *embracing the suck* echoed in Albert's mind. He was certain he'd heard that phrase before. Even the tone of the man's voice rang true, anger and all.

It took a few more seconds before a visual appeared in his mind, linking Bunker's face to a name from his past. "That's it! That's where I know him from!"

Dustin's eyes lit up. "Where?"

"From LA. The Kindred biker gang. Bunch of skin heads."

"The Kindred, huh? I'm pretty sure I've heard of those guys."

"The entire West Coast has, unless you're living under a rock," Albert said, letting the memory play out in his mind. "I told you I recognized him. Though I never knew the man had hair."

"I can't imagine him bald."

"Oh, he was. Completely. Like the others. I know it was their trademark, but still. It completely changes his look."

"Those nasty scars on his neck are pretty noticeable. I'm surprised it took you so long to place him."

"He didn't have them the last time I saw him."

"Must be burn scars. I wonder what happened?"

"He didn't like the ink, that's what happened. Swastikas don't exactly get you the red-carpet treatment. Not unless you're running in the proper circles. And I'm not talking about with Wall Street types, either."

"He must have really wanted them off to put himself through that."

"Or someone did it to him."

"You mean, like against his will?"

"Yep."

"I can't even imagine what that felt like."

"Oh, and by the way, his name wasn't Bunker back then either. It was Bulldog."

"Was he a slinger?"

"Nah. Just muscle. Damn good at it from what I heard. The man had a seriously nice hog and one of the hottest girlfriends on the planet. Can't remember her name though, but she could stop traffic. We're talking USDA Prime Choice. Fake tits and all."

"Figures."

"If I remember right, he used to ride with a mouth-breather named Grinder. If those two apes showed up for a collection, someone was going down. Big time."

"What the hell is he doing here?"

"The only thing I can think of is he went rogue. Otherwise, I can't see him running without his colors, or his bike."

"Or the girl."

"Her, too. Must have had to change his name and appearance when he left."

"I'm sure he had to."

Albert nodded. "Because once you're in the brotherhood, it's damn near impossible to get out. They'll bury you first."

"You think he recognizes you?"

Albert shrugged, pondering the ramifications if Bunker had. "I never spent a lot of time with him one on one. He might remember my street name as Tin Man, but not my face."

"Tin Man?"

"Yeah, the legendary meth cook without a heart."

"That fits, I guess."

"He was always busy providing perimeter security when my crew met with his boss, Connor Watts. Now *that* guy had a seriously bad temper. It seemed like every time we had an encounter with Watts, it almost ended in a shootout. Talk about stressful."

"Now I see why you want Burt involved."

Albert patted Dustin on the back. "I'm glad you agree, because you can never be too paranoid in this business. When you step balls-deep into that world, muscle and guns are the only things that keep guys like us safe."

"It's too bad you just pissed him off. Otherwise, he might have wanted to join our little business. If I had to choose, I'd take Bunker over Burt."

Dustin was right on both counts, but Albert wasn't going to admit it. There wasn't any point.

"Nah, I doubt it. He's obviously not the same man. Something's changed."

As it stood now, their future business prospects looked bleak with the Russians moving in. Access to the demand in town had been cut off, and transportation of the drugs to other cities and states would be difficult with checkpoints and roving patrols everywhere.

However, there was one alternative. If he could figure out a way to sell the crystals to the occupying force, then he could trade one set of addicts for another. It would also make him useful in the eyes of the Russians. And necessary. Both would keep him alive.

Albert had read somewhere that young, inexperienced troops are beyond anxious when in-country and living under the ever-present threat of snipers, IEDs, ambushes, and uprisings.

The unending pressure of being one of the hated occupiers takes its toll, resulting in drugs, alcohol, and women being a constant problem for their commanders. Especially since some of those same troublemakers were down on their luck outcasts, signing up to escape their past.

Our lives on this rock are a collective sum of our decisions over time, some good, others not. Those with weak moral fiber are doomed to repeat themselves, their relentless black cloud following them into service.

Let's face it, everyone needs a diversion from their own flawed existence now and then, usually when the pressure gets to be too much. That's how Albert made his living, tapping into that primal need to escape.

Sure, the article he'd read was focused on US troops overseas, but there was a chance it applied to the mighty Russian Army as well.

It's just human nature, he thought to himself.

Maybe his plans for Clearwater Red weren't dead after all.

CHAPTER 8

Several hours later . . .

Allison Rainey put a fresh towel on the floor in front of the fridge in her mother's kitchen. The defrost cycle had begun in earnest shortly after the customized backup generator Tuttle had sold her mom ran out of fuel.

Allison was certain the crotchety old fart had jacked up the price when Martha bought it from him the year prior, but the machine survived the EMP just like Tuttle claimed it would.

Yet the generator couldn't overcome the lack of fuel, despite its enhanced capabilities. That may have been the reason why Tuttle decided to sell his only generator—a move some might find strange. Then again, Tuttle was the pinnacle of strange.

At least the drip had slowed considerably since it first started, though the leak was still active, mocking her as if to say it was never going to stop. Only two dry rags remained in the laundry cabinet. Hopefully they'd be enough.

She turned her focus to the remaining dishes in the sink, resuming her casual hum to cover up what she was feeling inside. The impromptu funeral for Cowie and Franklin Atwater was finally over, and nobody was more relieved than she was.

Allison didn't know either of them well, but most of those in attendance did. Mainly Megan and Misty, their grief on full display, filling Allison's eyes with tears.

You don't have to be close with the deceased to be affected by their loved ones' anguish. It's natural to be sucked into the torment of a loss like that—unless of course, you had a heart of stone.

The new guy, Bunker, seemed to have that trait, his jaw stiff and shoulders broad. The man was a rock during the service, never leaving Megan's side the entire time.

Megan had held up fairly well during the emotional burial, but Misty was another story. The woman was a total wreck, kneeling before the grave of her dead fiancé, bawling her eyes out for what seemed like an hour. It was a tough scene to witness. For everyone.

Often times watching someone else's pain is worse than dealing with your own. Even the strongest person can break down when they see misery consuming someone they know, especially in the eyes of little ones.

The compassionate Sheriff eventually had no choice but to carry Misty across the road from Tuttle's, then haul her upstairs to Martha's bedroom. Misty fell asleep quickly, thank God, buried under a mound of covers and Kleenex.

The dishwater in the sink was no longer clean but the soap bubbles stood strong, caressing Allison's hands. The scrub rag in her hand was as dirty as the water, both symbolic of the world around them. The coldness of death had soiled a once-beautiful countryside, its relentless hunt for prey ongoing. The citizens of Clearwater were the primary targets, some more than others.

Everything was normal a few days ago, and now this—chaos and death swirling outside. However, just like her need for more water from the riser spigot outside, more funerals would be needed to cleanse the heartbreak she feared was headed to the town of Clearwater. In droves.

Megan appeared stable on the outside, but Allison could sense the child's pain. It was obvious: the girl's lingering stares at nothing. But that wasn't the only indicator. Megan's delay when answering questions was another clue. So were her occasional, random sniffs.

Megan was trying to show strength, but Allison knew it was only a matter of time before the child broke down, again.

Whenever it arrived, she prayed someone was there for her. Bunker or otherwise, it didn't matter. Megan would need a shoulder to cry on from one of the adults.

Allison might need a good cry herself, assuming the men failed in their duties to secure the area, or failed to run power from Tuttle's solar array to her mother's house, as they promised. Otherwise, the well pump would forever be useless, leaving her to fetch water the old-fashioned way.

When you've been spoiled by indoor plumbing all your life, it's difficult to go without. The same could be said for overhead lights and hot water. Oh, and a working fridge. All of it essential to feeling human.

She shook her head while her humming continued. What she wouldn't give for a hot soak in the tub right about now. Maybe a few scented candles, too, plus some classical music and a tall glass of Cabernet Sauvignon.

"Heaven in a ten-by-ten room," she mumbled.

"Thanks for the P, B and J, Mrs. Rainey," Megan said after Allison put another dish in the plastic tray on the counter. "It was good."

"Did you get enough, sweetheart?" she asked, wondering how long the ebony darling would hold it together.

"Yeah. But I'm not sure your son liked it very much. Or the new boy, Dallas."

Allison knew it couldn't have been easy for Megan when Dicky and Burt lowered the body of her father into the shallow grave behind Tuttle's barn. That type of finality really hit home, reminding Allison of her own father's funeral.

It was a little over six years ago—the entire congregation standing as one outside of the church. Once the coffin was in the hearse and it pulled away, a collective cry erupted. Watching the vehicle slowly make its way around the parking lot to the street was one of the hardest moments in her life. It was the end of her father, his remains heading down the street for cremation.

Allison broke out of her daydream and whirled around, realizing she hadn't heard the boys in the last few minutes. The two hellions were no longer in the kitchen, their chairs empty and pushed back at an angle from the table.

Their porcelain plates held partially eaten sandwiches, the peanut butter leaking out and mixing with the grape jelly in long smears. They must have snuck out while she was humming. She never heard a sound.

"Where'd they go?" she asked Megan, the girl's knee brace holding her leg straight along the side of the chair.

"I think they went to help Jeffrey get some eggs."

Allison smirked. "Oh, really now."

Her son Victor was many things, but he wasn't anything close to being helpful. Not unless he was getting paid to do so, like the last time he donned an apron and slung hash browns with her on the wood-fired grill in front of Billy Jack's Café.

It was the very same morning when Apollo snuck a twenty-dollar bill into her tip jar after the power went out. She had planned to return the money to the kindly Sheriff, but it was her only tip of the day. Everyone else seemed content to skip that part of the process, leaving her short on cash to pay for the ride home by the smelly mechanic, Burt.

Deputy Daisy walked into the kitchen with Allison's mother, Martha. Neither of them appeared gloomy or depressed, acting as if the dual funeral hadn't just happened—or a last-second shot by Bunker hadn't killed three masked men.

Allison figured the women were putting on a strong front for Megan. That, too, was human nature after a funeral, everyone preferring to move on and not dwell on the pain. No matter how traumatic the deaths, friends and family always rally around those suffering the most.

"What's wrong, Ally?" Mom asked, obviously sensing her frustration.

Allison didn't want Martha to sense her grief, so she wiped the concern from her face in an instant. She pointed at the table to change their focus. "The boys."

"I wondered how long they'd actually sit still. Looks like they hardly touched their food."

"Why am I not surprised?"

"Boys will be boys."

Daisy stood next to Allison in front of the wet dishes. "Can I help?"

Allison gave her a dishtowel to start drying. "Those two better not have gone far, or I'll have their heads."

"I'm sure they haven't," Daisy said, her tone confident and to the point. "Probably out helping Bunker and my boss."

"You know, just once it would be nice if a member of the male species did what they were supposed to do. That's all I ask. Just once. Is that so hard?"

Daisy finished another wipe down before stacking the dish on the counter. "You wouldn't think so, but we all know that's impossible when men have the attention span of a flea."

Allison laughed, bringing a twinge of peace to her heart. There's nothing quite like a fellow sister telling it like it is.

Martha took a seat at the table with Megan, choosing the chair formerly inhabited by her grandson, Victor. "You two need to relax. There are good men around; you just have to look a little harder. Sometimes it's difficult to spot the gems, with all the jerks in the way."

Allison rolled her eyes. "That's easy for you to say, Mom. You only had Dad to deal with the past forty-five years. Trying being a single mother in the world these days."

"I know, sweetheart. It's hard. But trust me, being married to your father wasn't always easy. I learned to say 'yes dear' even when I didn't want to. Remember that, girls. Once in a while, you just gotta let things go. Especially the little things."

"Different generation, Mom. Things are not the same anymore. There are no *little* things."

"You're right, the world is not the same, but people are. Sometimes, the best men are standing right there in front of you, only you're not paying attention."

"Right there in front of me? I think that's a little bit of an oversimplification. Don't you?"

"Not really. It doesn't take much to blind yourself to the answer, especially when you're focused on the wrong question."

Allison pouted, "I don't even know what that means, Mom."

There was a long pause in the room until Daisy cleared her throat. "Allison, can I ask you something?"

"Sure."

"I know you're not fond of men at the moment, but have you ever thought about getting something going with the Sheriff?"

"What do you mean? Like a date?"

"He's super sweet on you, in case you didn't know."

"Really? Gus?"

Daisy nodded, then smiled. "Why do you think he stops in every night after work to have dessert?"

"He's kinda cute and all, but I thought he just had a sweet tooth."

"Well, he doesn't. In fact, until you arrived in town, he'd been planning to get into shape and drop a few pounds."

"I had no idea," Allison said, seeing a vision of his beaming smile in her mind. He was a gentle soul, to be sure, but she'd never given him much thought. Until now. "He hardly ever says anything."

"That's because he's shy."

"The Sheriff? Shy? But he deals with people all day long."

"Yeah, he does. But don't let the badge and gun fool you. He's a big softy inside. Like a squishy teddy bear."

Allison didn't know what to say, so she said nothing.

Daisy continued. "In fact, he's one of the nicest guys you'll ever meet. Hell, if he was a little younger, I'd take a run at him myself."

"What does age have to do with anything?" Martha said from her seat.

Daisy paused before she spoke again. "It doesn't, really. But I know for a fact he only has eyes for Allison. Plus, there's the whole *no fraternization with a co-worker* regulation."

"Excuse me for saying this, Daisy," Martha said, her tone motherly, "but from what I hear, you don't exactly play by the rules when it comes to men."

"Mother!" Allison snapped.

Daisy latched onto Allison's forearm, squeezing gently. "It's okay, Allison. Everyone knows."

"I'm sorry, but sometimes my mom doesn't have a filter."

Daisy turned to face Martha, her hands working the dishtowel across a plate. "You mean Bill King?"

Stephanie walked through the back door only moments after the words flew from Daisy's lips. The conversation dried up an instant later, an eerie hush hanging in the air.

Stephanie stopped and put her hands on her hips. "You ladies were just talking about my ex, weren't you?"

Daisy nodded.

"It never ceases to amaze me how that jerk finds his way into almost every conversation. Even way out here."

"I'm sorry to bring him up, Steph. I know we had a deal."

"No, I get it. People need to gossip."

"It wasn't gossip, exactly," Allison said. "My mother was just being—"

Daisy didn't let her finish. "Actually, we were talking about the Sheriff and his crush on Allison."

"The Sheriff? Really?"

"Yep. Really."

"And Bill's name came up?" Stephanie asked, looking mystified.

"What did Mr. King do?" Megan asked, her sweet voice hanging in the air. "Was he bad?"

"Never you mind, little one," Martha said, snatching the boys' half-empty plates from the table. She grabbed Megan's, too, then carried the stack to the sink and dumped them into the brown water.

"Maybe we should talk about something else?" Daisy said to Stephanie, putting a handful of clean dishes into the cabinet.

"As long as it's not about my ex, then I'm good with it."

"I second that," Martha added.

"Then the ayes have it. Motion carried," Allison said without hesitation, beaming an ear-to-ear smile. "See now, ladies. That's how the newly formed Clearwater Women's Group handles its decisions. Collectively and without a second thought to anyone who relies on testosterone to get up in the morning, if you know what I mean."

Stephanie laughed.

So did Daisy.

Martha turned a deep shade of red before walking to the cabinet next to the leaky fridge.

"Speaking of which," she said, opening the door and pulling out a box of Band-Aids. She turned to Daisy. "I think you should take these and go keep an eye on the men. Someone is bound to need one."

Daisy laughed, then took the bandages.

"At least we don't hear any power tools outside," Allison said in a sarcastic tone.

"Good heavens, can you imagine?" Martha quipped, her grin in full bloom.

"Do you remember what Dad used to say? *If I'm not bleeding, I'm not trying.*"

Martha laughed. "Yes, every time he went outside, I swear."

Allison agreed. "When I cleaned out the garage after he died, I must have found a dozen extension cords that had been cut in half by the hedge trimmer."

"It's a wonder he still had all ten fingers when we buried him."

"We cremated him, Mother."

"I know. It was just an expression."

"Sort of like my testosterone joke a minute ago."

"Yes. Exactly."

Daisy motioned with the box of bandages. "I guess I'd better get out there before someone loses a limb."

"And if they do, pick it up and smack them over the head with it," Martha said, laughing after the last word left her lips.

CHAPTER 9

Bunker waited for Rusty to step out of the way before he finished the metal tie on the barbed wire. It completed another barricade at the end of Old Mill Road. "One more set after this and we're done prepping this side of the bridge. We'll need to keep them out of the way until we're ready for final positioning."

Apollo brought another 4x4 post into position, holding it at a forty-five degree angle. Rusty bolted it to a matching piece of lumber running the opposite direction. The two posts formed the letter 'X' lying on its side. Once a pair of ends was made, they'd string wire between them to complete the barrier.

"When we're done here, I should probably get back to Clearwater," Apollo said, his voice barely above a whisper.

Bunker needed him to stick around. "You really think that's a good idea, Sheriff?"

"No. But my duty is with the town. It's my job and I should be there. With everyone else."

"It's not going to be easy to avoid the checkpoints. Probably have a number of patrols out, too. If their orders are to shoot on sight—"

"I can get him there," Burt said before Bunker could finish his sentence. "Like I said before, I know a few shortcuts. Logging roads, mostly."

Apollo seemed to like that idea. His eyes locked onto Burt's. "Tuttle has some area maps we can use to plot a course around the roadblocks we know about. Going to need everyone's input."

Bunker wasn't sure how to respond. He didn't want either of the men to take off, but knew it wasn't his place to stop them. Despite the fact that the women and children needed maximum protection.

He decided to take a neutral, noncommittal approach, giving him time to come up with a plan to change their minds. "We'll figure something out once we get the perimeter secure."

Dicky lowered his rifle slightly and glanced back over his shoulder, his eyes meeting Bunker's. The huge man sent a head nod, bringing a welcome confirmation Bunker's way.

The TrackingPoint rifle looked good in the goliath's hands, his powerful grip keeping it secure and ready to fire. Bunker didn't know the man very well, but thus far Dicky had been easy to work with. He wasn't afraid to jump in and help with any project. Or take guard duty—Dicky volunteered before Bunker had to ask.

"Is this how you made them in the Army?" Rusty asked Bunker.

"I was in the Marine Corps, not the Army. That was Megan's dad. He was a master welder, if I remember right."

"Marines, sorry."

"It's okay, kid. I knew what you meant."

"So, did you?"

"Yeah, sure. Made my share of just about everything once or twice. It comes with the job. They teach us how to defend against all kinds of threats, and not just with a rifle. My favorite part was when we needed to improvise in the field. It never ceased to amaze me what your mind can accomplish when you're desperate."

"Or hungry, I'll bet," Apollo added.

"That, or trying to avoid hypothermia. The high-altitude wilderness training was the worst. Nearly froze the boys off that first night."

"Did you ever have to shoot anybody?" Rusty asked, catching the attention of Dallas and Victor as well. They stopped their work, turning their heads to listen.

"Yes, but it's not something I like to talk about."

"That had to be pretty intense. I'm not sure I could do it."

"My guess is that you could, if you had the right training."

"Maybe. But still, pulling the trigger has to be hard."

"For some it is, but they usually get over it if they want to stay alive. We had this saying, *The more you train in peace, the less you bleed in war.*"

"Makes sense."

"And trust me, we were always training. Sometimes, that's all we did for weeks on end."

"Sounds a little boring," Dallas said.

"At times, it was. But that is what's needed to protect this country. Our government spent piles of money making sure our minds and bodies were prepared for what we had to do. In the end, you have to act without hesitation, otherwise you have little chance to survive combat. There's no time to think. It has to be second nature."

Rusty nodded, but didn't ask another question.

Bunker continued, feeling the urge to share information about his father. He wasn't sure if the compulsion stemmed from the fact that none of these boys had a father around or not. But it seemed like the thing to do. "Then there are the truly great Marines. Those with the mindset to never give up, no matter what they face. Like my father. Before he became a firefighter, he was a member of SEAL Team Two. Men like him have this switch inside that kicks in when the shit hits the fan, always driving them forward regardless of the odds. But not everyone is born to fight," Bunker said, looking down at the letters tattooed on his knuckles: B-T-F. "Only a few have what it takes."

"How do you know if you're one of them?" Rusty asked.

"That's a good question. It starts deep within, somewhere inside your core. I'm not sure how to explain it exactly, but my father knew I had it. He was on me every day, always testing me to see what I was made of."

"Sounds harsh."

"Yeah, once in a while. But a man can accomplish anything if he is willing to push himself beyond his limits. I think that type of person makes the best warrior."

"It's sort of like my racing. I have a couple of friends who take way too many days off from training. I'm always out there riding, but it seems like I'm the only one. It's almost impossible to get them out of bed and away from their girlfriends."

"Exactly. Whether it's sports or combat, those who excel are dedicated to accomplishing the mission. And to do that, you must never stop pushing the envelope."

"To find your limits."

"Yes, because you don't know your limits until you fail, and that takes blood, sweat, and tears. That's what my old man taught me."

"You were lucky to have a dad like that."

"Though I did get tired of the constant preaching and pop inspections," he said, rolling his eyes. "Especially the dreaded almond duty."

"Almond duty? What's that?"

Bunker laughed after an intense memory flashed in his mind. "Every night when my father came home after his shift at the fire station, he'd inspect the ground around the almond trees. If a single nut was on the ground, there'd be hell to pay. The type of hell would vary, but when a former SEAL is dishing it out, you can bet your ass it would be tough."

"Every almond?"

"Shell or nut, it didn't matter. The ground had to be spotless. Those trees are the reason why I hate almonds to this day. I can't even stand to look at them, let alone put one in my mouth. I swear, I had nightmares about giant almonds crushing me for years, all because of those damn trees."

"I can see why."

"As I got older, the almond inspections didn't happen as often, but the punishment for failure went up. It forced me to overcome the anxiety that came with those random inspections, devising new and better ways to keep the birds out of the trees and the nuts off the ground, even in the wind."

"Were you a SEAL, like your father?"

"I planned to be at first, but then a different specialty found me. Something with a unique challenge attached to it. I decided to become a *sapper*."

"What's that?"

"Basically, it's a combat engineer. My job was to clear the way into battle for the infantry to follow. Most of the time that meant engineering a way into the combat zone using explosives and other techniques. To get past the enemy's defenses."

"Was your dad disappointed you didn't become a SEAL?"

"If he was, he never said anything. He knew I liked to be first into the fight. So becoming a sapper seemed like the logical choice. It's an important job. One that requires you to use your brains and your balls to clear a path for those behind you. Most of the time, we'd end up fighting alongside the grunts afterward, but there's something honorable about being first man in. Plus, we got to blow shit up."

"I can see why you liked it," Victor said.

"We also spent time fortifying our base defenses, plus looking for IEDs and other booby-traps. You'd be surprised how clever those booger-eaters can be over there. Almost anything can be turned into a bomb: bicycles, sidewalks, electrical transformers—you name it. For some reason, learning all that stuff really appealed to me. I'm not sure how to explain it exactly. It just fit."

Burt Lowenstein brought another stack of 4x4 posts from the barn, each cut off at the four-foot mark. The man had some serious pipes, his biceps bulging with every movement of his arms. His sagging gut was another matter; he obviously skipped the cardio portion of his workouts.

"That should be enough, Burt," Bunker said, pointing at the spot where he wanted them.

"You know, Bunker, I was doing some thinking about those Land Rovers behind the barn. Tuttle has a seriously nice torch I could use to make some adjustments. A little fortification, if you know what I mean. There's a shitload of steel plates out back."

"Good idea, but first we need to use the Rovers to push Tuttle's old trucks into position."

"I can do that. Where do you want 'em?"

Bunker pointed to the far end of the wooden bridge. "One on each side, funneling traffic to the middle. Once the Fords are into position, disable their tires and drive trains. If you can weld some of those plates onto the door panels, it'll be extra protection in case we get in a firefight."

"Tuttle's also got an old Massey Ferguson Combine out back, if you think it'll help. That harvester is from the '60s and built like a tank, but it should still run. At least it used to the last time I worked on it for the old man."

"What about the EMP?" Victor asked.

Burt shook his head. "Should be fine. No electronics in that beast."

Bunker agreed. "Just make sure you leave a path wide enough for a horse to get through. But not too wide. I don't want any vehicles making their way across the bridge."

"Why funnel them down the middle?" Victor asked.

"For easier kill shots. We need to concentrate our firepower in one spot, if they decide to come across," Bunker said. He pointed, aiming his finger at a mighty oak tree to the right, its branches thick with leaves. "If we build a hide up there, a sniper can cover that position with the TrackingPoint rifle. However, once the enemy zeroes in, he'll need an escape route. A fast rope down the back ought to do it. That wide trunk will provide excellent cover."

"I could reinforce it with some steel for protection," Burt said. "Then our sniper might be able to take out a few more of them fuckers."

Bunker liked that idea, except for one problem. "Might be tough hauling up all that weight."

Burt didn't hesitate. "We can use Tuttle's chain hoists in the barn. Just need someone to shimmy up there with the rigging to get us started."

"I can do it," Dallas said, raising his hand to volunteer. "I climb trees all the time."

"Then we should make two," Bunker said, pointing at another oak tree.

"For crossfire," Burt added.

Bunker nodded, wishing they had two of the M1400 TrackingPoints. "Redundancy is important."

Deputy Daisy showed up with a box of bandages in her hand. She held the delivery out.

Bunker locked eyes with the capable brunette. "Are those for me?" he joked.

Daisy gave the Band-Aids to Sheriff Apollo. "Actually, they're for all of you. Compliments of Mrs. Rainey."

"Martha obviously has the utmost confidence in us," Apollo said with a slight grin, taking the gift.

"We all do. Well, sort of," Daisy said with a smile. "How's everything going out here? Need any help?"

Bunker knew her last question was coming. Daisy wasn't shy about getting her hands dirty. Or bloody, for that matter. "Sure, we can always use another pair of hands. Just working through some logistics on how best to secure the area."

"What about explosives for the bridge?" she asked. "In case our defenses don't hold."

"I was *just* going to say that," Victor said, shooting a look at Dallas.

"That's a good idea," Sheriff Apollo said. "We might get ourselves into a position where we need to blow it."

Bunker didn't agree with Daisy's idea entirely. But it had some merit. "It would have to be as a last resort. Because once we cut ourselves off from the rest of the planet, we'll have no way across the river. Like with the sniper hides, it's important that we maintain at least one escape route."

Albert and Dustin arrived with bottles of water. The first one went to Bunker, the second to Daisy. She twisted off the cap and took a swig while the fat man's attention lingered on her figure.

Bunker waited for Albert to bring his eyes to him, but he never did. Bunker got the sense that it wasn't an accident. Maybe their altercation in the barn earlier had calmed the fire inside of Albert. Bunker hoped it did. For everyone's sake.

Burt spoke next. "If we rig up some ropes, we might be able to Tarzan our way across the river. If it came down to that."

"That's a terrible idea," Albert snarled, his tone sharp.

"You don't even know what we're talking about," Burt snapped. "Why don't you go hang out with the women, where you belong?"

"Guys. Let's keep it civil, please," Apollo said.

"We'd have to hide the rope in the trees," Dicky said, breaking his silence.

"And have some way to get to them," Rusty added.

Bunker shook his head. "In theory, that might work if the enemy doesn't spot them first. Otherwise, we're defending two entry points instead of one. Either way, I'm not sure it helps the women and kids. They'll struggle to make it across."

"So will I," Albert said.

"Me too," Dustin said. "It'll take too much upper body strength."

"Well, at least some of us could get the hell out of here if the bridge is taken out. It's better than nothing," Burt said.

"How much rope do you have?" Albert asked Burt, his flabby cheeks wiggling with each syllable.

Burt shrugged, his eyebrows pinched. "I don't know exactly. It's coiled up."

"Take a guess. Are we talking a hundred feet, or what?"

"More like a thousand. Tuttle has a bunch."

"What are you thinking?" Bunker asked Albert, trying to forget the heavy man's insults from the barn earlier. It wasn't easy to let those feelings go, but he needed to take the high road.

"A suspension walkway and a catapult. But we'd need explosives and a delivery system. Something we can use to launch the ropes over the river."

Burt scoffed. "Okay, genius, how do you anchor it on the other side? It's gotta hold weight."

"They're called grappling hooks, dumbass. You *do* know how to weld, right?"

"Of course I do."

"Good. Then all we have to do is shoot a couple of ropes across with hooks to catch on the trees. Then a couple of guys crawl across with lead ropes so they can secure everything. Then we pull the rest of the walkway across. Some wood planks and a little bush engineering should do the trick. Even the women and kids could use it."

"And your fat ass," Burt said.

"Yeah. Even me. I don't think it'll be that hard, as long as we use the proper amount of explosives. Hell, I could even mix some up, if I had the proper chemicals."

"He's a chemistry genius," Dustin added, his eyes searching for someone who was listening. "Tin Man is the bomb."

CHAPTER 10

When the nickname *Tin Man* landed on Bunker's ears, a memory stirred in his mind. It was a vision from his days in The Kindred biker gang, back when he provided security for his boss, Connor Watts, whenever Watts attended a business meeting.

The drugs-for-money exchanges always took place on the south side of LA in the abandoned warehouse district. Plus, they usually involved the crew of the infamous meth cook who went by the name *Tin Man,* a legend who pioneered the formula behind the purest form of ice ever to hit the streets, Clearwater Red. Occasionally Tin Man would attend the meetings himself, passing Bunker at the checkpoint he'd set up.

Bunker studied Albert and let his eyes take in every contour of the guy's round face. He'd only seen Tin Man a couple of times, but this unimpressive deputy could be the same guy.

Bunker also needed to consider the name of the drug, Clearwater Red, and the name of the town he'd stumbled into after the train incident. Was it purely coincidence that they matched, or was it another clue?

If Albert was Tin Man, he wasn't showing any indication that he recognized Bunker, or knew his secret past. Otherwise, Albert never would've gotten in his face in the barn over grave digging duty. Only an idiot would antagonize the head of security for The Kindred biker gang and expect to live through it.

Then again, there was a rumor floating around that Tin Man was a Tae Kwon Do expert. If that was true, Albert couldn't be the legendary meth cook. A man of his size would never be nimble enough to carry out the moves required.

No, it was more likely Albert knew of Tin Man's reputation and decided to impersonate him. To what end, Bunker couldn't be sure.

It would be easy enough to test Albert's chemistry skills by having him mix some of the improvised chemicals Bunker was thinking about deploying in their fight against the Russians. Assuming it came down to that.

Of course, that test would only happen if Tuttle had the necessary materials on hand, and Bunker could find a suitable ambush point. There was a lot to figure out before he brought his ideas to the rest of the group, but at least a plan was starting to form.

"We'll need Burt to fabricate some launch tubes," Apollo said, snapping Bunker back to reality.

"Not a problem," Burt answered. "Saw some steel pipe in Tuttle's bone yard."

"There's a huge stack of old pallets we could use for the boards," Dallas said. "They're in the back, just past the pile of fifty-gallon drums and some wooden spools."

"Spools?" Burt asked.

"Yeah, the kind the cable company uses on the back of their trucks for their wire. My dad made a backyard table out of one of them. Tuttle must have been collecting all that junk for a while."

"We'll need to find a place down river a bit," Bunker said. "If we need to egress quickly, we'll want a head start and effective cover."

"Guys . . . that's all well and good, but we still need explosives," Albert added, his eyes holding onto Bunker's.

Bunker nodded, noticing the odd look from Albert. He turned his attention to Apollo. "Did you notice any when you and Daisy were taking inventory?"

"No. But it wouldn't surprise me if Tuttle has them around here—somewhere. He seems to have everything else."

"Probably hidden," Daisy added. "When I was here the first time, he hinted at a secondary bunker. Not just the one in the barn."

"I know where we can get some," Victor said.

Apollo whirled his head around to peer at the longhaired boy. "Where?"

"At the stables. I know for a fact that Atwater has a cabinet full of stuff in his store. Plus, a ton of ammo. Even some guns. Nice ones."

"How exactly do you know all that?" Apollo asked, his tone reminiscent of a detective grilling a suspect.

"Ah, well, uh," the kid stammered, fumbling the words. "I think I heard Megan talking about it on the bus. You know, before it crashed."

"So, let me get this straight . . . a little girl, who you probably don't know very well, just so happens to mention explosives, guns and ammo on the bus? Out of the blue?"

"Yeah, Sheriff. But it wasn't to me. It was to one of her friends, I think. I don't know exactly. I wasn't super close when she said it."

Apollo raised an eyebrow and then shot a troubled look a Bunker.

Daisy cleared her throat. "Excuse me, gentlemen, but I think you're overthinking the problem. There's an easier solution for an escape route."

"Oh, yeah? What's that?" Burt asked, his delivery gruff and condescending.

"Since we're in the Rocky Mountains, I'm guessing there are some trees near the ledge. I heard they grow in these parts."

"Yeah, no shit," Burt quipped.

Daisy didn't seem to care about his attitude. "Couldn't we just cut a few of them down to use as the foundation for a bridge? I'm guessing one of you knows how to chop down a tree?"

Apollo pointed at one of his newly appointed deputies. "Seems to me Dicky worked at a logging camp a few years ago. I'm sure he can handle it."

"Yes sir, I did. In Alaska. Spent three summers running chainsaws."

The expression on Daisy's face indicated she'd expected that answer. "Just make sure they land where you need them. If they're tall enough, they'll span the gap, right?"

Daisy's idea about dropping trees gave Bunker an idea. Not for their escape route, but for setting up a Russian ambush. He filed the idea away, saving it until later.

"Absolutely, they'll be tall enough," Dicky answered. "We can pre-cut most of the branches, too. Just need to make a climbing harness so I can get up there."

Burt threw out his hands. "But we still have to get across. We can't just tightrope our way over a drop like that."

Daisy's piercing eyes scanned Burt from head to toe, pausing for a moment on his well-worn shoes. "No, of course not. But if you had sections of the walkway already built, then we could just slide them into position and nail them in place as we go."

Burt didn't respond.

Daisy finished her explanation. "I'd suggest making them a bit wider than we think we'll need so they'll cover the width of the tree spacing if Dicky's aim is off a smidge. Seems easy enough, assuming there's a chainsaw around here that still works."

"Dallas and I saw a few of them in the barn on a workbench," Victor said.

Bunker looked at Burt, needing to deliver a directive while he was thinking about it. "When you're finished with the Land Rovers, we'll need to park them on the other side of the river as part of our x-fill."

"After I fortify them, I'm assuming."

"Roger that."

"Should probably hide the keys somewhere close, too."

"Actually, no. I need you to rewire them with a quick start mechanism."

"A push button type thing?"

Bunker nodded, thinking of the Humvees in Afghanistan. "We won't have time to deal with keys."

"Wouldn't that make it easy for someone to steal them?" Victor asked.

Burt motioned with two fingers. "I could design it so a pair of buttons on the radio have to be pressed while you start it."

"That's a cool idea," Rusty said. "I didn't know you could do that."

"Sure. People do that all the time. Usually when they're tired of their cars getting jacked. I'll have to run all new electrical, though. But it shouldn't be a problem."

"Tuttle has a bunch of electrical wire in his workshop," Dallas said. "Big spools of it."

A new idea flashed in Bunker's thoughts after he heard the words *big spools of wire*. "Guys, I have a slightly different idea. It's based on all of your suggestions, which were excellent by the way. Instead of dropping those trees with a chainsaw, how about we use the Massey Harvester like a winch and lower a premade walkway into position."

"Like a drawbridge," Daisy added.

"Exactly."

Burt nodded, his upper lip tucked under. "I see where you're going with this. The harvester's weight should anchor everything in place, then we use its engine and the gears on the header out front to let ropes drop the bridge into place. It'll take a lot of welding to build the framework we'll need."

"Can you do it?"

"As long as I can find the parts in the boneyard, I don't see why not. Though I'm going to need some help if I'm gonna get the sniper hides built, the Rovers fortified, and the other stuff done any time soon."

"Rusty? Victor? Dallas?" Bunker asked, flashing a look at all three kids.

"Sure, happy to," Rusty answered. The other two nodded in earnest.

"But before I do, Bunker. Can I talk to you in private?"

Bunker nodded, then the two of them stepped away. "What's up?"

Burt's eyes tightened as he spoke. "I don't mind helping out, but I don't work for free."

"I can't pay you, if that's what you're asking."

"No, not exactly. I was thinking more about a trade."

"Okay, we might be able to arrange something."

"I want the TrackingPoint rifle when this is over."

Bunker didn't like the idea, but he didn't have much of a choice. Without Burt's skills, there was little chance any of them would survive an encounter with hostiles. He held out a hand for a shake.

When Burt grabbed it, Bunker said, "Agreed."

Burt let go of his hand, but didn't return to the group. "Oh, and there's one more thing."

"What?"

"I want to be the one in the first sniper hide. If I'm building it, then I get to take out the first Russian."

"Have you taken a shot like that before? At a human target?"

"No, but I've been hunting all my life. And just so you know, I rarely miss."

"Shooting a man is not the same as taking down a deer, Burt."

"Ah, bullshit. You aim. You fire. How hard is that? Especially when it's them or us. Trust me, it won't be a problem."

Bunker disagreed, but needed to soften his objection. "I've seen stronger men than you freeze in the heat of battle. It's not as easy as you think."

"Then they were a bunch of fucking pussies."

Bunker didn't respond.

"Look, it's simple. If you want all this welding work done, then that's the deal. It's non-negotiable."

Bunker paused, needing to consider all the angles. Burt seemed sure of himself, but trusting an untrained civilian with the security of the group was not the right move.

Yet, on the other hand, the TrackingPoint rifle would greatly increase the odds of success. "Okay, you have a deal. But I'll need to bring you up to speed on that rifle. Apollo, too. It's not like anything you guys have shot before."

"Why Apollo? I thought we just agreed on me?"

"As backup. Cross-training is important."

"Fair enough," Burt said after a pause. "As long as you don't try to fuck me out of this deal."

"My word is my bond," Bunker said, following Burt back to the group. However, before he could issue the next directive, Jeffrey arrived with a basket full of eggs. "What's going on?"

"They're talking about building a drawbridge," Dallas told him.

"Cool," Jeffrey said. "I wanna watch."

Apollo shook his head. "I don't think that's such a good idea, Jeffrey. Your mother's waiting for those eggs."

"But I wanna see."

"You need to run along now, son. Let the grownups handle this."

"But Victor and Dallas aren't grownups," Jeffrey whined.

Apollo hesitated for a moment before he spoke. "No, they're not, but they're helping Mr. Bunker and me, just like you need to go help your mom. We've all got our jobs to do. And yours is to help your mother."

Jeffrey dropped his head and turned away.

Bunker noticed a brown stain on the kid's hands, and across his clothes. "Hang on, Jeffrey. What's that on your shirt?"

Jeffrey stopped his departure. "Rust."

"From what?"

"This handle thing I found in the chicken coop. I tripped over it at first."

"What kind of handle?"

"It was round and sitting on a bunch of boards."

"Stacked up boards, or were they flat?"

"Flat. Like a door. I tried to pull it up, but it was too heavy."

Bunker flashed a look at Daisy. "Secondary bunker?"

CHAPTER 11

The armed escort tugged at Seth Buckley's arm as the Mayor was led down the corridor on the third floor of the Town Hall.

General Yuri Zhukov had summoned Buckley for an unscheduled meet-and-greet. They were headed to the largest office in the building—the one at end of the hall—Buckley's former office.

The guard grabbed Buckley by the back of the shirt collar and stopped him just short of the door. An empty nameplate holder stared back at Buckley.

A crisp Russian command found its way through the door from the inside. The door flung open and the guard forced him inside with a firm jab to the back of his neck.

Buckley took an off-balance step forward, landing in the grasp of yet another guard. The trim man with a huge, mangled nose led him to the front of the desk—an expensive desk that belonged to Buckley.

A high-ranking Russian officer with thick forearms and a square jaw sat behind the work surface. His rear end was nestled in the high-back executive chair, its leather plush and inviting.

General Zhukov's head was down, buried in a stack of paperwork. His right hand was busy scribbling across the paper with a pen, while his left worked a grip training device, squeezing the spring-loaded handles in rapid-fire succession.

Despite the squeaks of metal, the time between compressions held steady at about one every half second. Zhukov's short-cropped hair may have been laced with peppered gray, but he was obviously in terrific shape—at least his hands and forearms.

Buckley wasn't sure if he should speak, so he kept quiet and took the opportunity to look around his former office. All of his belongings were missing, including plaques, awards, certificates, artwork, knickknacks, and family pictures.

The bookshelves were empty, with only a smattering of dust remaining. The credenza was now to the right and turned around against the adjacent wall, its sliding doors facing the drywall.

Both visitor chairs were gone, probably to intimidate anyone who entered, forcing them to stand with nervous legs like Buckley. Nothing looked the same except for the placement of the desk and the brand-new chair he'd ordered from Amazon two weeks prior.

Two armed soldiers stood behind Zhukov, their eyes facing the picture window. The rumble and hum of activity outside told Buckley another convoy of supply trucks had rolled into town. He figured the two soldiers were keeping an eye on the truck deployment below.

Two equipment towers rose up into view beyond the glass, each recently erected by the occupying force.

Razor sharp concertina wire and other barricades were now encircling the town, with armed checkpoints established at every entry point. Sandbags, heavy trucks, machine guns, scanning equipment, spotters, snipers, and a slew of support troops kept watch on everything. Nobody was getting in or out, not without the Russians knowing about it.

Tri-color flags hung on buildings all over town, one dangling from the arms of the mammoth bronze statue commemorating Cyrus Clearwater, the town founder.

The flag's equal-sized horizontal white, blue, and red stripes may have looked plain and non-threatening, but that was not how they felt. Sure, the former Soviet Union's golden hammer and sickle was gone. So was the red star on top, but this version of Russia's flag still carried fear for anyone unfortunate enough to be trapped under its rule.

To the left of Zhukov was another man in a drab-green military uniform, only he wasn't carrying an assault rifle like the others. His lone weapon was on his hip: a black pistol in a holster. Some kind of satchel hung across his chest, its leather strap running from upper left to lower right.

Buckley could feel the weight of the man's eyes wash over him. He checked for a nametag on the observer's shirt. However, as expected, it wasn't there. None of the Russians he'd come across had displayed any form of ID, stenciled or otherwise.

He found that odd, given the number of troops in town. They couldn't have all known each other by face, could they? He didn't think that was possible and certainly not while in full tactical gear, including helmets and sunglasses. If he was right, then they had another method of identification. Something less obvious, but reliable.

The Mayor's desk contained at least a dozen stacks of folders and three rolls of white paper—each about three feet long. Buckley assumed they were maps, with Russian lettering on the outside. He could also see a bleed-through of various colors. Some were irregularly shaped, while others were blocky. Typical of a topographical map.

Zhukov looked up, his face stiff and focused as he continued the grip training. He motioned to the man on the left to move forward, which he did, snapping to attention once he arrived.

The General gave him a command in Russian, the syllables quick and to the point. The guard gave a single head nod in response before leaving the room with a hurried step.

There was no doubt who was in charge of this occupation. Likewise, there was no doubt about the precision and planning that went into this event. Nothing seemed to be happenstance or an afterthought.

Zhukov moved the hand squeezer to his other palm, never taking a second off. He sifted through one of the stacks before pulling out several files, each one with a streak of red ink running across the tab.

Other folders carried different colors: yellow, green, and blue.

Zhukov opened the first of the red-labeled folders and spun it around to face the Mayor. He cranked out a dozen more grip compressions, before he pointed and said, "Missing."

The left flap contained a photo of Daisy Clark, its edges held in place by a series of staples. She was in uniform and talking with a pair of elderly women on the street, both of whom carried shopping bags. Charmer's Market and Feed Store was the backdrop in the photo.

The right side of the folder held a light stack of papers. They'd been attached with twin hole-punches at the top and a metal fastener. If Buckley had to guess, he'd say there were about ten sheets of paper in total.

On top of the stack was a pre-printed form that featured various black-lined boxes of differing size and placement across the white. The words inside the rectangles were Russian, the strange symbols evident. So were the interspersed occurrences of the letter R, written in reverse.

Even though he couldn't read the foreign text, it was obvious the paperwork was some kind of dossier on the Sheriff's deputy. The snapshot was an action photo taken at a distance, not a still portrait as expected. Someone had been taking undercover shots.

Zhukov put the second folder next to the first and opened it, once again saying the word "missing." Like the first file, it was red-inked with a photo to the left and a writeup to the right.

Buckley recognized the full-color portrait of Gus Apollo. It was the same image of the Sheriff from the town's website. The Russians must have been trolling the Internet for information, where they grabbed the photo online.

The General continued, laying out folder after folder. Each was related to citizens he recognized: Dick Dickens, Stephanie King, Jeffrey King, Martha Rainey, Burt Lowenstein, Franklin Atwater, Megan, and the Mayor's grandson, Rusty.

Most of the images were action photos, again taken covertly at a distance. Dicky's and Burt's folders were redlined in ink, as were Daisy's and Apollo's, but the rest were color-coded in green. Buckley assumed the colors represented each person's threat level, with red being the highest.

Zhukov presented another series of files featuring residents who lived beyond the city limits, most in the surrounding forest. One was a redlined file, but the remainder were marked in green or yellow.

Another row of paperwork was put before the Mayor, this time with faces he didn't recognize. He assumed these were some of the remote families living off the grid, their photos taken in the forest.

After Zhukov stopped his presentation, he put the hand grip device down and leaned back in the office chair and said, "Need location."

Buckley hesitated. He needed to think this through. Every word he said from here on out might put people at risk.

He shrugged. "I don't know. Some of them are probably on vacation. People come and go all the time around here. It's not like we have checkpoints to log people in and out. This is the United States of America, or at least it used to be."

Zhukov brought his elbows up and put them on the armrests. He sat up with his back straight, then put his hands together and cracked his knuckles, his stare even more intimidating than before. "Location, Mayor. Now."

Buckley took a moment to study the open files once again. He noticed a few people were missing: Allison Rainey and her son Victor, plus the odd pair of temporary deputies, Albert and Dustin. They were not accounted for in the open files, either. Neither was Jack Bunker, but that wasn't a surprise since he'd just arrived after the EMP.

The incomplete set of files meant the Russian intel wasn't up to date or accurate, especially since they didn't have a folder dedicated to longtime resident and legendary fruitcake, Frank Tuttle.

Buckley wasn't sure if the Russian information gaps were a good thing or not, but it meant there was hope. They still needed him. Perhaps he could leverage their deficiencies to his advantage. To do that, he needed to play it cool and not show fear.

Zhukov snapped his finger in the air with a quick flip of his wrist.

An instant later, Buckley felt something hard press against the back of his head. He assumed the guard behind him was holding his rifle in a firing position, its sights trained on the back of his skull.

Buckley gulped, then took in a full draw of air. "As I said before, I don't know where these people are. Hell, I don't even know half of them."

Zhukov nodded at his guard, who promptly pressed the barrel of the rifle harder against Buckley's scalp.

Buckley knew that the longer he stood there in silence, the harder it was going to be to keep his panic in check. His lungs wanted to pump out oxygen at full tilt, but he managed to regain control of his breathing. "Look, General, if you shoot me, then I can't help you. And trust me, from the looks of it, you're gonna need my help."

Buckley pointed at the files on the desk to reinforce his words. "Not only with finding the missing people, but with maintaining order. People around here don't like being told what to do or where they can go. They *will* resist and I'm sure neither of us wants that. So let me help you, General. Give me some time to check around. Maybe someone knows where these people are."

Zhukov didn't answer but kept his eyes on Buckley, his face locked in a scowl. He picked up the grip trainer and went to work again with his fingers.

Buckley got the sense that these soldiers practiced their facial expressions for hours on end, all in an attempt to maximize their intimidation level without ever having to say a word. It was working, the tingle across Buckley's spine intense and growing. So was the tremble in his hands.

He brought his fingers together and began a rub—hand over hand—pretending to lather up with soap. He had no idea if Zhukov could sense his anxiety, but Buckley decided to continue his ruse.

Zhukov twitched his eyes, then sent his free hand into another stack of folders, this time pulling out a file with a streak of black ink along the tab. He stood up, his height rising several inches above Buckley's.

The General opened the file and put it on the front of the desk. The folder held two photographs, one attached to the left and one to the right. Buckley didn't see any paperwork associated with either image—just the snapshots.

Zhukov jammed his index finger into the photo on the left. As usual, the general kept his words to a minimum. "Identify."

Buckley studied the image. It was an overhead shot of some kind of forest camp. He counted six small buildings spread out across the landscape. Shacks possibly, he couldn't be sure.

He also thought a broken-down windmill was present, not far from two people near the entrance to one of the structures. The pair were standing apart, on either side of what he assumed was the door. Both of them had dark hair and clothing, and looked to be carrying rifles in their hands.

Buckley moved his eyes to the photo on the right. It was a snapshot of the same scene, only this time the camera's focal point was much tighter and held in a zoom, yielding a grainy portrayal of the two unidentified individuals. Their faces were blurry from the resulting pixilation, but the shadows told him one of them was shorter than the other.

A man and woman, he surmised, noticing the longer hair on the smaller figure. The man had dark splotches on his forearms. He thought the duo might be Bunker and Daisy.

Behind them was another figure several yards away, only this person wasn't standing. Buckley could see an outline of legs and arms surrounded by a brown and green fuzz. Someone must have been lying in the grass.

Buckley flipped the image up to see if another photo might be stacked underneath. There was. Again, it showed the same camp from altitude, only this time there were five people in front of the shack. One of them might have been a kid based on the much shorter length of the shadow. Wait, check that, two of them were children.

The person lying in the grass hadn't moved despite all the activity. Must have been a corpse. Or a very patient sniper.

Buckley brought his eyes to the Russian commander. "What am I looking at here? Where is this?"

"Camp. Identify," Zhukov said, sounding impatient.

Buckley shrugged. "Can't see their faces. Could be anyone."

Zhukov grunted, but didn't respond.

Buckley decided to continue, wanting to show confidence and strength. "You're going to need better satellite photos than this, General. Otherwise, I can't help you." He wanted to take a shot at the Russians for their inferior technology, but decided against it.

He knew US satellites could zoom in on a squirrel's penis from a hundred miles up, a fact he assumed the General knew all too well. Rubbing it in would accomplish nothing, other than getting him shot.

"From drone. Not satellite," Zhukov said, tossing the grip tensioner onto the desk again.

"Still, I can't see anything."

After a two-count, the General looked at his guard and motioned to the right with his head. The metal against Buckley's head pulled away, but the guard didn't, his boots still visible behind Buckley's polished dress shoes.

The door to the office swung open and in walked the observer from before. He wasn't alone. A female soldier was following close behind—a slender blonde with soft eyes and a petite, sculpted nose.

She was devastatingly pretty, despite the lack of makeup. Her cheekbones were her most noticeable feature, defined and alluring. So were her shapely lips and bronze skin. If he didn't know she was Russian, he would have taken her to be a Brazilian goddess. Someone you'd see dancing half-naked on a street during Carnival.

The blonde came forward with a field radio in her hand and put it on Zhukov's desk. The General had a short conversation with her in Russian, after which she turned to face Buckley. "General Zhukov would like me to translate for him. He finds English to be torture for his tongue." Her words were crisp and easy to understand.

Zhukov immediately snapped at her, his eyes fierce.

Her face tensed as she stammered to get the words out. "I misspoke, Mayor. The General finds English distasteful and inefficient."

"Okay, sure. I get it. Whatever the General needs," Buckley answered. "I have to say, your English is excellent."

"I studied English for three years at the university in Kiev."

"They taught you well."

"Thank you. The General arranged it for me. I owe him my career."

"I'm Mayor Seth Buckley. Pleased to meet you," he said in a friendly tone. Despite his trepidation, he thought it best to stay cordial and establish a possible friendship. Yet it didn't seem appropriate to offer his hand for a shake, so he kept it at his side.

She gave him a single head nod and a slight smile. "Valentina Zakharova, Communications Officer."

Zhukov interrupted the pleasantries with a two-minute diatribe filled with hand gestures, obviously frustrated about something. His eyes dropped to her small but shapely chest, lingering for a full second before they focused on something else.

Valentina nodded at her boss before speaking to Buckley. "General Zhukov has sent out patrols to locate the missing residents. It would be helpful if you could assist in the search by providing coordinates of each person's current location. Your assistance would help keep the situation calm."

Buckley shook his head. "Good thing you're here to translate because the General must not have understood me earlier when I said I don't know where they are. People come and go all the time around here. This is Colorado, not Russia. We don't keep tabs on everyone."

Zhukov responded in Russian.

Valentina translated. "The General says he understood you perfectly. However, he doesn't believe you. You are the Mayor and in command of this town."

Buckley couldn't hold back an involuntary snort. "In command? Me? Hell, half the people didn't even vote for me. If it weren't for a few extra votes in the runoff election three years ago, Billy Jack would have been elected Mayor, not me. So no. I'm not in command. Not like the General thinks. I wish I could help, but I can't."

"I understand. I will relay to the General that you refuse to cooperate."

His chest tightened before he threw up his hands. "Wait! Wait! That's not what I said. I'd like to cooperate, I just don't have the information he's looking for."

She paused, blinking her pleasant eyes as she stared with intensity at something over his left shoulder.

Right then, the hairs on the back of Buckley's neck sent a shiver down his shine when he realized she was looking at the guard behind him.

He sucked in a short gulp of air and held it as he followed her gaze to check the location and status of the guard behind him.

The slender man hadn't moved, still holding the same position as before. Buckley wasn't sure why she was looking at the guard in that manner. Must be her concentration look, he figured, letting out the breath from his lungs.

The observer in the corner walked to Valentina. He leaned forward to whisper something into her ear in Russian. She nodded a few seconds later, then spoke to Zhukov, though the length of her communication seemed to be twice as long as what Buckley had just told her about his desire to cooperate.

Perhaps she was adlibbing. Hopefully for the better, trying to get his point across to the short-tempered General. Then again, the observer had just intervened with the murmur in her ear. Who knew what he told her?

When she finished relaying her message, Zhukov scoffed before he shot out from behind the desk. He began to pace the room, his hands locked together behind his back. At the end of each run, he'd look at Valentina and hold her eyes, like a father deciding on a punishment.

Buckley kept an eye on the deliberate steps of the commander, waiting for the man to say something. Buckley thought he'd been believable and had laid out a good case for his continued involvement. However, with legendary Russian arrogance filling the room, there was no way to know how the General might react.

It was also possible that Zhukov knew more than he was letting on. If that were true, then this was probably some kind of test. A test Buckley might have just failed by holding back key information.

Those drone photos could have been part of Zhukov's fishing expedition, only showing Buckley the long distance, grainy shots to sample his willingness to help. The test theory would explain why the Russian tech seemed inferior, when in fact it wasn't.

Then again, maybe the shots weren't taken from a Reaper-type, high altitude attack drone. It could have been one of the smaller, portable copter-types. If so, then maybe it was hovering at high altitude and those images were the best it could generate. That alternative explanation made sense as well.

Regardless, Buckley could have made an educated guess as to the whereabouts of the residents in the photos. Even though he didn't know the exact location of the missing persons, he could have sent the Russian patrols in the right direction. Or offered up Daisy and Bunker as the armed persons in the camp photos.

He weighed the odds of each of his theories as the General made his fourth pass. His gut was telling him that the Russians were actually in need of help. Otherwise, he'd be dead by now. A Russian commander doesn't have one of his guards hold a gun to a prisoner's head and then not pull the trigger when the answer isn't what he was expecting.

No, they needed him alive. He was almost sure of it. Someone had to fill the obvious gaps in their intel, and he was the best candidate. That's why they brought in the Mayor of Clearwater. The commander of the town in their eyes.

If Buckley could prove his value, the occupiers might bring him into their inner circle. He knew they'd never trust him, but maybe he could pick up some cross talk or hints about their plans. Then he'd need to figure out a way to get a message to the Sheriff, Daisy, or Bunker. Assuming any of them were still alive.

Part of him hoped his friends had decided to head away from Clearwater. Somewhere safe and not within the reach of the Russians. However, his gut knew better. Those three would never abandon the town. Or their friends. Even Bunker—the man he knew the least about.

Zhukov stopped his pacing and returned to the desk. He sat down in the swivel chair and spoke to the observer at length. The observer nodded mostly, but he did get in a few words before he turned and headed for the office door. A few seconds later, the man was gone from sight, the sound of his boots making quick work of the hallway outside.

The General brought his focus to Valentina. She stepped forward, her posture snapping to attention. Zhukov relayed his orders; her eyes locked and focused.

When the General finished speaking, he waved a quick hand at her before turning his attention to the paperwork on the desk. The man's eyes never came Buckley's way, almost as if Buckley wasn't standing in the room.

Valentina spoke to the guard, again in Russian, then turned her stunning face to Buckley, pausing before she spoke. "The guard will escort you out of the building."

The guard latched onto Buckley's arm.

Buckley tried to pull away, but couldn't. "So that's it? We're done here?"

She gave him a single head nod. "The General is a busy man. You are dismissed."

The guard spun Buckley around and hauled him toward the office door.

Buckley glanced back at Valentina, hoping to glean some information from her before he left his former office.

Valentina's beauty was on full display, filling the room with splendor, but that's where the information ended. Her eyes were devoid of emotion, not giving up a single detail or any impression he could use.

He should have expected as much. These Russians were cold, calculating, and well-trained.

The guard brought him through the door and into the all-white hallway he knew all too well. He'd traveled this same corridor a thousand times before, only this trip was different. He'd just failed biblically. Sure, he'd taken this walk after a failure many times, but never after a fiasco that might affect the lives of everyone in town—and a few who weren't.

He thought he'd kept his cool and played the situation correctly. The Russians' failure was a clear opportunity to work himself inside, but apparently his tactics were wrong. He must have missed something. A hint. A phrase. A look. Otherwise, the guard wouldn't be pulling him along like a prisoner heading for the gallows.

Just then, Bill King appeared at the far end of the corridor. A guard was escorting him as well, but they were heading the opposite way.

The facts lined up in an instant. General Zhukov must have summoned the Silver King Mine owner to his office. A man who would do anything to save his own ass. Or the ass of someone he cared about. Like his son Jeffrey.

A twinge hit Buckley's chest after he realized what he'd missed. The Russians didn't need to rely on him after all. There was another person in town with the stature, the brains, and the balls to work out a deal, and probably sell out everyone else in the process.

The adrenaline soared in Buckley's veins, giving him the strength to pull free from the guard. He flew at King and pushed the slender blond man against the wall with the force of a linebacker taking down a quarterback.

King's back smacked into the wall with a thud.

Buckley's chest was pumping with fire when he looked up and let the words fly from his lips. "Don't you dare, Bill!"

King grunted, then brought his hands up in an attempt to free himself from Buckley's grip, but his effort failed.

Buckley felt a strength he'd never felt before, wanting to pull back a fist and land a punch in the center of this man's face. He wasn't sure where this anger was coming from, but it was long overdue. "You can't do this, Bill! Those are our friends out there! People you've known a long time!"

"Yeah, and one of them is my son."

The guards pulled them apart, tossing Buckley to the floor in a heap. His shoulder slammed into the base of the wall, sending a sting of pain into his body.

King adjusted his shirt collar, while shooting a look of superiority down at Buckley. The man turned and continued his trek to the General's office with determination in his step.

Valentina was in the hallway, just outside the office door. She must have seen everything, yet her face looked numb. Almost like she'd expected the altercation to happen.

CHAPTER 12

Bunker waited for Sheriff Apollo to pull open the wire mesh door of the metal fencing that surrounded the chicken coop in Tuttle's back yard. Once the hole was large enough, Bunker slipped inside the structure Tuttle had built as a Faraday cage.

Daisy was right behind him, the two of them heading for the secondary door that led to the actual chicken coop.

The birds went wild as two sets of legs invaded their space, clucking and running in random directions. Bunker couldn't believe the raw pandemonium, wings flapping and feathers flying.

"Can you imagine doing this every day?" he asked after his mind flashed a scene of old man Tuttle hobbling his weary bones through the two sets of doors.

Chickens are a high maintenance food source that require regular attention. Building a secondary cage around the coop made little sense, not when you must feed, water, and fetch eggs daily. That's what a normal person would think. Of course, not everyone in Clearwater saw Tuttle as normal. He was anything but.

However, the farther Bunker dug into Tuttle's life, the more he believed Tuttle wasn't simply a crazy old man like everyone thought. *A mad genius* might be a better term, even if Tuttle had a tendency to go overboard.

The working theory was that Tuttle had built this wire structure to appear crazy, when in reality he was hiding something. Something important enough to bury under a mound of chicken shit. On face value, the idea seemed absurd, but after Jeffrey showed up with rust on his hands, they decided to investigate.

Bunker figured Apollo was thankful for his wide hips and extra girth, relegating him to doorman duty since he'd never fit. Yet, given the look on Apollo's face, Bunker was sure the Sheriff wished his nose wasn't downwind. The stench of feces was strong, permeating the yard.

Daisy tapped Bunker on the arm and pointed to the left. "Jeffrey said it was over there, near the watering station."

When a rooster came at Bunker with its beak in attack mode, he swatted at it with a backhand. The bird dodged the swipe, but didn't back down. It came at him repeatedly, each time landing a blow near the bandage wrapped around Bunker's forearm. "Damn, El Chappo is pissed."

Apollo laughed.

"Maybe I can herd him into a corner. Hang on," Daisy said, moving her feet quickly with hands outstretched. The bird changed direction and ran the other way.

"See if you can keep him there," Bunker said, sending his hand into the straw. He fished in the sticky mess until he found a ring of metal, then reported, "Got it!"

A second later Bunker had the door open, its hinges complaining in a squeal of metal on metal. The straw and other clutter clung to its surface, no doubt held in place by the abundance of excrement.

Even if the man in black hadn't gunned down Tuttle, Bunker didn't think the chicken coop would've been kept any cleaner. There had to be a month's worth of crap on the floor, literally. Given the mess inside the home, Tuttle obviously didn't prioritize neatness. It was going to take a firehose and a scrub brush to clean off his shoes.

"What's down there?" Apollo asked.

"Not sure. Can't see the bottom. The hatch is angled."

Daisy joined Bunker, her eyes focused on the opening below with her hands on her hips. "Huh, not what I expected. I figured there'd be a regular ladder like what we found with the weapons cache. Not those metal rungs."

"It reminds me of a submarine hatch I once climbed into, though this one doesn't smell like the ocean."

She laughed. "Yeah, I'm guessing there weren't too many chickens onboard a sub."

He smiled, feeling the need for a little humor. "Well, not the kind that still have their heads."

"Do you think he stocked this one with guns and ammo, too?"

"Probably. You never want to keep them all in one place." Bunker bent down and knocked on one of the all-white walls. A deep-toned hollow sound answered back, his knuckle test vibrating across the steel. "Just what I thought."

Daisy knelt down and ran her fingers across the metal. "Nice powder coat."

He nodded. "Some serious cash went into this."

"Prefabricated?"

"That would be my guess. Rust-proof and air-tight."

"What else do you think is down there?"

"Only one way to find out," he said, holding out his hand. "Ladies first."

She shook her head. "Not today, Bunker. Age before beauty."

"Well then, I guess we have more chickens running around here than I thought."

She smacked his arm with a light swat. "Hey watch it, buddy. El Chappo's not the only one who bites."

Bunker couldn't hold back a grin. "Promises. Promises."

Daisy didn't answer.

Bunker let go of his smile, then turned his attention to the trap door when something new caught his eye—something he hadn't noticed before—a steel plate underneath, glued to the boards instead of screwed.

He wasn't sure why Tuttle decided to give the illusion the door was made of wood, but he was happy to see a trio of hydraulic-assisted hinges connecting the thick plate to the walls. Otherwise, the door would have been much harder to open and more dangerous when someone climbed down—like him.

"Watch the door for me," he told Daisy, swinging around to put a foot on the top rung of the down ladder.

She held the door as he descended using the thirty all-white metal rungs, each welded to the walls and spaced about a foot apart.

If he had to guess, he'd estimate the walls to be running at a thirty-degree angle. The design made the climb safer but seemed to be a waste of engineering. A vertical shaft would have been much more efficient and easier to build, especially for something buried thirty feet deep.

The instant his foot landed at the bottom, a series of lights snapped on behind him. He found himself standing on a wood plank in an eight-foot tall tunnel made of corrugated steel. It looked like a giant culvert—the kind of pipe you'd find buried under a roadway to carry runoff water from one side to the other.

He was at the far end of the tunnel, where a bright yellow sign had been hung on the wall next to the ladder. It was about a foot wide and had a set of black, upside-down triangles and the words FALLOUT SHELTER stenciled on it.

A hand-carved wooden plaque hung to the right of the warning sticker. It said *MUD ROOM*.

Directly behind him was a single showerhead hanging from the ceiling. It was centered over a drain in the floor. The words "Decontamination Station" flashed in his mind.

To the right was a stainless steel, thirty-gallon garbage can with a lid on it, plus a whiskbroom and dust pan. Beyond the dust pan was a two-foot piece of plywood with a dense patch of nails sticking up in the center, their tips covered in dried clumps of mud.

"Wait, that can't be right," he muttered. There was no mud above the hatch—only chicken crap, so mud couldn't have been on the nails. That meant it was dried shit, scraped off by Tuttle after running his shoes over the sharp points.

Bunker took advantage of the bed of nails to rid his shoes of a sticky layer of feces, then washed them off with a blast of water from the showerhead. He used the broom and dustpan to quickly sweep up the mess he'd made, then walked across the wooden plank posing as a floor. His destination—the other end of the tunnel.

The corrugated steel corridor came to a stop at a two-way junction. His choices were to turn left or right, then take another corridor like the one he was in.

The two connecting tunnels had overhead lights, each appearing to be about twenty yards in length. He figured they took another sharp turn at the far end, but he couldn't see it from his position.

Bunker returned to the down ladder and craned his neck up. "You gotta get down here and see this."

Daisy climbed down in seconds, her face smothered with anticipation when she arrived. "What is this place?"

"Some kind of underground bunker. I'm not sure if Tuttle built this himself or not, but it looks to be huge."

She held out a hand. "Lead the way."

He pointed to the nails and then the showerhead. "You might want to clean off your shoes first. Close quarters and all."

Daisy did as he suggested before they ambled to the two-way junction, with Bunker leading the charge. He went left and walked to the far end of the connecting tunnel, where it took a ninety-degree turn to the right as expected.

When Bunker found the end of the next tunnel, he came upon a closed door. But not just any door. This was a sealed hatch, much like what you'd find between compartments on a nuclear submarine.

He grabbed the handle in the middle and spun it until the door released. He pushed it open and went inside, stepping over the lower edge of the bulkhead.

The next section wasn't round like the tunnels. It was rectangular and spacious, with heavy beams supporting the steel walls and ceiling in two-foot increments—no doubt engineered to support the weight of the dirt outside.

"Holy crap!" Daisy said after she stepped through the hatch and found her way next to Bunker.

"That's an understatement," Bunker said, taking in the scene before him. The walls and ceiling might have given off an ugly industrial look, but the rest of the space was better appointed and modern. Well, Frank Tuttle's version of modern.

Plush, tan-colored carpet covered the floor from wall to wall. In the middle of the room were a pair of leather couches and a love seat. Three La-Z-Boy chairs completed the seating area, along with two floor lamps and a central coffee table, complete with a glass top. The eight-foot-long dining table in the far corner was a nice touch. So was its overhead chandelier and stable of high-back chairs. A stereo system and flat panel TV hugged the wall in front of the couch, providing a prime viewing angle.

There was even a fancy, curved bar in the corner. The mirrored wall behind it held a shelf full of booze. Bunker counted at least twenty bottles, mostly whiskey based on their familiar labels.

Rows of glasses hung upside down from a wooden rack, directly above a handful of knickknacks sitting on the bar's surface. One of them was a miniature statue of a fat man wearing a white apron. Below the figurine was a placard that said, "Frank's Bar and Grill."

"Now this is what I call a man cave," Bunker said, his tone energized. "Cave being the operative word."

The black and white artwork on the walls failed to match the expensive carpet and modern furnishings. They were military photographs from the 1940s, if Bunker had to guess, each protected in a simple wooden frame.

The action scenes were all different but portrayed the same theme—a beach landing, with troops and equipment storming the sand.

The massive room reminded Bunker of Senator Gray's game room in Laguna Beach, California. He'd only been to the career politician's house on Rivera Drive once with his boss, Connor Watts, but it was a memorable visit. If Bunker remembered correctly, the Senator purchased the mansion for sixty million and wasn't shy about sharing that fact with just about everyone he met.

Bunker spent most of that night standing watch outside of the home, while Watts and Gray drank copious amounts of alcohol and smoked Cuban cigars in celebration of their newfound alliance. When the two-man party was over, Bunker hauled his boss back to their clubhouse to sleep off a wicked hangover.

Tuttle's country version of the Senator's room was almost as nice, if Bunker chose to ignore the bland steel construction. Oh, and the black and white artwork. Senator Gray preferred Picassos.

Bunker and Daisy continued forward, passing the seating area before opening the hatch on the opposing wall. They went through another tunnel that took them to the sleeping quarters.

This section was round and made of corrugated steel like the connecting tunnels, only triple the diameter. Its layout was much more efficient than the living room, with three sets of bunk beds lining the walls on both sides.

Daisy hesitated for a second, pointing at each bunk bed in rapid succession. "This sleeps, what? Eighteen?"

"Tuttle must have been expecting company."

She fiddled with the mattress on the upper bunk closest to her. "The kids are gonna love this."

Just past the third set of beds was a shower, tub, and dual toilets. None of them had privacy walls or curtains.

Bunker pointed at the first toilet. "Yeah, but I'm not so sure about this. I don't know about you, but certain things need to be done in private."

"I won't argue with you there."

The next compartment was the kitchen. It wasn't nearly as spacious as the main room, but featured top-of-the-line Viking appliances and a matching full-sized, built-in double-door fridge—all of them Cobalt Blue.

"I don't know who designed this place," Daisy said, "but I would've added in more counter space and storage. Feeding eighteen people won't be easy."

Bunker pointed at the intersecting point of two of the floorboards. "Looks like storage is underneath."

Daisy bent down and put the tip of her finger inside a plastic recess taking the place of one of the corners. She pried the floorboard up, revealing a two-foot-wide storage space underneath.

Inside were at least two dozen #10 long-term food cans lying on their side with labels facing up. Mostly pasta and potatoes, though there were a number of veggies, too.

Bunker turned the knob on the faucet in the sink and ran his hand under the stream. "Instant hot water. Nice touch."

"I got first dibs on the tub," Daisy quipped. "Heaven knows I need a bath."

Bunker laughed. "You mean the tub without a curtain?"

"Yeah, we'll have to solve that little problem first."

"If not, we can find a volunteer who'll gladly stand guard for ya. I'm pretty sure Albert's been checking you out."

Her face went tense as she wagged her index finger at him. "Oh, don't even go there, Bunker. Not unless you wanna see me pull my gun again."

Bunker smiled, then opened the door to the fridge. He scanned its interior. The shelves were stocked, but not with food. Bottled water and cans of beer were the only two items. The contents of each shelf alternated from one type of beverage to the other, filling every square inch with inventory.

"The man obviously loved his beer," Daisy said in a jovial tone.

"Don't we all."

"At least it's not that crappy light beer. Might as well drink water at that point."

Bunker appreciated her taste for what he considered God's beverage. Though he did enjoy his share of whiskey, too. "Nothing quite like a cold one. Especially on a hot summer day."

She put her hand inside and snatched a can, then held it in his direction. "My treat."

His mouth watered when he thought about popping the lid and downing it quickly. The cool mountain freshness of this particular brand would have been heaven. "Nah, I'll pass. We got too much work to do. Need to stay sharp. Maybe when this is all over, we can indulge in some serious brain cell killing. But for now, we need to keep moving."

Daisy put the can back on the shelf and grabbed two bottles of water. She gave one of them to Bunker. "I figured as much. But I needed to be sure."

"So, what? That was a test?"

"Yeah, but not just for you," she answered, removing the cap and taking a few swigs of water.

"I see. You wanted to slam one, too."

"Was thinking about it."

Bunker took a drink, swallowing hard in preparation for another round. "Like I said, later."

She paused, tilting her head a bit. Her eyes ran soft before her lips grew into a smile. "It's a date, then."

"Copy that," he said, holding back the rest of what he wanted to say. He took a step toward the next compartment, but stopped his feet when he noticed the puzzled look on Daisy's face. "Something wrong?"

Her eyes darted around the kitchen. "Can I ask you something?"

He worried it was going to be a personal question after her comment about a date. "Yeah, shoot."

"How exactly did Tuttle get all this stuff down here? It's not like the fridge or stove could fit through that hatch."

"Good question. Must be another entry point somewhere."

"Yeah, maybe," she said, pausing. "But he still couldn't have hauled them down the narrow tunnels. Or pushed them through those bulkheads. They're too small."

She was right, leaving only one answer. "Must have been pre-installed before they lowered this section and buried it."

Daisy nodded. "Makes sense."

"I'm sure that's why he spent the money on these high-end appliances."

"Because replacing them would be next to impossible."

Bunker agreed. "He needed stuff that would last."

They continued their exploration of the subterranean base, working their way out of the food prep area through another airtight blast door.

Tuttle had planned this horseshoe-shaped complex well, every section spaced out and protected from the previous. It was almost as if he was expecting some kind of catastrophic event to take place underground.

Whether that be a fire, a virus, invasion, or something else, Bunker wasn't sure. The fire extinguishers hanging on the walls before and after each blast door had him leaning toward fire. Regardless, he was impressed with Tuttle's madness. A madness masquerading as genius, if Bunker chose to look hard enough.

After a ninety-degree right turn, they traveled into another rectangular section containing a generous supply of equipment and hardware—both large and small—everything from nuts and bolts on up to refrigerators. A workbench sat to the right, with a sheet of pegboard hanging behind it on the wall. Hand tools, saws, and tape were the most prevalent items, each hanging from a hook.

"Looks like you were right," Daisy said, moving her feet toward the stack of Cobalt Blue appliances in the corner. Tuttle had two of everything. "These are the same models we saw in the kitchen." She looked at the blast door again, her hands up and spaced apart. "Still won't fit."

"He's using them for parts."

She nodded after a short pause, then her voice dropped in pitch and developed an accent, as if she were trying to imitate a country man. "A man's got to have backups, Daisy."

He laughed, appreciating her theatrics. "Tuttle?"

"Yeah. Something he said to me a few days ago."

"Well, he's right. Redundancy is important."

"He obviously believed it."

"I can't imagine how long he's been at this."

"Or how much he spent."

"I guess when you live alone and never leave your homestead, you can get a lot of work done."

"If the walls don't start talking to you first," she said, laughing.

Electrical panels covered the wall opposite the bench, with a handful of conduit piping linking them together. The three Tesla Powerwall v2.0 battery units installed down the center caught his attention. "I was wondering when we'd run into his battery array. Looks like he went all out."

Daisy didn't respond, her head down and feet moving for the exit door of the section. He wasn't sure if something was pulling her forward, or she simply wasn't interested in Tuttle's tech. Either way, he decided to follow her lead.

The next corridor had a blast door at the far end as expected. However, this tunnel had a feature not found in the others—a junction at its midpoint. It branched off to the left, which was odd since every turn they'd taken since the first intersection was a ninety-degree right. Bunker assumed the series of right turns would complete a closed horseshoe shape that would take them back where they started.

"Hmmm. I wonder what's down there?" Daisy asked, standing shoulder to shoulder with Bunker.

"If I had to guess, another way out. The main hatch can't be the only access point. Not if Tuttle planned this as well as I think he did."

"Which way should we go?"

"Straight ahead. Let's see what's in the next compartment. If my bearings are correct, it's the last section before we head back to where we started."

She marched ahead without hesitation, her hands making quick work of the spin wheel in the center of the door. She opened it.

Bunker waited for her to step inside, but her feet didn't move. He put a hand on her shoulder, letting her know he was in position and ready to proceed. She still didn't advance. "Something wrong?"

She nodded with her knees locked, her eyes never wandering from the view into the next room. "Uh . . . we might want to take a minute and think about this."

Bunker pushed in next to Daisy, leaning past her arm. He peered inside, his vision filling with stacks of wooden crates and barrels—dozens them— each with black lettering stenciled on their sides.

It took a few seconds for his brain to catch up to what his eyes were reporting: TNT, gunpowder, charcoal, and Tannerite.

When his mouth finally joined the party, he said, "Now that's a stockpile."

Bunker stepped over the bulkhead and took position to the right. He wanted to swing his head around to check on Daisy, but couldn't pry his eyes from the four containers labeled IMX-101.

It wasn't long before he heard footsteps coming his way, then a rustle of air wandering in from the left.

"What's IMX?" she asked.

"If I'm not mistaken, it's a new high-grade explosive I've read about. Something new since I served."

She took a step toward the door. "Sounds dangerous."

"Actually, just the opposite. It stands for Insensitive Munitions Explosive. The Army wanted something much more stable in their arsenal. But I didn't know it was already in the field."

She bent down and picked up a series of clear plastic bags, each filled with powder inside. "What's all this for?"

Bunker could see their labels as she picked them up in pairs: Red Iron Oxide Fe_2O_3, Barium Nitrate $BaNo_{3/2}$, Sulfur, Potassium Nitrate KNO_3, and Aluminum Power, 30 Micron. "Base chemicals to mix, in case he ran out of the final product."

"You can buy all this stuff?"

"Everything but the IMX. It's military-issue only."

"How did Tuttle get his hands on it?"

"He couldn't. Not unless he had a source inside the Army."

"Or former Army. Like Franklin," Daisy said.

"I suppose, but that would mean they were involved in some kind of black market sales of munitions. Does that sound like them?"

She paused for a moment, then shook her head with vigor. "Tuttle was a little unhinged, but he wasn't a criminal. Neither was Franklin."

"Are you sure?"

Her eyes lit up. "Positive. There's no way either of them was an arms dealer."

Bunker couldn't stop the next set of words from leaving his lips. He felt compelled to take a shot at his own past. "Sometimes, people aren't what they appear to be. Even close friends."

"Yeah, I know. Tell me about it," she said in a steady tone, raising one eyebrow in the process. "But not Tuttle and Franklin."

"Then this must be something else."

"It has to be," she added.

"At least now we know why he designed this place with the blast doors," Bunker said, taking an unplanned step toward the first container of IMX. He didn't know why, but he suddenly felt the need to check its contents.

Daisy grabbed his arm, stopping his advance with a firm squeeze. Her tone turned deliberate, matching the intensity in her eyes. "Maybe it's time we head out, Jack? This stuff could be unstable."

Bunker let her words soak in and resonate, his mind still churning through the potential uses of the IMX. Her concern was understandable, not having his experience around explosives.

The desire to inspect the stash vanished from his chest. "You're right. This can wait."

She nodded, her eyes turning soft. "We need to check that connecting tunnel, then get back to the Sheriff. I'm sure he's starting to wonder what's going on down here."

Bunker agreed, reversing course. He led the way out of the chamber, taking a quick right at the midpoint of the previous tunnel.

A chemical odor hit his senses about halfway to the next blast door. He stopped and held up a closed fist out of habit. "Do you smell that?"

"Yeah, chlorine," Daisy said after a hand came up to her nose. "But why would Tuttle have chlorine? It's not like he has a pool."

"To decontaminate water, among other things."

"He must have a lot of it," she said, blinking a few times before she spoke again. "Maybe we should turn around?"

He thought about it for a moment, but his curiosity overruled his logic. "You wait here. I'll check it out."

She didn't argue. "Be careful."

The chlorine scent continued to grow, but it wasn't enough to stop his advance. In fact, the increase was only a slight amount, making him wonder if the odor had drifted into the hallway from its source.

However, that theory didn't make sense, not with a closed door in front of him. The seals should have kept the smell from seeping into the tunnel, assuming it was an airtight door.

If he was correct, then only one explanation remained—someone must have moved through here recently, bringing along the chlorine cloud. Probably from the supply room he figured was on the other side.

He opened the door and stepped inside to find another mud room, about half the size of the first one they'd encountered beneath the chicken coop. As expected, a series of metal rungs led up to the surface at a thirty-degree angle. This room also had a decontamination shower, but the shoe-scraping board with nails was missing.

"A second entrance," he mumbled before calling out to Daisy. She came to his position in seconds.

He pointed at the ladder. "The chlorine is up there."

"Wait a minute," she said, taking a step back. "If these doors are sealed—"

"My thoughts, exactly," he said, stopping her in midsentence.

"Then someone else was just down here."

"One of the boys, I'm guessing. You know how they like to explore."

Bunker climbed the ladder and opened the hatch at the top. The chemical smell tripled as soon as the air from above landed on his nostrils. He minimized his breathing while climbing out. Daisy was right behind him, her shirt collar pulled over her nose.

A small wooden shed about eight feet across and just as wide surrounded them. Sunlight poured in through a series of cracks in the boards along two of the walls, showering the room with streaks of light.

Bunker took a visual inventory, counting seventeen buckets of chlorine tablets, twenty-two gallons of liquid chlorine, and sixty bottles of pure ammonia. All of them pushed up against one of walls.

Daisy pointed at the exit door, her eyes watering. She coughed. "Let's get out of here."

Bunker agreed and followed her through the door where a grassy pasture met his feet.

The back of Tuttle's trailer was a least a hundred yards away, with the pole barn standing proudly to the right. The chicken coop was on the left as expected, confirming Bunker's suspicions about the horseshoe shape of the underground complex.

The Sheriff and several others were huddled around the chicken coop, their backs to him. Two of the gawkers were Victor and Dallas. He figured one or both of them had just been in the escape hatch.

"That was intense," she said, coughing three more times. "I can see why he stored all those chemicals way out here. If the wind shifted, the smell would completely overtake his house."

"I don't think that's why he did it."

"What do you mean?"

"He wanted to keep trespassers away."

She turned and looked at the small shed, then at the chicken coop. After another round of coughing, she said, "To conceal the escape hatch."

"Smart, if you think about it."

"Just like hiding the entrance under the chickens."

"Roger that. None of this is by accident."

"Obviously. But I never expected ammonia," Daisy said. "Pure ammonia at that."

"Seems to me, if you dilute ammonia in water, it can be used as fertilizer."

"That would mean he's stocking it as backup to the ammonium nitrate in the barn."

Bunker smiled, his tone turning light as he delivered his best rendition of Daisy imitating Tuttle. "A man's gotta have backups, Daisy."

CHAPTER 13

Mayor Buckley stood with sore knees in front of the window in the back of the Sheriff's Office, his lungs struggling to process the ever-thinning air of the building.

Three Russian checkpoints were visible inside the city limits, carving up the streets into designated control sectors, each with razor wire and barricades. Troops with assault weapons stood at the ready, their eyes watching everything around them. Most of the soldiers were older, with grizzled faces from years of service. The younger men looked unsure, their heads twisting at the slightest noise.

The pain in his heart doubled as he watched a three-man team in tactical gear escort a man, his wife, and two children from one point to another—all four civilians under the threat of a bullet. Other citizens roamed free, though everyone knew their activity was under watch by the eye in the sky.

Construction of the video monitoring system began once the signal towers were in place to track the transponders injected into everyone's neck. General Zuhkov's men quickly deployed a centralized, tethered hot-air balloon with a remote-controlled gyroscopic camera attached. The technology wasn't daunting to say the least, but it was efficient to deploy and covered a wide area. Too much high-tech would be complicated to mobilize and maintain, which is why Buckley figured they'd chosen the simpler balloon route.

The Russian tech meant a central monitoring station was operational in town. Buckley hadn't seen it yet, but it didn't mean it wasn't there. He thought it would be within cabling distance from the mobile generators, their diesel engines purring in the background.

The latest trucks to arrive were a pair of flatbed tractor-trailer rigs. Their cargo—a skid-mounted water treatment plant made by a company called Evoqua. Buckley presumed the equipment was a combination of filtration and reverse osmosis, designed to keep the Russian troops safe from contaminated water.

The need for a purified water source made sense, given their unwelcome presence. It wouldn't take much for a lone saboteur to poison an unprotected water supply, taking out a large group of soldiers without firing a shot.

Water and food are just as important as guns and ammo when you're the invading force. He thought about the logistics of their arrival and realized water would have been too heavy to transport. Plus it would have run out quickly, leaving the invaders at the mercy of the town's water supply. That left only one choice—mobile equipment for onsite filter and decontamination before the water touched the lips of their men.

The buzz of activity continued outside, with scores of citizens and troops doing what they needed to do to survive one more day. So far, no shots had been fired—on either side—but he worried the situation might soon change.

Clearwater may have been a peaceful town that rolled up its sidewalks at night—a town where life eased forward at its own leisurely pace. Even so, these were Americans under duress. Proud. Resilient. Free. It wouldn't take much to spark an altercation, which is why he figured the inoculations had been launched first.

FEMA's contagion alarm was a masterful stroke of genius, designed to add a layer of control to what would surely be an angry population. At the time, everyone in town was thankful for FEMA's help, lining up willingly for what they thought was a life-saving inoculation.

Of course, that perception changed once the residents realized it was only step one of the Russians' occupation plan. As it stood now, anyone considering resistance would think twice with lethal explosives and tracking devices buried in their necks.

He wondered if the FEMA plot would have been successful if Bunker and Apollo had still been in town. Buckley obviously wasn't prepared for the misdirection, nor was he paying close enough attention when it unfolded right in front of him. Bunker and Apollo might have made a difference, noticing that something was off with the FEMA rollout.

All Buckley could do now was stand back and let the Russians expand their grip of terror. He was outgunned, outmanned, and outsmarted by a band of arrogant Slavs who'd arrived from a land far away.

He used to be the man in charge of all things Clearwater-related. A man people respected and looked up to on a daily basis. But that status evaporated the instant the Russians snuck into town.

Their show of force had everyone cowering to their demands, including him. There was one exception though—Bill King, the Silver King Mine owner. The same man who had his own private audience with the General.

There was no way to know what transpired in that meeting, but his gut told him that King wouldn't hesitate to sell out everyone in order to save his life and that of his missing son. He might have managed to turn a profit in the process, too.

Buckley leaned his butt against the edge of Apollo's desk, giving his back and his legs a rest. Thus far, the Sheriff's Office hadn't been commandeered by the invaders like the Mayor's Office had been. However, that didn't mean General Zhukov had forgotten about this space.

His men had already searched the office, removing the pistols, rifles, ammo, tear gas, gas masks, batons, Tasers, Kevlar vests, riot gear, and other equipment. Basically, anything that could be used against their forces, including the letter opener in Daisy's top drawer.

The Sheriff's Office was now a useless relic, with only historic significance behind its name. Much like he felt at the moment. Obsolete. Moth-balled. Forgotten.

A triple knock came at the door behind him. "Mr. Mayor. We need to speak with you," a man's voice said in perfect English. His tone was deep and gravelly, indicating someone of advanced age.

Mayor Buckley chose to ignore the visitors since the hail was devoid of a Russian accent. He needed whomever it was to go away and leave him be.

The knock rang out again, this time turning into heavy bangs on the door. "Mr. Mayor. We know you're in there. We need to speak to you."

Buckley exhaled, letting his shoulders slump as a dull headache began to establish a foothold in his brain. The pounds hit the door again and again. Finally, Buckley decided to speak. "Go away. I'm busy."

The man's voice changed its pitch and its cadence. Someone else was speaking now, the tone softer and younger. "Seth, it's me, Stan Fielding. I've got my two girls with me and we really need to speak to you. It's urgent."

Buckley didn't respond as more fist pounds hit the office door, then all went quiet. The Mayor relaxed, thinking Stan and the other man had given up.

Thirty seconds of silence ticked by, then the pounding and verbal demands started up again. It was clear Stan and company weren't going away.

Buckley needed to take action; otherwise, the incessant noise would soon send his headache into orbit. "Enough already, Stan. Come in. The door is unlocked."

The hinges creaked before footsteps entered the workspace. Buckley turned to make eye contact with Stan, but his focus found the innocent faces of the man's twin redheads, Barb and Beth. Their freckled, pre-teen faces were round and puffy, as if they'd been crying only moments before.

Four other people had followed in behind Stan and his girls—two older and two younger, all men. Their expressions were identical—they wanted answers.

Stan held up a white sheet of paper, waving it as if it were a priority communique from the

President of the United States. The other visitors did the same, their hands clutching single sheets of paper.

"Have you seen this?" Stan asked.

Buckley suddenly found the energy to reengage his former life as Mayor. He walked out from behind the desk and met Stan halfway. "What is it?"

"Work assignments," Stan said, giving the paper to Buckley. "For everyone on my street."

Stan turned sideways and held out a hand toward the pair of men on his right. "These are my neighbors, Jack Koehn and his eldest son Don." He moved his arm again. "This is Phil Wright and his son Bret."

"Pleased to meet you," Buckley said in his mayoral voice. He held out a hand for a shake, but there were no takers.

Stan continued, "The Russians are going door-to-door with dogs to confiscate our weapons and ammo. Then they're handing out these notices before they move on to the next house. Everyone is scared, Mayor. You need to do something."

Buckley wasn't surprised by the confiscation of weapons, not after they'd done the same thing to the Sheriff's Office. He was more concerned about the piece of paper Stan had just given him.

His eyes scanned the words on the page. Unlike the dossiers he'd seen on Zhukov's desk, everything was in English, with the name of Stan's street printed in bold letters at the top. Below it were four columns of names—resident names—grouped together and listed by surname, with a number immediately after it.

Stan's last name was near the bottom of the first column: *FIELDING: 3*. Two other families were listed ahead of his, bringing the count of persons in their group to ten. Above their names was the heading: *Ore Transport. Sector 4. Shift 2*.

"What am I looking at here?" Buckley asked in an effort to stall, even though he knew what this paperwork represented.

"We're all supposed to work the mine, starting Monday. Even my girls."

"Why would they need to assign workers? Bill King has plenty of men for that already."

"This isn't for the Silver King Mine."

"Why would you say that?"

"One of my neighbors speaks a little Russian and overhead some of the soldiers talking. They plan to bus us daily to the abandoned Haskins Mine."

"The old phosphate pit?"

"My girls can't be working in a mine, Mayor. It's too dangerous. You have to stop this."

Buckley's mind took a minute to process the information, not wanting to believe what he was hearing. "Your neighbor must have misunderstood what they were saying." He held up the paper and pointed at the task assignment printed above Stan's group. "Why would the Russians need workers for *Ore Transport Duty* at a phosphate mine? There's no ore. It doesn't make sense."

Stan looked at the other men standing with him, then brought his eyes back to Buckley. "We think there's something else in that hole. Something important enough to risk invading the United States."

Buckley gulped after remembering something Bill King had said earlier, when the business owner let it slip that at least one uranium mine was still operating in Colorado, and it was a lot closer than anyone realized.

Anyone except the Russians, apparently.

CHAPTER 14

"Do you think Sheriff Apollo will let me have a gun?" Victor Rainey asked the big man, Dicky, whose powerful hands were holding the precision-guided TrackingPoint rifle in a firing position. The tree line beyond the Old Henley Bridge was the target of the rifle's scope.

Dicky brought the high-tech weapon down from his shoulder, then took a swig from one of the three water bottles sitting behind the barbed wire barricade. "You'll have to ask him. I'm not sure what he'll want to do."

Victor flipped his head to the right, sending the longest part of his hair to the side. "Don't you have some pull with him? I mean, you're a deputy. Doesn't he listen to suggestions?"

"Actually, kid, I'm only a temporary deputy. So no, I don't have any influence with the Sheriff. Like I said, you need to ask. Not me. I just do as I'm told. Something I'm guessing you need to learn to do as well."

A high-pitched squeal of hinges rang out from behind Victor's position, then the hollow ping of steel hitting steel. He turned his head in a flash. As did Dicky, both searching for the source of the noise.

The Sheriff was on his way from Tuttle's front gate with a pair of rolled-up papers in his hands. The Mayor's grandson, Rusty, was walking with him, the handlebars of his high-end mountain bike in his grip.

"Looks like you'll gonna get your chance," Dicky said, his tone terse and to the point.

Victor swallowed hard, forcing down a knot of saliva. "Not exactly what I was hoping for."

"I know, but if you want to get somewhere in this world, you need to take ownership of your actions. That means manning up when the situation calls for it. Like now. What's the worst that can happen?"

"He says no."

"Then he says no. At least he'll know you want to help. It's a start."

Victor nodded as he waited for the Sheriff to arrive. Dicky was correct. Nobody was going to give him any respect unless he did something to earn it. He wasn't sure if asking for a gun was all it would take, but he planned to ask.

"Any activity?" the Sheriff asked Dicky when he arrived.

"No sir. All quiet."

"I figured as much. No news is good news," the Sheriff said, tapping Victor on the back with one of the papers. "Right, sport?"

"Yeah, no news is good news."

Apollo pointed at the bicycle. "I thought having Rusty's bike down here was a good idea to speed up the notification process."

"Yes sir," Dicky said, sounding more like a soldier than a deputy. "Much faster than running. Every second counts."

"What do you think, Victor?"

"Sure. I guess. If that's what you need. But seems to me that using the walkie-talkies you found would be better."

"Bunker and I discussed that, but we decided to save the batteries."

"They're rechargeables, aren't they?"

"Yes, they are. But charging them takes time and power away from other things—more important things. We also don't know if the frequencies are being monitored. If they are, it wouldn't take long to get a fix on our position, and we can't afford that. So we decided to keep them off, for now."

The Sheriff motioned to Rusty.

Rusty gave the bike to Victor. "Just don't wreck it."

Victor took the bike by the handgrips, his foot fumbling for the kickstand.

"You do know how to ride a bike, don't you?" Rusty asked, his brow furrowed.

"Yeah. No problem. Everyone knows how to ride a bike."

"But this isn't just any bike."

"I know. I'm not stupid."

"Good then," Apollo said before Rusty could respond. "If anything pops up, let me know immediately." He held up the rolled paper. "We're heading inside to go over these maps with Bunker. There's something interesting I need to show him."

"Good luck, sir," Dicky said, nudging Victor on the shoulder.

The Sheriff brought his eyes down to Victor. "Is there something else?"

Victor's lips started to answer before he was ready. "Ah, yeah, well, uh . . . I was wondering if I could maybe get a gun? You know, to help protect the bridge and all that. Like Dicky."

The Sheriff shot a glance at the towering guard before returning his focus to Victor. "Do you think you're ready for a gun, young man? It's a lot of responsibility."

Victor felt emboldened by the man's question. He decided to deliver his words like Dicky would have done. "Yes sir, I am. A hundred percent."

"I appreciate your gumption, son, but the answer is no. I don't feel comfortable with a weapon in your hands. I'm sure your mother would agree with me. And so would your grandmother."

"But you don't understand. Grandma showed me how to shoot last summer with her .22. It's not hard. I hit every can at least once. Ask her."

"I'm sure you did. But chances are, you need a lot more practice. Shooting cans is a lot different than being an armed guard."

"What, you don't trust me?"

"It's not that, Victor. There are procedures in place to make sure someone's ready to carry a gun. Especially someone your age. But even more importantly, I'd need to run it by your mother first, and I think we both know what she's gonna say."

"Yeah, you're just like everybody else. You don't trust me."

Apollo didn't respond.

"Look, I apologized, but I guess that doesn't count for anything."

Apollo took a second before he spoke. "You mean for what you did at the bus accident."

"I said I was sorry. If I had known what Bunker was going to do, I would've stuck around. But I didn't. He was just some guy who showed up out of the blue. How did I know he wasn't going to push the bus over the cliff?"

Apollo gave the maps to Rusty, then cradled Victor with an arm around the shoulder. He pointed at a flowering bush ten yards away. "Let's have a little chat, shall we?"

The two of them moved away from the group, then Apollo spoke again, this time with a much softer voice. "I know you don't think anyone trusts you, and maybe they don't, but that's because of what you did."

Victor shrugged. "I said I was sorry."

"And we all appreciate that. But it takes more than just words to earn trust."

Victor wasn't sure if he should say anything, so he didn't.

"Trust is about honesty and how you conduct yourself when it really matters. You have to show responsibility and quit taking the easy way out. That means no more lying and no more stealing. I know your mother is at the end of her rope with you."

"I didn't steal anything."

"Yes, you did. Be honest."

Victor held his tongue.

"We all know you broke into Franklin's store and stole his gun."

"That wasn't me. That was someone else."

Apollo dropped his head and shook it before he made eye contact again. "You see, this is exactly what I'm talking about. When you lie, people don't trust you. No matter how many times you apologize afterward. Do you hear what I'm saying?"

Victor nodded.

Apollo continued, his tone more serious than before. "It's time to grow up and be accountable for what you did. So right now, I need you to be honest and answer me. That was you in Franklin's store, wasn't it?"

Victor considered his options, pausing before he answered. "Yeah, Sheriff. It was me. I broke in, but I needed a gun so I could protect my mom after what happened. Wouldn't you have done the same thing if you were me? It's not like my dad is around anymore to protect us. So I had to."

"Okay, some of that is justifiable, but why did you destroy the office?"

"What? I didn't destroy anything."

"Rusty told me about what you did. He was there. The place was a complete mess."

"All I did was take the gun under the desk. I didn't touch anything else. I swear. Took me like ten seconds, then I was outta there. I knew right where it was from what Megan was saying on the bus."

Apollo didn't answer.

Victor continued, "It must have been the men in black. They showed up right after I got there. That's how I lost the gun, when I started running."

"They chased you?"

"Well, sort of. I'm not sure. I didn't stick around to find out."

"I see," Apollo said, his eyes indicating he was deep in thought. A handful of seconds drifted by before the man spoke again, this time tugging Victor by the arm. "All right, come with me."

Apollo directed the next question to Rusty. "When you first arrived at the horse stables, was the front door open to the store?"

"Yes sir."

"Did it look like force was used, or did someone use a key?"

Victor knew what the Sheriff was suggesting and decided to tell his side of the story first. "I crawled in through a window in Franklin's office. He always leaves it open."

Rusty looked at him. "That was you?"

"Yeah, but I never trashed the office. That part is a lie, Sheriff."

"There were papers everywhere. I saw it," Rusty said, his tone elevated.

Apollo held up his hands. "Easy boys. Nobody is accusing anyone of anything. I'm just trying to understand what happened."

Victor could sense the Sheriff's distrust. "I already told you, Sheriff. I went in through the window and took the Colt that was under the desk.

When the men in black came into the store, I went back out the window, but lost the gun in the bushes or something."

"Maybe someone needs to head back there, Sheriff, and take another look? I'll go if you need me to," Dicky said.

Apollo didn't hesitate, shaking his head. "I don't want anyone leaving without an escort. But since we only have one horse, our choices are limited."

"What about the Land Rovers?" Rusty asked, giving the maps back to Apollo.

"We'll only use them if our camp is overrun. Otherwise, they sit right where they are."

Dicky nodded. "Too much noise."

"Exactly. We can't risk using them unless we know precisely where the Russians are. No, I'm afraid horseback is the only choice. For now."

"It's too bad we only have one," Dicky said.

Apollo shot a nod at Rusty. "Let's go have a chat with Bunker." He looked at Dicky and Victor before he departed. "Stay sharp, men. Everyone is counting on you."

"You got it, sir," Dicky answered.

Victor waited until Rusty and the Sheriff were out of sight. He looked up at the giant. "You believe me, right?"

"I'd like to. But at this point, the jury is still out."

Victor dropped his head. He knew most of this was his fault, but some of what happened wasn't. "It seems like no matter what I do, I get in trouble. Even before we moved here, it was the same thing. Everyone judging me all the time. Even when I didn't do shit. It was always my fault. But not this time. All I was doing was trying to protect my mom. That's all. It's just not fair."

A heavy silence hung in the air for what seemed like a minute.

"Hey, I'll tell you what," Dicky said, holding out the rifle. "You hold this and stand guard while I go take a major leak. All that water is running right through me. My back teeth are floating."

Victor took the gun and smiled. "Really?

"Yes. But don't let me down."

"I won't. Thanks for trusting me."

Dicky pointed to the rifle. "That's the safety. It won't fire as long as it's engaged."

"Okay, got it."

"But let me be perfectly clear," Dicky said, pointing at the stand of trees on the other side of the bridge. "The safety stays on unless you see the entire frickin' Russian Army coming through those trees. Not some rabbit, or a bird. Am I making myself clear?"

"Crystal. Safety stays on."

"You'd better have both feet intact when I get back. Hands, too," Dicky said, turning to head toward the tallest oak tree in the area—the same tree Bunker had selected for the first sniper hide.

Victor leaned his weight under the heavy rifle and held it up to his shoulder. The scope was a million times bigger than the one mounted on his grandma's .22. He looked through it. The image was clear and bright, allowing him to see every detail across the bridge.

Right then, something Dicky said tore into his mind. It was his earlier statement to the Sheriff about the need for more horses.

Victor's thoughts filled with an idea. One that would surely earn him the respect of everyone in camp. Even the Sheriff.

He brought his eyes around to check on Dicky's position. The man was almost to the base of the oak tree, his hands working the front of his pants. A few seconds later, Dicky was behind its wide trunk and out of sight.

Victor leaned the rifle against the wooden posts of the barricade, being careful to brace it so it wouldn't fall over. He grabbed one of the water bottles and twisted off the cap. After a quick swig, he used the remaining liquid to fill the orange water container hanging on the downtube of Rusty's bike.

He gripped the handlebars and flipped the kickstand up with his toe. A few seconds later, his butt was on the seat and his right foot on the pedal, ready to take off for the far end of the bridge, and beyond.

If he hurried, he figured he would be back before dark. However, he needed to buy himself some time so Dicky wouldn't miss him and send out search parties.

Victor turned his head in the direction of the tree masquerading as an outdoor toilet. "Hey Dicky! I gotta pee, too, and check on my mom. I'm gonna ride back to house. The rifle's right here for ya."

"Okay. Grab some more water while you're there."

"Will do."

CHAPTER 15

Sheriff Apollo unrolled one of the maps he'd brought to Martha Rainey's house from the hidden bunker beneath Tuttle's barn. He held it down with a spread of his hands, its footprint spanning almost the entire length of the dining room table.

The second map was still rolled and standing in the corner of the room, its center bound by a rubber band. He was saving it for later, once he had a chance to test a theory he was working on regarding Tuttle's maps.

Bunker stood across the middle of the table from Apollo, sandwiched between Stephanie and Daisy, both of them leaning forward, eyes glued to the map.

Apollo made a mental note to pull Bunker aside later and have a discussion about the new information he'd uncovered about the theft of Franklin's Colt 1911 and the subsequent appearance of the men in black at the store.

He also needed to verify Victor's testimony with Megan—the part about the girl giving up the secret location of the gun. Something was nagging at him about the words Victor had used. Most notably, his statement about the office window *always being open*.

Victor couldn't have known that fact unless Megan told him on the bus, or he'd been using that entry point to break in on a regular basis. Either way, Megan needed to confirm.

Albert was next to Daisy, looking nervous, with his skinny friend Dustin on the other side of him. Both men stood erect, with their arms folded across their chests.

Martha Rainey took position at the head of the table, just as the matriarch should do, with her daughter Allison manning the opposite end of the six-foot-long mahogany surface.

The Mayor's grandson Rusty hovered only inches beyond the reach of Apollo's right elbow, with Dallas and Jeffrey pushed in close on his left, their hands pressing down on the map.

Megan Atwater and her knee brace sat in the dining chair in front of Stephanie King, her eyes wide from the mounting excitement. Megan glanced up and sent Bunker a smile over her shoulder. He reciprocated with a grin of his own, then put a soft hand on the top of her back.

Misty Tuttle remained upstairs after her breakdown during the burial of her fiancé. Apollo could still feel the run of tears on his arms, having carried the distraught woman up those same steps earlier.

"This is what I was telling you about," Apollo told Bunker, shooting a long, extended look at the map on the table.

Martha put a candleholder on the end of the map in front of her, while Allison used a thick photo album to secure the other.

Apollo pulled his hands away and gave Bunker a black magic marker from his pocket. He'd found it in Martha's kitchen drawer.

Bunker removed its protective cap, then flashed a look at Burt and Albert. "Where did you see the convoy?"

Burt pointed at a road cutting through the mountain range on the left, just above a bridge symbol printed in black. "It was about here."

"Actually, it was here," Albert said, aiming his finger an inch lower. "We hadn't quite made it to the bridge."

Bunker looked at Burt with one eyebrow raised, obviously waiting for confirmation.

The mechanic's eyes tightened for a few seconds before he answered, moving his finger on the map to match Albert's correction. "I hate to admit it, but Albert's right. They set up the roadblock here, just past the bridge. We were coming up a rise on this side when he spotted them."

Bunker drew the letter 'X' where Burt had indicated, smothering Mason's Bridge in ink.

Dustin smiled. "Yep. That's where we were." He pointed about a quarter inch to the right. "The boulders we hid behind were over here. I'll never forget that moment for as long as I live. Talk about intense. Especially the tanks."

"How many tanks?" Bunker asked.

"Three, I think."

Bunker nodded. "Sounds about right. What did the chassis and turret look like?"

Dustin shrugged. "Not sure. They looked kind of old, but we weren't exactly close."

"Does it matter?" Apollo asked.

"Yeah, it does. If it's a classic T-72, it might not have reactive armor. If it's newer, then all bets are off."

"With our luck, it'll be the newer model," the Sheriff said.

"I wouldn't say that. The T-72 may be old, but it's still their most popular main battle tank. There are literally thousands of them still around, so I wouldn't rule it out. Those things are damn reliable," Bunker said, looking at Dustin again. "Did you see rectangular, raised objects covering the hull? They'd look like pillows, or wedge-shaped packs around the turret."

"I don't remember any of that," Dustin answered. "But Burt got a better look at them."

Burt nodded. "Flat hulls, for sure. Plus they had steel drums attached to the back. Two of them."

"For extra fuel," Bunker said before looking at Apollo. He nodded. "I'm betting T-72."

"That's good, right?"

"Possibly."

Stephanie King spoke up next, her finger aimed at a spot not far from the first roadblock. The map legend in the corner indicated its distance was only a handful of miles away. "I think this is where we stopped for a potty break. Right, Daisy?"

Daisy took Stephanie's hand and moved her finger an inch closer to the first roadblock. She brought her eyes up to Bunker. "Do you think it was the same convoy?"

Burt spoke before Bunker could respond. "Did you see any tanks?"

Daisy shook her head. "No, just a few trucks. But they could have been there, and we just didn't see them."

"Tanks are kinda hard to miss," Burt replied, his tone sharp and to the point. "Unless you're asleep."

"Burt's right," Bunker said, tracing his finger along the roadway. When he came upon another bridge named Royal Palace Bridge, he stopped.

Dallas joined the conversation, tapping his finger next to Bunker's. "That's the first roadblock I saw." The kid moved his finger down another inch on the map. His voice cracked when he said, "My parents' house is here. At least it used to be."

Bunker drew a second X on the map to cover the Royal Palace Bridge, then put a hand on the kid's shoulder. "We'll find them, I promise. Just need to be patient."

Dallas nodded, sniffing. His hand went back to the map, touching two different points. "The other roadblocks I ran into were here and here." Both of his touches landed on landmarks, the first being Kay's Crossing Bridge and the other Union Towers Bridge.

Bunker drew two more X's, each over the designated bridge. He looked up at Apollo. "Where did you find Misty and her boyfriend?"

Apollo took a second to find his bearings on the map, looking for a waterway that followed the river flow he remembered. When he found a match, he put his finger on it. "Dicky, Rusty, and I were here."

Bunker's eyes followed the river upstream several miles, then his finger landed on the paper next to another landmark. "I wonder if they were headed to Rickman's Bridge before they spotted Misty and Cowie," he said, circling the bridge and drawing a question mark inside the ring.

"No, they weren't," a new female's voice rang out from behind Apollo.

Apollo turned his head.

It was Misty Tuttle, her feet landing at the base of the stairs. The bedsheet wrinkles on her right cheek were distinct, no doubt due to some serious sack time. Her eyes were puffy and her hair was a tangled mess, sticking up at odd angles.

Misty ambled across the floor and squeezed in next to Allison. "The Russians weren't headed to some bridge. They were hunting for us. They wanted us dead."

"Why?" Bunker asked, sounding skeptical.

Apollo didn't wait for Misty to answer. "Because allegedly, they'd stolen a formula from the Russians."

"We did steal it. Well, actually, Angus stole it, but I convinced him we needed to get it here, to NORAD. I have an old friend who works there," she said with conviction. Her hand traced a path from Colorado Springs to Clearwater. "I wanted to see my dad while we were in the area, but they found us first. Almost like they knew we were coming."

"What kind of formula?" Albert asked.

"It's probably a new kind of bomb," Burt added. "The news likes to say the arms race is over, but they're full of shit."

Misty shook her head, looking frustrated. "No, it's not for a bomb. Why do men always assume it's a bomb? That's exactly what my friend in NORAD asked me when I first texted him about it."

"Well, it *is* the Russians after all," Albert said, shrugging. "That's what they do. Develop new and better ways to kill the planet. Just like we do."

Misty seemed to ignore Albert's statements. "It's for something called Metallic Hydrogen."

Albert sucked in a breath, his eyes flying wide. "What did you say?"

"Metallic Hydrogen. They've figured out a way to make it."

"That's not possible," Albert snapped. "The pressures required are enormous. Plus, you'd need to keep it super-cooled."

"What's Metallic Hydrogen?" Dustin asked Albert.

"A theoretical phase of hydrogen," Albert answered, his eyes never leaving Misty's face.

"I hate chemistry," Burt mumbled, though Apollo heard it clearly.

Albert continued. "Basically, it would be a new kind of liquid metal, made entirely of hydrogen. A   Quantum   Fluid   with   nearly   unlimited superconductivity. At least, that's what the theoretical physicists said in the article I read."

"Sounds like a bunch of gobbledygook to me," Burt said.

"We're talking cutting-edge stuff. One of the scientists went on to say that if we could solve the manufacturing process, we might be able to use it to create a quantum bridge that could tap directly into zero-point energy. Of course, the man was just speculating, because nobody has a clue how to actually make Metallic Hydrogen. We just don't have the technology."

"Well, they do now," Misty said. "They're making it in Russia as we speak. And from what Angus told me, they've figured out a way to avoid supercooling it. It has something to do with a rare Earth element found in only certain parts of the world."

"Are you talking about some kind of subatomic stabilizer?" Albert asked.

She shrugged, the corners of her mouth turning south. "I don't know. Angus mentioned a new kind of nano-particle, but it was all over my head. I wish I could remember more."

Albert looked at Apollo, his voice charged with intensity. "If she's right, do you know what this means?"

Apollo shook his head.

"It means the Russians would have access to almost unlimited amounts of free energy. Something they could sell to the rest of the world at a fraction of the cost of oil."

"Holy shit! They'd put the Middle East out of business," Dustin said.

"And the United States," Bunker added. "We have more oil reserves than anyone."

Burt smirked. "I'm not sure putting all the oil companies out of business is such a bad thing."

"Except for all the jobs we'd lose. And tax dollars," Bunker said.

"I'm betting it would crash the stock market, too," Albert added.

Dustin laughed. "Rich people always hate it when someone tries to turn them into poor people."

"Once the oil companies are out of the way, Russia could raise the price to anything they wanted," Martha said.

"And control the world," Albert said.

"So this is all about money?" Allison asked.

"It usually is," Bunker answered. "Money and power, though most of the time they are the same thing."

"He who controls the energy has the power," Albert said, his tone deliberate. "In more ways than one."

Misty continued, "Angus stumbled across a classified file while he was working as a contractor in one of their joint research labs in Australia. When he told me about it, we decided to get this information to my friend in NORAD. Someone needed to know about it."

"Why NORAD, if it's not a bomb?" Burt asked.

Misty rolled her eyes. "Weren't you listening? I had to tell someone in the government, and he's the only one I knew. Plus it was close to my dad's house. That way I could kill two birds with one stone."

Kill being the operative word, Apollo thought. Franklin and Cowie—two unintended victims of the techno-invasion. "That explains why they were hunting for you, but it doesn't explain why the Russians decided to invade the US." He looked at Bunker, hoping for insight.

Bunker nodded, slowly. "Unless the two are related somehow."

Daisy spoke next. "Maybe that's what the Morse Code signal was for."

Apollo nodded, though he was still having a hard time processing the meaning of the new information. "If those coordinates were to deposits of the rare elements—"

Bunker finished his sentence. "—it would be worth the risk of invasion."

"I need to get a look at that formula," Albert asked Misty. "It might not be what you think it is."

Dustin patted his friend on the back. "Tin Man will figure it out. He always does."

"Tin Man?" Allison asked.

"Just a nickname from high school," Albert said in a downtrodden voice, shooting a look at Bunker. "Something I'd like to forget, but some people won't let it go." He moved his eyes back to Misty. "That formula? Can I see it?"

Misty shook her head. "I don't have it. Angus kept it hidden. He said it was safer if I never laid eyes on it."

"So let me get this straight. You never actually saw it, yet you came all this way and almost got yourself killed in the process, for something that might not even exist," Albert said in a patronizing tone, shooting a look of doubt at Apollo.

Misty's voice shot up a level. "Angus wouldn't lie about something like this."

Albert huffed. "Well, he *was* a spy working for the Russians. Not exactly a ringing endorsement for the truth."

Burt nodded. "Albert's right. Spies are experts at lying. That's what they do. All day, every day, to everyone. Even you."

"Like I told you guys, he was a contractor. Not a spy."

"Same thing," Albert quipped. "He obviously was part of all this, somehow. Nobody is that innocent. Especially if they're working in some secret advanced research lab with the Russians."

"How many times do I have to say it? He wasn't a spy!"

Burt laughed. "You do realize that if he was a spy, he'd never tell you. So you really don't know for sure."

"Neither do any of you!" Misty shot back. "But I know my Angus. He was a good man who just wanted to do the right thing."

"We should search his clothes," Apollo said.

"They're upstairs. In the hamper," Martha said, "waiting to be washed."

"Seriously, who washes the clothes of a dead man?" Burt asked.

"Habit, I guess," Martha answered.

"I'll get 'em," Rusty said, leaving the table an instant later.

Daisy tapped Bunker on the shoulder. "Maybe you should show everyone what we found in those pouches."

Bunker paused for a few moments, then reached into his pocket and pulled out several brightly colored items. They looked like playing cards, except for the extra angles cut into each of the four corners. He tossed them onto the map, sending them into a spray of color.

"Pokémon cards?" Dustin asked in a stunned voice.

"Dude, you can't be serious," Albert said to Bunker.

"I know. It seems ridiculous, which is why I hadn't brought it up before now. But the men in the miner's camp had these sewn inside their pants. Someone put them there for a reason."

"Yeah, some nut job," Martha Rainey said. "Sounds like something Tuttle would do."

"Mother!" Allison said before looking at Misty. "I'm sorry. She didn't mean it, Misty. Sometimes my mom just says things without thinking."

"It's okay. I know my dad can be a little eccentric," Misty said, her eyes tearing up. "I mean, could be."

Bunker continued. "Bottom line, these cards are no accident. Neither was the observation drone in the miner's camp. Someone planned this."

"And sent an assassin to Tuttle's place," Daisy said.

Bunker looked at Daisy, then at Apollo. "This is all connected somehow."

Daisy turned her eyes to Misty. "Do you think the men in black went to your dad's place looking for Angus?"

Misty choked back the answer, only nodding in response.

"God damned KGB," Burt snapped.

"Actually, it's the FSB," Albert said. "They took over for the KGB."

"Sorry guys, but you're both wrong," Bunker said. "The FSB is for internal security. The SVR handles foreign security. Then again, if this was under the control of their military, the GRU is responsible."

Apollo didn't want to mention the obvious, so he kept his mouth shut. In the end, Misty got her dad killed, regardless of which Russian intelligence service was involved. An assassin was in his home, torturing him for information he didn't possess.

An extended silence sucked the oxygen out of the room until Jeffrey grabbed one of the cards and held it up to the light of the chandelier. "Cool. There's a—"

Stephanie snatched it from his hands and put it back on the table. "What did I tell you about asking first?"

"Sorry, Mom."

Bunker gave two of the cards to Jeffrey. "Knock yourself out, kid."

Dallas took one of the cards from Jeffrey, then reached into his pocket and pulled out a device that looked like a small gun. He pressed the lever on the handgrip, sending out a brilliant blue and yellow flame from the opposite end. He aimed it at the lower corner of the card. "Ever see what happens when you burn one of these?"

Apollo grabbed the pocket torch from Dallas before the card caught fire. "Where did you get this?"

"Found it in Tuttle's kitchen."

"No more fire. You hear me?"

"Yes sir. Sorry."

"And no more snooping." Apollo gave the mini-torch to Bunker, then walked to the corner and grabbed the remaining map. He brought it to the table and held the roll up to grab the group's attention.

Apollo let his eyes wander around the table, making eye contact with everyone. "There's something else I want to show you all, but I've been saving it until after we had our discussion. I didn't want what's on this map to influence anyone's input."

"Come on, Apollo. Let's see it already," Burt snapped, making a stab for the roll.

Apollo pulled the map back, keeping it out of Burt's reach. "Before I show you what's on this map, everyone needs to prepare themselves."

Burt rolled his eyes, his waist bent forward with both hands on the table. "Jesus Christ, Apollo. What's with all the drama?"

Apollo slid the binder from the middle of the roll and uncoiled the map, spreading it over the one already on the table. He kept his hands on the corners so it wouldn't spool up on itself. He peered down at the lines and ovals written on the map by Tuttle. "Anything look familiar?"

Bunker grabbed a corner of the new map and pried it up. He scanned the map underneath, then brought the corner down to look at the top map once again. He repeated the process three more times, then said, "The marks I made are almost identical to the ones on top."

"What does this mean?" Stephanie asked Apollo.

"It means Tuttle knew this invasion was coming. Or at least, he was trying to figure out how it might be done. That's why he marked up the top map. This is no coincidence."

"Are you serious?" Martha asked.

"Now we know why he had all the supplies in the barn," Daisy said.

"And the weapons in the two underground bunkers," Apollo added.

"Let's not forget the Faraday cages, too," Bunker added. "He knew something was coming.

"For a while now," Albert added.

Misty looked at Martha, flaring her eyebrows as she spoke. "Still think my dad was a nut job?"

Martha's face turned soft, her head lowering a bit. "I'm sorry. I never should have said anything. Sometimes my mouth gets the better of me."

"You know Martha, living across the street from you was never easy for my dad. I didn't get many letters from him while I gone, but when I did, your name always came up. So it wasn't just your mouth. He knew you were watching everything he did. Nobody likes to be spied upon. Especially by some old witch who lives across the street."

"Hey, you can't talk to my mom that way!" Allison said, walking toward Misty.

Apollo grabbed her, keeping the women apart. "Easy now ladies, let's not do something we'll all regret."

"This doesn't concern you Sheriff," Misty said, her tone sharp.

"I said I was sorry. I hope you can forgive me," Martha said, pulling her daughter back from the Sheriff's grip. "I couldn't help it. It's not easy living out here all alone."

"Found 'em!" Rusty yelled as he made his way down the stairs with a wad of clothes in his hands. He plopped them onto the table, breaking the tension in the air.

Allison backed off. So did Misty, almost like the heated exchange never happened.

Bunker, Apollo, and Daisy began a hand search of Angus' shirt, pants, and shoes, turning pockets inside out, checking seams, and yanking out soles.

A few minutes went by before the trio came to a collective conclusion, one that Apollo announced to everyone else in the dining room. "Nothing here, folks."

"I told you this was a wild goose chase," Burt said.

"It must still be on him," Albert said, locking eyes with Apollo. He tilted his head, sending a signal that resembled a question.

Bunker nodded. "He's right."

"No. No. No," Misty said, holding up her hands and taking a step back from the table. "You're not digging him up."

"We have to, Misty," Apollo said.

Misty shook her head, looking like she could breathe fire. "No, I won't let you. It's sacrilegious."

Apollo looked at Daisy and Stephanie, then shot a nod at the staircase. "Ladies? A little help, please."

The women didn't hesitate, moving to Misty and grabbing her arms. Misty fought against their control, twisting her body in defiance.

"I'm sorry, Misty, but there's no choice," Daisy said as she and Stephanie led the emotional woman up the stairs and out of sight.

"That was intense," Dustin said to Burt.

"Too bad the Sheriff didn't let them throw down," Burt answered. "My money was on Allison."

"Like in the market, with Grace. You should have seen it. That was a pretty good cat fight," Dustin said, turning to Albert. "Right?"

Albert ignored the comment, focusing on Bunker instead. "It's your turn with the shovel, dude. Dustin and I dug the last round of holes."

"Follow me," Bunker said, leading the group out of Martha Rainey's house and across the street to Tuttle's.

The shovels were still leaning against the back wall of Tuttle's house when they arrived, only a few feet from the fresh graves they'd dug next to Tuttle's. He scanned all six gravesites with his eyes. "Anyone remember which one it is?"

Martha pointed at the first grave. "That's where I buried Tuttle."

Dustin aimed a hand at the second. "That's the black cowboy's."

Rusty walked from Martha's position to the far end of the graves. "These last three are the guys Bunker shot."

Bunker nodded, then stood over the lone unidentified grave. It was the third one from Martha's position. "Then this is where we start." He lifted the shovel above his head and brought it down with force, penetrating the darker colored dirt at its midpoint.

His eyes came up to Burt. "Grab the other shovel. We've got work to do."

CHAPTER 16

Apollo slid the top half of the body onto the ground, while Burt took care of the legs, both men sidestepping the gravesite just uncovered. Albert and Dustin took a step back to make room next to the hole.

The clean bed sheet they'd used to wrap the deceased was now a brownish color, with moisture splotches and other defects marring the all-white tapestry of the cloth.

Bunker began to unwrap Cowie, starting with the end of the sheet nearest to the head, then unwinding the material in a diagonal pattern.

Dallas and Rusty took positions next to Bunker. The boys' willingness to help suggested they weren't fazed by the exhumation process. Not in the least.

Apollo couldn't say the same for himself, wishing they didn't need to dig up the corpse. His apprehension wasn't because of some religious belief. It was more about respect for the dead.

Once a body was in the ground, he believed that's where it should remain. After all, that's why they call them "the remains." However, countless lives were at stake and the only clues to the madness behind the Russian invasion might lie with this cadaver.

Burt held the lower half of the body off the ground, while Bunker's hands completed the sheet removal process. Once the man's naked body was exposed to the air, Bunker gave the soiled bed sheet to Apollo.

Apollo coiled the material into a loose ball, then put it over the man's privates. Sure, a dead man can't feel embarrassment or become chilled from a draft, but it still was the right thing to do.

"What are we looking for?" Burt asked Bunker. "He's obviously not carrying anything."

"My guess is the formula is hidden on him."

Burt threw out his hands and shrugged in an exaggerated motion. "Okay, but where?"

"Check the bottom of his feet and between his toes. If the formula is still with him, it's not going to be obvious. Could be very small, too."

"We have to think like a spy," Albert said. "Check inside his lips and eyelids."

Dallas whispered something into Rusty's ear. The two boys laughed.

"What's so funny?" Burt asked, his hands prying apart each set of toes on the right foot.

Rusty shook his head, his lips not willing to answer. Dallas was still laughing, though it was more of giggle.

"Come on, out with it. What's so funny?" Burt asked, his tone serious.

Dallas pointed at the bundle of cloth covering Angus' midsection. "Check his butthole."

Burt shook his head, then looked at Bunker. "Everyone's a comedian around here."

"Actually, Dallas might be on to something," Dustin said. "Seems like the perfect place to me. Nobody would ever want to check there."

"Why am I not surprised?" Albert asked in a cynical tone.

Bunker shook his head at Dallas. "Maybe I shouldn't have taken you back to your father's house. I'm starting to think too much desensitization is not a good thing."

"He's right, boys. This is no time to be joking around," Apollo said.

Dallas dropped his head, his tone somber. "Sorry."

Apollo knew the boys were just being boys, using humor to cover up their anxiety. "Let's stay focused, shall we."

"But I wasn't exactly joking. It's possible, right?"

Bunker sounded frustrated when he said, "Sure, just not likely. If he has it on him, it would be someplace a little more accessible."

"At least they're getting along okay, which is pretty amazing under the circumstances," Martha said to Apollo, nodding at Rusty and Dallas. "More than I can say for Rusty and Victor."

"Among others," Bunker interjected, his focus landing on Albert.

The big man locked eyes with Bunker, but didn't respond. Nor did his facial expression change, obviously not wanting to address the comment sent his way.

It was clear something was going on with Albert and Bunker. Apollo wasn't sure what was fueling the tension, other than their near fisticuffs in the barn earlier. He thought their heated exchange was a thing of the past, but their odd looks, head turns, and cryptic comments seemed to indicate their distaste for each other hadn't eased.

"Dallas, why don't you and Rusty go check Tuttle's bathroom," Bunker said.

"For what?"

"See if you can find some shaving cream and a razor. We've got some hair to remove. I'll need scissors, too."

Dallas laughed again. So did Rusty.

"It's not for that," Bunker said, looking less than amused. "We need to check his scalp."

"Good idea," Albert said in a deliberate tone, his eyes never leaving Bunker. "I'm sure there are plenty of guys who've hidden stuff under their hair. Stuff like scars. Birthmarks. Lumps. Hell, I'll bet even a few tattoos. Nobody would ever suspect it, either."

Bunker hesitated for a good three seconds, his eyes lingering on Albert. Then he motioned at the boys with a quick wave of his hand. "Go on. Get the stuff we need."

Dallas and Rusty took off a moment later, taking a path between the end of the trailer and the barn.

* * *

"Wait! You don't have to do this," Mayor Buckley screamed, his feet churning at top speed across the grassy square. Deputy Rico was only a few feet behind him, both men trying to stop what was about to take place in front of a growing crowd of Clearwater residents.

"Ready . . . aim . . ." a Russian soldier yelled in broken English. A three-man squad stood before him, their rifles aimed at an equal number of prisoners, each on their knees with hands tied behind their backs. The commander's accent was thick; so were the blindfolds covering each of the captives' faces.

Buckley called out again, his lungs gasping for air. "Don't do this! Please!"

A second later, the order to fire was given. Gunshots rang out and brain matter exploded when the invaders' bullets let loose with their rage.

The crowd turned away, gasping in unison, the unarmed prisoners toppling over in death.

The energy in Buckley's legs vanished in an instant, stopping his gallop with a slam of the ground into his knees. A stabbing pain filled his heart, his mind unable to comprehend what he had just witnessed.

"No! No! No!" he screamed in a fading voice, his lungs starving for oxygen.

Rico plopped down next to him, the expression on his face mirroring how Buckley felt. Rico covered his eyes with his hands and began to sob. Slowly at first, then more tears came to him as the seconds ticked.

Buckley wanted to console Rico, but the rage in his chest convinced him to get up and keep moving. Answers were needed and he couldn't get them from his current position.

He resumed his trek with weak, unbalanced strides, his eyes unable to look away from the blood-covered corpses. When he arrived, two guards turned their rifles on him. The third grabbed Buckley by the suitcoat and stopped his advance with a straight arm.

"What did you just do?" Buckley asked, his voice charged with grief.

Valentina came into his vision from the right, seemingly out of nowhere. "These men were charged with sedition and sentenced accordingly."

"Sedition? What are you talking about?"

"They refused to report for work duty, then resisted arrest when the General's security team took them into custody. One had a concealed knife. A forbidden weapon."

"So you just shot them? In cold blood?"

"All resistance will be met with swift justice."

"On whose authority?"

"General Zhukov's."

"Take me to him! I demand to speak with him this very instant!"

* * *

Bunker drew the razor across the crown of Cowie's head, his hand holding the razor at a consistent angle. The shaving cream gave way under the even pressure, the edge removing the hair in one pass.

He wouldn't quite classify the remaining hair as stubble, but it was close after the scissors had done their job to give him better access. He figured another swipe or two and the man's head would be completely bald.

The process reminded Bunker of his days riding with The Kindred. Every morning he'd stand in front of the dingy mirror and drag a razor across his lumpy head. The sound and vibration of stubble ripping across his scalp was a unique sensation, one still fresh in his memory.

Martha Rainey came around the corner of the trailer. "That didn't take long. Find anything?"

"Nothing yet," Bunker said. He brought the razor up and positioned it for another draw. About halfway through the next pass, something appeared beneath the shaving cream. It was an all-black tattoo, but not one he'd seen before. This one was perfectly square and filled with patterns of dots and squares.

"A QR code?" Rusty asked, his voice an octave higher than usual.

Dustin looked just as surprised. "What the hell?"

Albert folded his arms across his oversized gut before raising an eyebrow. "There's a first time for everything."

"Wow, I didn't expect that," Apollo added.

"None of us did," Bunker said, his eyes drawn to the detail of the artwork.

"What's a QR code?" Martha said, her question defining her age.

"It stands for Quick Response code," Albert answered.

Dallas added, "Normally you use a smart phone to scan it, then it takes you to a website on the Internet."

"Didn't Japan's auto industry invent it?" Dustin asked.

Albert shook his head. "I don't think they invented it, but they were the first to use it widespread. At least before the Internet crashed their party."

"Well, that's pretty frickin' useless," Burt said. "No Internet. No website."

"Angus obviously didn't expect the EMP," Bunker said, running through the logistics in his mind. The man must have created a special webpage somewhere on the Internet that contained the Russian formula, then had a tattoo artist draw the code on his head. "It's damn fine artistry."

"Time to fill the hole back up. Then I need some food," Burt said, looking at Martha.

"Look, just because I'm a woman doesn't mean I'm stuck with all the cooking duties."

Burt laughed. "Your daughter then. She's had plenty of experience at Billy Jack's."

Martha stopped her approach next to Bunker, then answered Burt. "You'll need to take that up with Allison. But I'm pretty sure she'll tell you the same thing."

"To go fuck myself," Burt said in the middle of a chuckle.

"You said it, not me," the old woman answered, leaning in close to the tattoo. She held her eyes on the matrix of squares for a few beats. "Are these supposed to be all black?"

"Yep, just like any other barcode," Albert answered.

Martha stood upright and said, "Well gentleman, I hate to tell you, but that's not a QR code."

"How the hell would you know?" Burt snapped. "A minute ago, you didn't even know what it was."

Martha pointed at the upper left corner of the tattoo, drawing Bunker's focus. "You see here, the center of that larger square is not black like everything else."

Bunker studied the dot before he spoke again. "Looks black to me."

She scoffed. "No. It has a tinge of burgundy to it."

Bunker shook his head. "I don't know. Black is black."

Albert laughed hard.

"What's so funny, dude?" Dustin asked.

"Most people don't know this, but women can see shades of color that men can't. More so in the red spectrum. It's all about them rods and cones."

"Okay, if it has some red to it, what does it mean?"

Bunker answered Dustin, "It means I need a magnifying glass."

"What are you thinking?" Apollo asked.

"A microdot."

"Something a spy would use."

"You'll need more than a magnifying glass," Albert said with confidence.

"A microscope?" Dustin asked.

Albert nodded. "Got one back at my place."

Bunker agreed with their line of thinking. "Just need transportation."

Apollo spun to face the fenced-off area of Tuttle's back yard where Tango stood with his snout buried in the short grass. "I'm guessing four-legged transportation. Not four-wheeled."

Bunker laughed. "We'll need to map out a route. Figure I'll do some scouting while I'm out there."

"I can help with that," Burt said.

"Actually, you need to get back to work on the projects. There's a lot more welding to do."

"Hey, wait a minute."

"A deal is a deal, Burt. That TrackingPoint rifle isn't free."

"If we follow the routes Tuttle put on the map, I'm hoping we can get you where you need to go," Apollo said.

"Time to gear up," Bunker said, getting to his feet.

"All the gear is in the bunker below the barn," Apollo said.

"I'm glad you've decided to stay," Bunker said to the Sheriff. "Someone needs to keep an eye on things till I get back."

"It's not that, exactly. I still need to head back to town, but since we only have one horse, I'll wait for now. Besides, I don't think Tango wants my fat ass on his back, too."

Bunker smiled. "Or mine, either."

"Yeah, as if."

"What about my mom and sisters?" Dallas asked. "You promised."

"Don't worry, I'll look for them. They're probably in town, if my hunch is correct."

The kid nodded, but didn't respond.

Bunker held out his hand. "I'll need that photo you found."

Dallas took it from his pocket and unfolded it. The scorch marks on three of the corners obscured some of the scene, but the rest of the image was useable. Well, mostly useable, if you discounted the heavy crease down the middle. The kid had obviously opened and closed the photograph a number of times, cherishing the lone surviving memento from the house fire.

Dallas gave it to Bunker with a trembling hand. "Mom's hair is black now."

Apollo cleared his throat. "You might want to talk to Daisy before you go. I'm guessing she needs someone to swing by her trailer and feed her cat, Vonda. I left food and water out when I was there before, but I'm sure it's running low by now."

"I'll take care of it."

Burt huffed. "You guys are worried about some cat?"

Apollo ignored Burt's jab, still speaking with Bunker. "I'm sure she'll appreciate it."

"I'll make the rounds with everyone before I head out. Make sure they're all on the same page."

"Well, that and say a few goodbyes. Just in case. God forbid."

"Copy that."

Martha pointed at Cowie's bald, naked body. "I think you're forgetting something, Bunker."

"Oh yeah. Right." Bunker moved to Cowie's feet, then motioned to Burt. "Grab the other end. Let's get him inside."

CHAPTER 17

"Where are we going?" Mayor Buckley asked Rico Anderson after they entered the main entrance to Charmer's Market and Feed Store.

Rico didn't respond.

Buckley hadn't planned to visit this establishment today, not with a pending meeting with the Russian General on the horizon. But Rico convinced him to follow along, claiming it was Priority One.

The mercantile owner, Grace Charmer, waved a quick hello as Rico led the Mayor past the front registers in silence.

Buckley nodded back at her.

The nervous, red-faced look on Grace's face sent a chill down his spine, almost as if the old woman had just been sentenced to life in prison for mass murder. It was the strangest feeling. One that Buckley couldn't shake.

"Hopefully everyone is here," Rico whispered, his feet marching down the center aisle. The man's step was deliberate. So were his words.

"For what?" Buckley asked, his gut telling him the stockroom door was their destination. It stood between the grain bags and the animal feed piled along the rear wall. He remembered those stacks well, he and Rico carrying the inventory through the store when the Wal-Mart supply trucks arrived in town.

Rico stopped, then glanced around with hunched shoulders and determined eyes, obvious paranoia fueling his movements. "Not here, Mayor," he said, his voice barely a purr. "Wait for thirty seconds, then follow me in through the back door."

"Why?"

"Could be sympathizers around. Can't be too careful."

Buckley nodded, even though he had a long list of questions boiling in his brain. Especially about the word *sympathizers*.

He looked around to see what had Rico spooked. Three customers occupied the same aisle as he did, two of whom held baskets in their hands. The other was behind a full-sized cart, all of them seemingly busy with their shopping duties.

Unlike the chill he'd received from Grace's body language, everyone else in the store appeared engrossed in their own worlds. Nothing out of the ordinary.

Buckley stood firm as Rico turned and walked away, continuing his original path down the center aisle. At the end, he took a ninety-degree right.

Buckley could see the top of the Hispanic's jet-black hair moving above the racks as Rico made two lefts, then a right. A handful of seconds later, the door to the back room opened and Rico's head disappeared from sight.

"Afternoon, Mayor," one of the residents said as she slipped past the Mayor with her shopping cart leading the way. One of the front wheels fluttered in epileptic mode, shuddering side to side in a lightning quick wobble.

Buckley recognized the overweight eighty-year-old woman. She was Jane Flacco, a round-faced senior who always kept her gray hair short—short enough to resemble a recruit fresh out of Basic Training. No makeup either—a scary thought to say the least.

"Afternoon, Jane. How's George doing these days?"

She tucked in her upper lip before she spoke again. "Meaner than a God damn snake. That's how he's doing."

Buckley expected a negative response since this woman never seemed content about anything, except when she took down the prize at Bingo and ran with gusto to the front of the hall to collect. The sight of all of her extra weight flopping and wiggling was a sight he could never un-see. "I take it his gout is acting up again?"

"Yeah, that and the fact that he's a total pain in my ass. I've had hemorrhoids I liked better."

Buckley held back a laugh, remembering the celebration party involving the Flaccos from the year prior. "Didn't you two have an anniversary recently?"

She nodded. "Sixty-one, if you can believe that."

"That's quite an accomplishment, Jane. Congratulations."

She shook her head. "Just between you, me and the lamppost, I'm pretty sure that ass-hat of a man won't make it to sixty-two. But you didn't hear it from me."

Buckley smiled out of courtesy, having heard her same rhetoric a number of times over the years. Yet the Flaccos were still alive and still married, despite their loathing for each other.

He figured the very nature of their tumultuous relationship was the one thing keeping them both alive. That communal hatred gave them something to look forward to when each new day arrived.

Buckley had learned over the years that most people only need a single reason to crawl out of bed and keep plowing forward, even if it's one filled with nausea for another.

Mrs. Flacco snatched two items from the shelf in front of her and put them into her half-full shopping cart as Buckley started a silent count to thirty.

One of her items was a shovel and the other was a length of braided rope. The rope landed on top of a bear trap. The shovel nestled in next to a king-sized container of lighter fluid, its metal moving the plastic bottle over an inch.

The rest of her cart was full of items that Buckley could classify as weapons, if he didn't know the woman: framing hammer, black-handled axe, crowbar, and a blue nail puller. Not a single morsel of food.

She pointed at the front windows of the store. "You gonna do something about all those cock-sucking Russians? Those assholes are really starting to piss me off."

Her heavy tone didn't catch him off guard, but her extra foul language did, sending his tongue into a stammer. "Uh, well, yeah . . . I'm working on it."

"Well then, work faster. Some of us don't have all day."

"I'm doing my best, ma'am."

When Buckley's count hit thirty, he found his way to the back room where Rico was waiting inside with two additional members of the Sheriff's full-time deputy team: Zeke Dawson and Russell Thompson.

"Good to see you guys up and about," Buckley told them, their eyes glassy and movements slow. The roadway bandits did a number on them, but at least they'd found some shoes to wear. "I didn't expect Doc Marino to release you so soon."

"He didn't," Zeke said. "But we couldn't wait any longer."

"What's going on?" Buckley asked, his eyes landing on each man in succession, hoping for some insight into this clandestine meeting.

Rico waved his hand. "Follow me, Mayor."

Buckley did as he was told, following Rico through the mess of empty boxes covering the storeroom floor, then into the small break room along the back. Rico stopped in front of the door-sized refrigerator on the left.

The stainless-steel model had been built into the wall and featured a pair of magnetic Green Bay Packer stickers along its front. Below them was a series of football schedules from the previous three years.

Buckley expected Rico to reach for the handle on the door, but that was not what happened. The man's brown-skinned hand went under the cabinet on the right, where his fingers yanked on something. Buckley heard a dull noise that sounded like a latch giving way.

Zeke grabbed the back edge of the fridge and pulled with an outstretched arm. The entire unit swung open, frame and drywall included.

The depth of the steel fridge reminded Buckley of a bank vault door opening. Behind it was a short passageway that led to another door.

"Seriously?" Buckley muttered.

"Leads to a panic room, sir," Rico said, stepping inside the chamber first. "Grace's husband had it built when they remodeled this store."

"Grace said he barely got it finished right before he died," Zeke added. "Poor bastard."

"After you, Mr. Mayor," Russell said, extending a hand toward the opening.

"I take it Grace knows about all this?"

Rico didn't hesitate with the answer, his face looking even sterner than before. "Absolutely. She's the one who offered the space, so all of us could meet in private."

Buckley went inside. "All of us?"

Zeke and Russell followed, closing the secret door behind them.

Rico opened the next door, then stood aside as if he expected the Mayor to react. Three men were huddled inside, standing around something about four feet high and covered in a padded moving blanket.

Two of the men had their backs to the door, so Buckley couldn't see their faces. One had extra-long gray hair pulled back into a single ponytail that hung down to the middle of his back. The other was a tall, shorthaired blond with a thick waist and broad shoulders.

The third man was facing Buckley. It was Bill King, the Silver King Mine owner.

Before Buckley could blink, his feet took off in a sprint, bringing him to King's position in a flash. Buckley hands came up on their own, planning to wrap the traitor's throat in a stranglehold. However, before his fingers made contact, the stout man with short blond hair spun on his heels and jumped in front of Buckley.

When Buckley's eyes took in the man's face, his heart skipped a beat. It was Bill King's convict of a brother, Kenny.

The man's powerful hands latched onto Buckley's chest, stopping his approach. "Easy there, Mayor."

"Kenny?"

"Hey Seth. Miss me?"

"When did you get out? I thought your parole hearing wasn't for another month, at least."

"Got released early," he said, his tone grizzled and deep. A grin crept up on his lips. It was slight and maniacal, but a smile nonetheless. "On account of bad behavior."

"Actually, he escaped," Rico said, without a hint of concern. "After the EMP hit, the Department of Corrections lost containment of the facility. He just made it here this morning."

"Sneaking past the Russian checkpoints wasn't easy, but here I am," Kenny said. "It pays to know every nook and cranny of this town. Russians missed a few."

Buckley took a step back when a series of flashbacks from Kenny's drug trafficking trial flooded his memories. The Mayor had taken the stand as one of the federal prosecutor's character witnesses, feeling obligated at the time. He looked at Rico, then Zeke. "Why isn't this man in handcuffs?"

Kenny stepped forward, holding his wrists together. "If you're man enough, Seth, go for it. Nobody here will stop you . . . except possibly me."

Rico stepped between the two men. "I think you need to hear him out, Mayor."

The longhaired man on the left finally turned around to reveal his identity.

Buckley recognized the leather-skinned entrepreneur with several teeth missing from his crooked mouth. "Billy Jack? You're involved in this?"

His country twang filled the room when he spoke. "Like Rico said, you need to take a minute here, Mayor. We got a lot to discuss."

Buckley turned for the door behind him, but Zeke intercepted his departure. "Please, Mr. Mayor. This is important."

Buckley froze, needing a moment to think about the dynamics at play. Blood adversaries were working together, including members of the Sheriff's Office, and nobody seemed concerned. Kenny King was not a man to be taken lightly. By anyone.

Zeke motioned for Buckley to turn around.

Buckley spun, just as Kenny put his hand on the crown of the blanket covering the item next to him. He removed it with a yank to reveal an unconscious woman strapped to a chair with her head hanging limp.

The petite blonde had blood dripping from cuts on her cheeks and above her badly swollen eye. The large slit across the front of her military uniform revealed her porcelain skin, almost to the point of exposing her breasts.

It was the General's interpreter, Valentina—beaten and unconscious.

"What the hell is going on here?" Buckley asked.

"Getting some answers," Kenny said. "The old-fashioned way."

"By torturing a woman?"

Kenny's eyes turned fierce. "No, Mayor. We're extracting information from the enemy. In case you haven't noticed, the town is crawling with them."

Buckley shook his head, his mind running through a number of retaliatory scenarios the General would unleash because of their actions. "You guys can't do this!"

"The hell we can't. This is war, Mayor," Bill King said, breaking his silence. He pointed at the exit door. "Right now, outside this store, people are dying in the streets. You were there, Mayor. They just gunned down some of our friends. People who voted for you."

"Still, this isn't right," Buckley said, pulling the hanging piece of Valentina's shirt up. "She's just the interpreter. This woman didn't pull the trigger."

"No, she didn't, but she's still guilty as hell," Kenny said, taking a step closer to Buckley. "Trust me, I know guilty, Seth. I was surrounded by it for years after you and Fielding testified against me."

"Look, I was just doing my job. You left us no choice. We had to protect this town from the evil you were selling."

"And now, I'm doing my job," Kenny said. "Like you, I'm just protecting this town from the evil the Russians are selling. After you let them stroll right in and take over, I might add. What kind of man just stands by and let's that happen?"

"A coward. That's who," Bill King snapped.

Buckley looked at Bill first, then at Kenny. "I'm sure you don't know this, but your brother had a private meeting with General Zhukov. He sold us all out, like a traitor."

"Nice try, Buckley. But you don't know what you're talking about," Bill said.

Buckley pointed at Bill, his eyes still locked on Kenny. "I was there. I saw him. He's working with the Russians. You can't trust him for a second."

Bill shook his head, his voice calm and cool. "All you saw was me in the hallway, but you have no idea what was said in that meeting, if anything. You're reaching, Buckley. It's pathetic and weak."

"I'm pretty sure I know what was said. It's what men like you do to save your own ass. You'd give up everyone you know without a second thought. Even your brother."

Bill pointed at the door. "Are you forgetting I have a son out there somewhere?"

"That's exactly my point. To save him, I'd bet my last dollar that you gave up Bunker and Daisy when the General showed you the photographs. Even your own brother, if it came down to him or you."

"What photographs?"

"From the drone."

"That's enough," Kenny said to Buckley. "You're wasting your breath, Mayor."

"What I'm telling you is the truth," Buckley said. "You guys are being misled. You can't trust anything that man has told you."

"Even if he did try to save Jeffrey, none of that matters now," Kenny said, his eyes turning to the bleeding Valentina.

"Wait—" Buckley said, trying to get through to Kenny and stop this madness. "I don't think you realize who she is."

"I know exactly who she is," Kenny said without missing a beat.

"You don't understand. She's not just some Russian you've grabbed. She's part of the General's personal staff and I get the strong impression she's important to him. More than just professional, if you catch my drift. If you do this, he'll take it out on the town. Tenfold."

Kenny spun to grab Buckley by the neck with force. "I said that's enough! We're doing this. End of discussion. Am I making myself clear?"

Buckley couldn't breathe with the man's powerful grip squeezing his windpipe.

"You're either with us or against us, Mayor. You need to decide before I lose my patience. And trust me, that's the last thing you want to happen right now."

Buckley nodded in a panic.

Kenny let go after a three-count, his chin locked in a forward position with clenched teeth.

Buckley gasped a sudden, deep breath, then bent over and coughed before his lungs recovered.

"Now, where was I?" Kenny said to the group, his eyes turning to the captive in the chair.

Rico grabbed the Mayor by the bicep and spun him around. The Deputy shook his head and sent a silent message with a flare of his eyes not to push the situation.

Buckley wasn't about to give up. Not yet. There had to be a way to stop this, but he needed to try a different tactic.

Bill King was a liar and a cheat. There had to be a secret to expose. Something that might allow him to get through to Kenny and the others, but he needed to dig to find it. Dig like a Special Federal Prosecutor, combing through political files in search of a crime. One had to exist somewhere, if he probed hard enough. If nothing else, if he kept the attention on himself, maybe they'd stop their assault on Valentina before they killed her.

Right then, his mind replayed the steps Rico had taken when they'd first entered the market. They were careful and guarded. Plus, the deputy had used the term *sympathizers*, which brought a new question to Buckley's mind. One he sent Kenny's way. "How did you get Valentina in here without anyone noticing?"

Bill King tilted his head, then raised an eyebrow at his brother.

Kenny nodded in response, as if to give his approval to answer the question.

"The Russian bitch wandered into the store on her own. Grace took her down in the back when nobody was looking. Then she came to me for help."

"Grace?"

"She's a true American Patriot. Unlike others I know," Bill said, aiming his barbs at Buckley. "Kenny was cleaning up after his long walk home when Grace showed up. She filled us in on what happened, then we came here to get answers."

Right then, another flashback rose up from Buckley's memory. The vision showed Grace standing by the register with that strange look on her face. A guilty, downtrodden look. "I still can't believe Grace started this."

Bill laughed. "Didn't think the old bag had it in her. Obviously, I was wrong."

Buckley took a moment to run it through his mind. Granted, Grace was a little high-strung and had attacked Allison with the broomstick shortly after the EMP took down the grid, but a disagreement over stolen Pepsi was lightyears away from attacking a Russian officer.

Grace's look of guilt could have been the result of any number of things. Probably from letting these miscreants use the back of her store for torture. "I've known Grace for years. She'd never do this." He shook his head with force, letting his words hang in the air for a beat. "No. I don't believe a word you're saying. Not for a second."

"It really doesn't matter what you believe, Seth. What's done is done," Kenny said.

Buckley looked at Zeke and Russell, then turned his eyes to Rico. "You guys okay with this?"

Rico's eyes tightened. "It's them or us, Mayor. We've got to make a stand before it's too late."

"I get that, but this isn't the way. We can't start torturing people. It'll only make things worse. There has to be another way."

Kenny shoved at Buckley's chest. "I suppose you just wanna stand around and talk the Russians to death."

"Yeah, as a matter of fact, I was waiting to have a chat with General Zhukov. To lodge a complaint about the executions. I'm sure I can reason with him. We have to try."

"I thought as much. That's all you politicians ever want to do is talk, talk, talk," Kenny said, rolling his eyes. "The minute they pulled the trigger and shot our people in cold blood, they declared war. The gloves are off, Mayor. It's time to take back our town."

"I get that you want revenge. We all do. But do you really think you have a chance against the Russian Army?"

"Fuck the Russians. Americans don't back down from anyone."

"You need to stop and think here," Buckley said, throwing up his hands. "What are you gonna fight with? They've confiscated all the weapons."

Bill King shook his head, laughing. "If you really think they found all the weapons, you're dumber than you look, Mayor."

Buckley paused, unsure how to respond.

"And don't forget, our family owns a mine. Weapons aren't the only thing we have," Kenny said.

"Explosives?" Buckley asked.

"More than you know."

Buckley felt a glimmer of hope spring up inside. "But that still doesn't change the situation.

How many lives will be lost trying to kill them all? Ten? Twenty? A hundred?"

"I doubt we'll have to kill them all," Zeke said. "We just have to make them miserable enough that they'll want to leave. It's about destroying their morale, Mayor."

"Hit and run," Kenny said. "We know where they are, but they don't know where we are. Or who we are, either."

"Home field advantage," Bill King said.

Kenny slapped his brother on the back. "We hit them hard and fast before we disappear into the woodwork. Then repeat."

Russell Thompson added, "It's what happened in Afghanistan. The Russians eventually withdrew after a bunch of sheepherders broke their will."

"It's still a huge gamble. You're putting everyone in danger."

"They obviously need us for slave labor, so the last thing they'll want to do is kill off their workers," Kenny said. "We can take advantage of that."

"They'll hunt you down."

"But they'll never find us. They don't know this town like we do."

Buckley pointed to the side of his neck. "I don't think you realize that we, unlike you, have trackers in our necks. And explosives."

Kenny scoffed. "Damn it, Seth. You'll believe anything, won't you?"

"I'm not following."

Kenny pointed at his brother's neck. "Show him, Bill."

Bill turned his head, exposing the left side of his neck.

Buckley counted six stitches. "You removed it?"

"Didn't have to."

"Because there's nothing there," Kenny said. "They went through all that injection bullshit to convince everyone not to resist. You really didn't think any of that was real, did you?"

Buckley didn't answer right away, shrugging. "Seemed legit to me."

"That kind of technology only exists in a James Bond movie, Mayor. None of it was real."

"I'm pretty sure it does exist. We just don't know about it yet. It's not that far-fetched, with how fast technology is advancing these days."

"Even if it did exist, it would cost a fortune to use it on a mass scale like this."

Kenny had a point, but Buckley still didn't believe the man would risk his brother's life like that. "So let me get this straight. You just took a knife and started digging around your brother's neck, hoping the implant was fake?"

"No, dumbass. Your girlfriend Valentina told us," Kenny said, pointing at the small dinette table in the corner. The First Aid kit was sitting on its surface and had its lid open. A bloody knife sat next to it, with some gauze covered in blood. They'd obviously used it to patch Bill up after cutting into him.

Bill King pointed at his neck. "Doc Marino's handiwork."

"He's in on this, too?"

"Oh yeah, he knows what's at stake."

"Anyone else I should know about?"

"No, that about covers it."

Kenny took a step forward. "I want to keep this small and efficient. Otherwise, the Russians will find out that we know about their fake injections."

Buckley wanted to respond, but couldn't after his mind filled with a scene of a bloody massacre in the town square. Bullets flying everywhere. Bodies ripping apart. Children screaming.

In his vision, he found himself walking through the grass in horror, the eyes of the dead looking up at him. "Aren't you forgetting the balloon outside? They're watching everything we do. They'll know she came in here and never left."

"No, they won't," Rico said without hesitation. "It's centered over the square and their cameras can't look directly down."

"We're in a blind spot," Kenny added.

"You can't know that for sure."

Kenny pointed at the unconscious Valentina. "That's why you extract information from those who do know."

Rico nodded. "She said they're using it mostly for intimidation."

"And to watch the perimeter of town," Zeke added.

"A sniper can take it out easily," Russell said.

"It's time someone stands up to them," Bill King said, now shoulder to shoulder with his brother. "And you, you God damn son-of-a-bitch—we're tired of your leadership. So consider this your recall election."

"I thought we had an understanding, Bill."

"What, like we're friends or something?"

"More like a coalition for the good of the town."

Bill huffed an angry breath. "Not after you testified against my brother in open court."

"Look, I wasn't the one accusing your brother of anything. That was Stan. I was only providing background information."

"More like character assassination."

Kenny grabbed Buckley by the shirt collar, pulling him forward until the two of them were nose to nose. "Don't think for a second that I've forgotten a single word of what you and Stan said on that stand, Mayor. I've had years to plan my revenge."

Buckley gulped as the shirt around his chest tightened under the man's grip.

Rico put his hand on Kenny's wrist. "We're going to need everyone, Kenny. We have to pull together, despite our differences."

Kenny hesitated for a few seconds, breathing heavily. He let go of the material with a shove. "Trust me, there will come a time when I take my revenge against all those who stood up against me."

"Welcome to the Resistance, Mayor," Zeke said, moving in front of Kenny.

Rico and Russell joined him in a show of solidarity.

CHAPTER 18

Bunker filled the remaining pouches on one of Tuttle's tactical vests with ammo magazines, then packed his rucksack with a slew of supplies for his reconnaissance mission. He wasn't sure what he'd face once he left the compound, but he needed to be prepared.

Tuttle had stocked the bunker with just about everything a warrior could need, though most of the weapons and gear were civilian models, not the same high-end military-grade equipment he'd trained with. But it would do. At least the Steiner 8x30 binoculars were first-rate, their built in rangefinder and compact size a welcome addition to his load-out.

He planned to travel weapons-light for speed and agility, needing only a reliable semi-auto handgun and a tactical rifle. He figured a Glock .40 and a 7.62 should be sufficient, mainly because if he found himself in a situation where he needed more firepower, then he'd probably be surrounded and outgunned by a Russian strike team.

Tuttle had mounted a red-dot Vortex scope on the AR10. He took a moment to consider upgrading to a high-powered model, but decided to keep the optics as-is. Long-range marksmanship wasn't his specialty, so the CQB setup was preferred.

Where he was going, a Close Quarters Battle was the most likely scenario he'd face. Hopefully, it wouldn't come to that, but he took along extra batteries for the scope and magazines just in case.

Daisy arrived in the supply bunker, her hands buried in her pockets. "Looks like you're just about ready."

"Just need to pack a few more items. I'll head out at dusk."

"Under the cover of darkness. Smart." She snatched a head-mounted device from the stack next to her and tossed it at him. "Don't forget this."

He caught the night vision goggles in his left hand. "Thanks." He put the Gen2 device into his pack, along with a change of civilian clothes and a Colorado Rockies ball cap.

"Think you'll need those?" she asked.

"I might have to blend in as a civilian and I can't do that wearing this," he said, glancing down at his forest-green camo and rattling gear.

She hesitated before she spoke again, her eyes watching every movement of his hands. "The Sheriff and Burt have mapped out a plan for you. They're waiting in Martha's dining room."

"Tell them I'll be there in a flash."

Daisy moved closer and wrapped her arms around his neck, then kissed him on cheek. It was only momentary peck of her lips, but there was feeling behind it.

"What was that for?" he asked in a whisper.

Her hug grew tighter. "Just wanted you to know how much I appreciate you stopping by my place and checking on my cat."

Not the answer he expected, but it made sense. At least the situation didn't spin sideways and get emotional. "No problem. I'm headed that way."

She let go of the embrace, her eyes focused on the floor around his feet.

Bunker wondered if his lack of reciprocal hug offended her. "Is there anything else you need me to do, while I'm there?"

Her eyes came up and met his. "Just make sure the gas is off."

"Consider it done."

"There are bowls in the cupboard by the sink. Vonda won't overeat, so go ahead and leave extra food and water for her. That should hold her for a while."

"I can bring her back if you'd like."

"No. She'll just slow you down."

"Are you sure?"

Daisy shook her head, though the shrug that followed looked tentative. "She's only a cat, Bunker. It's not worth the risk. We've got way more important things to deal with right now."

Her callous answer was unexpected. The woman had a big heart, that much was clear, but he figured she'd react like most pet owners—overly attached and willing to risk life and limb to save the animal.

"Will do," he said, letting the question go so he could shift focus back to his packing.

"Stephanie and Megan are getting Tango ready."

"Excellent. One less thing I have to worry about."

"Speaking of worry . . . I don't think either of them wants you to leave. Things could get a little weird before you head out."

Bunker didn't respond, needing a moment to think.

"At least that's the impression I got when I stopped by to check on their progress."

"Did they say something?"

"No. Just a feeling."

"Okay. I'll deal with it. Thanks for the heads-up."

A suffocating silence hovered in the room as Bunker stared at Daisy and she at him. There was another topic he needed to cover with her, but he wasn't sure if this was the right time.

Daisy spoke before he could decide. "All right, then. I guess my job here is done." She turned and walking away.

"Hey Daisy?" he asked in a delicate tone.

She stopped and turned in an instant, her eyes filled with anticipation.

"There's one more thing I need to say."

"Okay, shoot."

He cleared his throat, waiting for the words to line up on his tongue. "Thanks for believing in me. I know we've had our moments, but your trust in me means more than you'll ever know. I won't let you down."

She smiled, her tone turning confident as her face flushed red. "I know you won't. Otherwise, I'd have to hunt you until the end of time, *Bulldog*."

He sent back a smile, appreciating her not making this goodbye any more difficult than it already was. They both knew the mission was dangerous and some words were best left unsaid.

* * *

"Where's Victor?" Sheriff Apollo asked Dicky when he arrived at the guard station at the end of Old Mill Road.

Dicky pointed in the direction of Martha Rainey's house. "He went inside a while ago. Should be back anytime. Hopefully, he'll remember the water."

"Ah, no. He's not inside."

"What do you mean?"

"His mother sent me here to check on him."

"Shit," Dicky said, looking down at the empty spot of dirt formerly occupied by Rusty's bike.

Apollo shook his head, not wanting to ask the next question. "Tell me he didn't take off?"

Dicky shrugged, then pointed at the oak tree designated for the sniper hide. "I was over there taking a whiz when the kid told me he was heading back inside to check on his mom. I thought that's where he went."

"Jesus, Dicky. How could you let this happen? I assigned him to this spot so you could keep an eye on him."

Dicky dropped his head. "Sorry, Sheriff. I fucked up."

Apollo thought about continuing the reprimand, but chose not to because it wouldn't change anything. Besides, this failure was his for trusting Victor and leaving the flight-risk kid with a volunteer deputy. "Do you have any idea where he went?"

"No sir. Just what he told me. I thought he rode the bike back to the house to check on his mom."

Apollo paused, putting on his detective hat. A set of tire tracks angled around the barricade and led to the bridge. "What were you two talking about right before he took off?"

"Nothing really. He was feeling down after you refused to give him a gun. I know he thinks that nobody trusts him, so I put him in charge of this station when I went to take a leak. I thought it might cheer him up."

"Anything else?"

"That's about it."

"When was this exactly?"

"Right after you left earlier."

Apollo ran through the conversation with the kid, replaying the words exchanged. "I laid into him pretty good, didn't I?"

"He needed to hear it, boss. Otherwise, he'll never grow up."

"Yeah, maybe so. But I didn't need to be so harsh."

"At least he admitted to the break-in. That's a start."

"I suppose it is. But if he thinks none of us trusts him, then there's no telling why he took off."

"I'm sure he's just trying to find a way to prove himself. I was like that back in the day, always trying to figure out where I belonged."

Apollo agreed. "It's not easy at that age, especially when you don't have a father figure around."

"Down deep, I think he's a good kid."

Apollo felt a knot form in his stomach as he peered over his shoulder, his eyes landing on the Rainey homestead. If Victor took off because of what Apollo had said, then whatever happened to the boy was his fault.

He let out a slow breath, his mind a whirl. "I better go have a chat with Allison."

"I can go explain it to her, Sheriff. You shouldn't have to. This was my bad."

"No, this one's on me."

"Are you sure? Because I don't mind taking the heat. I was in charge and he skipped out on my watch."

"I appreciate the offer, Dicky, but I got this. It's my job as Sheriff," Apollo said, the pain in his abdomen intensifying. "Stand watch until I send Daisy here to relieve you. Won't be long. She's helping Bunker get geared up."

"You got it, boss. Again, I'm sorry."

CHAPTER 19

Apollo took Allison Rainey by the crux of the arm and led her away from the other members of the compound who were standing around the dining room table in Martha Rainey's house. The area maps were spread out across the surface and ready for Bunker, but he hadn't arrived yet from Tuttle's place.

"Where's my son?" Allison asked, her tone tense and suspicious. The depth of concern in her eyes was obvious, almost painful.

Apollo needed to soften the news and find a way to explain his complete and total failure. The last thing he wanted was to inflict undue emotional trauma on the woman he'd been planning to ask out on a date ever since she landed in town. He swallowed hard, then licked his lips in a stall maneuver until he found the proper words. "That's what I wanted to talk to you about…"

"Is he hurt?"

"No, no, no," he stammered. "That's not it."

The volume in her voice shot up a level. "Then what is it, Sheriff? Is he dead? Oh my God, he's dead, isn't he?"

Martha Rainey joined the conversation an instant later, touching her daughter's forearm with a soft hand. "What's wrong? Is it Victor?"

Allison nodded, looking at her mother with fright in her eyes. "Yeah, something's terribly wrong. I can sense it. But I can't get the Sheriff to tell me anything." Her eyes swung to Apollo. "Why won't you tell me?"

Apollo opened his mouth to answer, but Martha beat him to it, not letting a millisecond of silence drift by. "You need to tell us, Gus. Right now. This very instant!"

"I'm trying to—" Apollo said, wishing they'd let him respond before their mounting hysteria ran them over. "Victor took—"

"Damn it, he stole something again!" Allison snapped, throwing up her hands. She shook her head at her mother. "I told you he'd do it again. I told you. It just never stops with that boy."

Martha's eyes softened, compressing some of the wrinkles along her temples. "It'll be okay, honey. It's not your fault. You're a good mother."

Allison stuck out her chin and pinched her lips before she answered, her breathing more exaggerated. "If I'm such a good mother, why does he keep doing this?" She paced a bit, her feet moving in a circle, tears beginning to show on her cheeks. "I thought we were making progress. He promised me."

Apollo brought his arms up to stop the woman's trek, but Martha got in the way when she wrapped her arms around Allison's neck and spoke into her ear. "Trust me, Allison. You've done everything you can. None of this is your fault."

Allison's arms were hanging limp, not returning the embrace. "Yes, it is my fault. I'm his mother and I'm responsible for everything he does. I just wish I could get through to him, Mom, but he's just like his father—stubborn, and he doesn't listen to anyone. I don't know what I'm going to do with him."

The hug ended before Allison shifted her focus to Apollo. "He's going to jail, isn't he?"

"Hang on a minute. I never said that," Apollo answered, trying to break through the madness running amok.

"But he stole something, didn't he?"

"Yes, as a matter of fact," Apollo said, taking a step closer to Allison. He needed to penetrate the panic surrounding her and explain, "but you need to listen to me—"

Martha put out an arm, pressing her palm on Apollo's chest before he could finish his sentence. "We appreciate your concern, Sheriff, but this is a family matter now—a *private* family matter. You need to step back and let me deal with this."

Apollo pushed her hand away. "All right, just stop. Both of you! You're getting way ahead of yourselves here."

Martha's lips ran quiet and her eyes shot wide.

Apollo continued while there was a moment of silence in the room. "Both of you need to shut the hell up and let me talk."

Allison looked stunned.

Martha folded her arms across her chest and stood more erect than before. "I suppose that's an order?"

"If it has to be an order to get the two of you to listen, then it's an order. But for heaven's sake, let me talk for a minute."

Apollo peered at the others by the table. Each of them was staring at him, their faces covered with shock. "Everything is okay, folks. No need to be concerned. Just a little situation, but we've got it under control."

He took a moment to make sure Allison and Martha were listening before he continued. "What I was trying to tell you is that Victor borrowed Rusty's bike and went for a ride."

"A ride?" Martha asked before pointing toward the front of her home. "Now? With everything that's going on out there?"

"Yes, he took off and we're not sure why. But there's no reason to start a panic, ladies."

"When did he leave?" Martha asked.

"A while ago."

"And you're just telling us now?"

"I would have told you earlier, but I just found out myself."

"You need to go look for him, Sheriff," Allison said, grabbing him by the hands with a tender wrap. Her fingers squeezed his, grabbing his attention. "He shouldn't be out there all alone. It's too dangerous."

Her skin was smooth and supple, just like he'd imagined. Her touch was a distraction to be sure, but he managed to push through it and regain his focus. "I plan to. But first, I wanted to let you know that he's missing. But we'll find him, you have my word."

* * *

Bunker opened the front door to Martha's house and waited for Daisy to enter first. When he stepped inside, he found Apollo standing to the left with Martha and Allison. The Sheriff's hands were holding onto Allison's, all three of their faces flushed red.

Jeffrey, Stephanie, Rusty, Burt, Albert, and Dustin stood to the right, holding position near the dining room table. Their faces looked numb. So did Megan's, her butt planted in the same dining room chair as before.

Bunker looked at Apollo, the tension in the room thick and palpable. "What did we miss?"

"I need to go take care of something, then I'll get right on it," Apollo told Allison, ignoring Bunker's query.

She nodded, then let go of his hands.

Martha wrapped an arm around Allison and pulled her close.

When Apollo arrived at Bunker's position, he said, "There's been a development."

"The Russians?" Daisy asked.

"No, it's Allison's son," Apollo said, the volume in his voice less than before.

"Did he get hurt?" Bunker asked, lowering his voice to match the Sheriff's.

"No. He took off with Rusty's bike while Dicky's back was turned. I had them both on guard duty."

Daisy took a step closer, leaning in close to Apollo. "Did he run away?"

"Not sure. But we're going to need to send out a search party."

"How long ago was this?" she asked.

"Too long, unfortunately. I just found out when I went out there to check on things."

"Why didn't Dicky say something?"

"He didn't know, apparently. Victor waited until he was behind a tree doing his business, then pretended he was taking the bike back to the house to check on his mom. That's when he took off. Tracks head across the bridge."

"Why would he do that?"

Apollo took in a slow breath, then let it out. "I think it has something to do with a little chat he and I had with about him stepping up and taking responsibility."

"Franklin's 1911?" Bunker asked.

"That, and other things. I might have been a bit too rough on the kid."

"So the boy got pissed and just took off?" Daisy asked.

"I'm afraid so."

"It's possible he might come back on his own, Sheriff," Bunker said. "I'm not sure sending out a search party is the right move. Not with me leaving."

"He might, but I promised his mother we'd look for him. We got a kid out there who needs our help."

Bunker nodded. "Then we'd better hurry before it gets dark."

"Dicky and I will handle it, Bunker. You need to get moving as planned."

"What about me?" Daisy asked.

"I need you to relieve Dicky."

"10-4."

Apollo looked at Bunker. "Burt and I have outlined some waypoints for you. The map's on the table."

"Okay, show me what you got."

CHAPTER 20

"Excuse me, General," Colonel Sergei Orlov said in Russian after knocking, waiting for clearance to enter the newly acquired office of his commanding officer.

General Yuri Zhukov was not a patient man by any stretch, but Orlov hoped today might be the exception. Then again, maybe the General would deny this unscheduled meeting, one Sergei preferred not to have with the ruthless leader.

Usually Sergei stood in the corner of the General's office in silence, waiting for orders. It happened recently when the guards dragged the Mayor in for a light interrogation. Then again when the Silver King Mine owner tried to negotiate his way out of the occupation.

It was degrading for an officer who had achieved the rank of Colonel to stand at attention for hours on end, but it was an honor to serve Mother Russia in whatever capacity she needed. And right now, she needed him to suck it up and support the narcissistic, overconfident General during *Operation Gospodstvo*.

It was the single most important mission in Russian history, one that drew his full attention the instant he learned it involved taming the American beast on American soil.

What kept him moving forward in this demeaning role was the knowledge that once their battalion had acquired what it needed, they'd return home with the spoils of a victorious mission. His name, and the names of his junior officers, would live on in the history books for all those who came after.

Sergei tried hailing his commander again, this time raising his voice and knocking four times instead of three. "General Zhukov. I have important information."

"Enter," Zhukov said in Russian, his voice thready. His words sounded painful.

Sergei adjusted his uniform, making sure every crease was perfect before he stepped through. When his feet landed inside the threshold, his eyes found a naked man lying face-down on a massage table. A white terrycloth towel covered the man's midsection, leaving his upper back and sandy-white calves exposed to the Colorado air.

A rail-thin American woman in an all-white outfit chopped at the man's back with the downward edge of her hands. The reddish glow in the blonde's cheeks intensified as she worked the area just above the towel in a rapid-fire motion, pounding the stress away.

Sergei wasn't sure how the narrow-hipped resident could work her hands with such speed and precision, but the woman was obviously a professional.

Typical, Sergei thought to himself, having witnessed the General's taste for blonde women and massages before. Russian Foreign Intelligence had developed detailed files on every Clearwater resident and he was certain the General used the SVR-gathered information to select this woman as his personal masseuse.

Sergei had his share of body hair, but nothing close to that of the General's. It looked like the masseuse was pounding at a Persian rug instead of someone's spine.

He cleared his throat, keeping the conversation in Russian, not only due to its classified nature, but because the General despised English. He couldn't blame his boss. He wasn't fond of it either, but like he preached to his men, it was part of their duty.

Technically, learning to speak English was an order that came from the highest levels of the Kremlin—one every officer in this command had accepted without question. It wasn't easy preparing for this most prestigious mission, not when a year of endless language sessions was involved. "General, sir. Sorry to interrupt."

The masseuse stopped her hands when the General raised his head and brought his eyes to Sergei.

Sergei felt the eyes of the woman on him. He turned to confirm, seeing her tuck two unruly strands of hair behind her ears, exposing more of her face.

She was attractive, but much too thin for his taste. He preferred women with wide hips and a little meat on their bones. Yet he knew she was just the type of woman the General preferred, having witnessed the man's selection process before. The man loved to sample the local cuisine. Both with his lips and other body parts.

"Can't you see I'm busy?" the General snarled.

"Sorry, sir. But this can't wait."

"Make it quick, Colonel."

"Sir, the information I carry is classified." Sergei could have provided more information to his commander, but decided against it. Their pre-mission briefing had been explicit and clear—a small percentage of Americans speak Russian. He wasn't to assume his conversation was secure when speaking his native language.

Zhukov waved at the masseuse to leave the room. The woman didn't hesitate, backing away and taking one of the hand towels from a stack next to her. She folded the towel in half, then used it to dab the beads of sweat on her brow as she walked to the office door and disappeared outside.

The General rolled to his side and sat up. The towel fell from his lap when he stood up and strolled behind his desk, never bothering to cover up.

The leather chair squeaked when Zhukov's naked backside slid across the upholstery. He flashed a scowl. "I don't have all day, Orlov."

"Sorry, sir," he said, handing the General a single sheet of paper containing eleven items on the Daily Action Report. "An incident has been reported that warrants your immediate attention."

He watched the General's eyes, waiting for them to land on the last item. The other notices were fairly routine, given the nature and location of their mission. He'd seen it all before when in-country. So had the General.

Flare-ups with residents and troop misconduct were predictable when dealing with command and control of foreign civilians. The newest recruits were usually the problem. It developed like clockwork, usually within days, leading him to classify the troops in one of two groups: those who were overly committed to their first assignment, or those struggling with their own inner demons.

Not every Russian who puts on the uniform can handle the relentless pressure of being in-country, especially when you're looking into the eyes of innocent women and children.

However, when an officer goes missing—a female officer—everyone takes notice, even the new recruits. Patriotism trumps morality every time. Especially when it's the General's interpreter. He'd hoped to have a resolution before stepping into this meeting, but his pair of investigators came up empty.

"When was this reported?" Zhukov asked.

"Forty-five minutes ago. Officer Zakharova failed to appear for a scheduled duty assignment. Our initial search came up empty."

Zhukov slammed the paper down on the desk. "That's unacceptable, Orlov! Find her! Tear apart this town if you have to. Task whatever resources you need, but I want her found. Now!"

"Yes, sir."

* * *

Burt Lowenstein stood next to Bunker and across the table from Apollo and Dicky as he put his scarred finger on the map. Mechanic work ages a man's hands quickly, leaving them broken, bruised, and beyond salvation. Constant grease and soap were only part of the problem. Wrench slippage near an engine block caused far more damage, tearing skin from bone upon impact.

Burt traced a path along a series of black lines he'd drawn on the map earlier, purposely avoiding the red circles Tuttle had added when the old coot was still alive.

"This is the way I'd go, Bunker. It's the safest route back to town."

Bunker nodded slowly, then pointed at a clearing bordered by mountains on all sides. "What can you tell me about this?"

"That's Patterson's Meadow. But you'll want to avoid it, too." Burt drew a line from north to south, taking Bunker's eyes through a narrow gap in the topography. "It's a death trap, with only one way in or out. A guy could get himself killed in there."

The answer didn't appear to faze Bunker, almost as if that was the answer he was expecting.

"What's with all the circles around the meadow?" Stephanie asked, putting a hand on Bunker's back as she leaned in next to him.

Burt saw her smile at Bunker, then rub her hand across his back. The man didn't seem to notice. Or else he chose not to react to her friendliness.

"Daisy thought he might be planning to build a cabin on it," Apollo said from across the table. "But we really don't know for sure."

"Okay, I get that," Stephanie said. "But why highlight all the bridges and the other stuff?"

"It's important to know the area, especially the egress points," Bunker said, his tone slow and even, sounding as if he was running it through in his head.

Apollo nodded. "If a forest fire hit, his options would be limited."

Bunker walked to the other side of Burt, leaving Stephanie's hand dangling. "I'm going to need to take a closer look at it."

Burt wasn't sure why. The meadow was much too close to town to be used as any type of base camp, if that's what Bunker was thinking.

Stephanie put her finger on the lines representing the highway near it. "At least it's close to some pavement. I don't know about you guys, but driving these dirt roads would get old after a while."

Burt disagreed with the buxom beauty. The clearing was much too close to the paved highway— would be easy pickings for the Russians. He'd choose something more remote.

Bunker put the tip of his finger on Burt's original path, then drew an imaginary line from it to the mouth of Patterson's Meadow. "Is there anything to worry about in here?"

"Not really. Just avoid the highway." He took the protective cap from the black marker and added another line to the map. "This logging road is one of the nicer ones in the area. The Forest Service maintains it regularly."

"How wide is it?"

"It's pretty wide. At least forty feet. Maybe more. The ATV riders fly up and down it all the time. At least they used to whenever I was out there hunting. Those assholes always scared off the game in the area."

"Wide enough," Bunker mumbled, his eyes locked onto the map.

"Wide enough for what?" Burt asked.

"It's not important," Bunker said, straightening his posture. He rolled up the map. "How are the projects coming along?"

"I'm getting there, but it's a ton of work," Burt said. "All I can say is that you better come through with that rifle. Otherwise, you and I are gonna go a few rounds."

Apollo answered instead of Bunker. "No reason to go there, Burt. A deal is a deal. It's yours when this is over."

Bunker's eyes darted around the room. "Has anyone seen Albert? I need to have a chat with him."

"He's down the road, hanging out with Daisy," Dicky said.

Apollo rolled his eyes. "Why am I not surprised?"

"I don't know how she puts up with it," Burt said. "Even I don't drool that bad."

Apollo looked at Bunker. "While you're doing that, I'm gonna check on Allison and her mother before Dicky and I head out to look for Victor."

"I'm sure they'll appreciate that. Just don't overcommit on the search. Can't risk everyone's security for the sake of one troubled boy."

Apollo's eyes signaled he agreed with the assessment. "There's a fine line. But we gotta try."

"Good luck," Bunker said, holding out his hand for a shake.

"Keep your head down out there," Apollo said, grabbing his hand and shaking it twice. Dicky did the same. The two men left the room in a rush.

Bunker looked at Stephanie. "You wouldn't happen to know if Martha has a pen and some paper around here, would you? I've got a laundry list to write."

She pointed at a curved entry table hugging the wall by the front door. "Try the drawer. That's where I'd keep them."

CHAPTER 21

Fifteen minutes later . . .

Bunker grabbed the assault rifle leaning against the wall by the front door of Martha Rainey's place and loaded a magazine from his vest with a firm shove of his hand. He headed outside with the map lashed to his rucksack using the Velcro straps along the side.

Shortly after his feet hit the pavers outside, a tug landed on his right arm. The force was enough to turn him sideways.

"You got a minute?" Stephanie King asked, her son fiddling with the Pokémon cards a few yards away. Dallas was huddled with Jeffrey, shining a flashlight at the underside of one of the cards.

"Sure, but I need to get moving. The sun is almost down." Bunker didn't see Megan, but he knew she was around somewhere. He planned to say goodbye to the ebony child who had captured his heart.

"So . . . you're really going to do this?" Stephanie asked in a defiant tone.

"I'm coming back, Steph. Don't worry."

"You say that, but you really don't know for sure. It's dangerous out there."

Bunker held up his rifle. "That's why I have this."

She hugged him without warning, her ample chest pressing hard into his tactical vest.

He brought his arms up and wrapped his forearms around her back. He put his free hand on her back and rubbed, making sure she knew he appreciated her concern. "I know you're worried, but this is what I'm trained to do."

"But it's the Russians."

"Trust me, they have no idea who they're dealing with."

"Please be careful. We need you to come back in one piece."

"I will," he said, as the hug continued.

"Jeffrey would be heartbroken if you got yourself killed."

"Yeah, I'm pretty fond of that boy, too," he said, debating whether to say the next three words lining up on his tongue. He decided to set them free. "What about you?"

She leaned back from the embrace but didn't answer, her face only inches from his. Her watery eyes never moved. He stopped his breath as her stare lingered for what seemed like a minute, their lower bodies pressing together.

"You two gonna kiss, or what?" Dallas asked.

The words broke through the awkwardness to end the stare-down. Bunker pulled his arms away and stepped back.

Stephanie did the same, looking like she had an hour's worth of words she was holding back.

Bunker exhaled, letting the breath he'd been holding escape.

Someone tugged at Bunker's pant leg.

He looked down.

It was Jeffrey, hovering only a foot away, with Dallas next to him. The freckled boy brought his hand up with the deck of Pokémon cards in his clutch. "These are yours, Jack."

"No Jeffrey, you hang on to them until I get back. Someone needs to keep them safe."

The boy nodded, then spread the cards out in his hand. He took one from the stack and held it up. "I want you to have this one."

"For good luck," Stephanie said a millisecond later, her tone pushy and to the point as usual. She snatched the card and gave it to Bunker.

Bunker knew he couldn't refuse. He took it and studied the colorful scene. The cartoon character portrayed a demon-looking squirrel creature with a fiery tail. "Which one of them is this?"

Jeffrey's face lit up with excitement. "That's Charmeleon, my all-time favorite."

"He looks fierce."

"He is. But there are a bunch of other characters I like, too. My second favorite is Metapod. But Parasect is cool, too. Oh, and Arcanine. He's really fast."

Bunker never paid much attention to the Pokémon craze. Why should he? He didn't have any kids and Pokémon wasn't a high priority for the members of the brotherhood. The Kindred had other hobbies, so to speak, usually with names like Candi or Jasmine. "How many are there?

"Over eight hundred."

"Wow, that's a lot more than I thought," Bunker said, figuring this kid was a collector. He seemed to know a lot about the Pokémon phenomenon. "How many do you have?"

Jeffrey held up the cards Bunker had given him. "Just these. Mom won't let me collect them."

Bunker smiled at the boy, then slid the Charmeleon card into one of his pockets. "Thank you, sport. I'll be sure to keep this one safe for you."

"Don't forget my mom and sisters," Dallas said.

"I won't," Bunker answered, figuring he'd run across them along the way. Most likely in town, with the other residents. When you're the occupying force, a centralized detention zone is the most efficient strategy to maintain order.

Stephanie leaned forward and whispered in Bunker's ear. "I'm sure Jeffrey would like a hug."

Bunker nodded. He bent down on one knee and waited with arms outstretched. Jeffrey knew instantly what to do, flying into Bunker's embrace.

After their hug ended, Stephanie said, "Megan wants to say goodbye, too. She's waiting for you by the corral."

Bunker stood. "She's not by herself, is she?"

"No, Rusty's keeping an eye on her."

"I'll head there shortly." Bunker turned his feet toward the end of Old Mill Road. "Wish me luck, everyone."

Stephanie didn't answer as Bunker walked away.

Neither did Jeffrey or Dallas.

CHAPTER 22

Bunker waved a quick hello at Daisy when he arrived at the guard station by the Old Henley Bridge, but didn't send any words her way. He aimed his focus at Albert instead. "Can we talk a minute?"

The fat man paused before he nodded, then walked with Bunker using his trademark waddle.

When Dustin started to follow, Bunker held up a hand. "Why don't you hang back a minute, Dustin?"

"Oh, okay. Will do."

After twenty yards or so, Bunker stopped and turned, keeping Albert in a direct line between him and Daisy.

"I sense a question coming my way," Albert said, his tone confident.

"You could say that."

"I'm all ears."

"I think it's time for the two of us to clear the air."

"About what?"

"About something you and I have been dancing around for a while now."

Albert blinked, but didn't respond.

Bunker ran through a half-dozen variations in his mind about the question he wanted to ask, before deciding to keep it simple and direct. "Are you really Tin Man?"

Albert's breathing stopped as he angled his head to the side, staring at the ground in silence.

"It's not that hard a question," Bunker said, recognizing the stall maneuver. "It's either yes or no."

Albert brought his eyes to bear, letting out the inhale he'd taken in. "Are you really Bulldog, enforcer for The Kindred?"

Bunker couldn't hold back a short chuckle. "I think you already know the answer to that question."

"As do you, to mine."

Bunker should have expected the non-committal rhetoric Albert was slinging. If he was Tin Man, then he'd probably spent his share of time in front of curious law enforcement—as had Bunker. That type of intense scrutiny hardens your resolve, teaching you to remain calm and choose your words carefully, if you decide to speak at all.

Detective teams are masters at spins, lies, and deceit, able to say almost anything to entrap their suspect. Self-incrimination is one of their most powerful tools.

Only those suspects who keep their wits about them while being grilled in the hot seat will survive the hours, sometimes days, it takes until the public defender makes an appearance. For those who rode with The Kindred, a hired barrister would arrive within an hour to end the questioning and ensure the gang's secrets remained a secret.

A smirk landed on Bunker's face.

The corners of Albert's mouth turned up. Yet it wasn't a grin. It was more of an *I'm smarter than you* look.

Bunker decided to change tactics, choosing a flanking maneuver instead of an all-out frontal assault. "Look, you and I both know you're not Tin Man."

"Then why are you asking?"

"Because we're a long way from the streets of LA and these people deserve better, one way or the other."

"I'm sure that's true. But since I don't have a map in front of me, I'll defer to your expertise on the matter."

Bunker shook his head. "So the dance continues."

"Are we done?" Albert asked, looking bored.

Bunker wondered if there was another way to confirm Albert's identify. The heavy man wasn't going to give a direct answer.

Right then, his mind connected with a memory from the past. Rumor had it the legendary meth cook possessed certain physical skills that would be easy to confirm without wasting time on any more words.

Bunker made a closed fist and threw a punch at Albert's head.

Albert responded in a flash, bringing his hands up in a lightning-quick defensive maneuver, deflecting the punch with a hook block. The big man countered by closing the gap between them, moving into Bunker's center position with a twist of his body.

An instant later, Albert locked Bunker's outstretched arm in a wedge position, then leveraged his considerable weight to drive Bunker to the ground on his back.

Albert brought a knee down on Bunker's chest, while simultaneously unleashing a swift right jab that stopped less than an inch from Bunker's nose.

"Satisfied?" Albert said a moment later, his eyes focused and fierce.

Daisy ran to their position. "What the hell is going on?"

"Just testing a theory," Bunker said from the prone position, the rucksack pressing into his spine.

Albert withdrew his fist, then stood up before extending an open palm.

Bunker grabbed it, letting Albert pull him to his feet.

Daisy moved between the two combatants with her arms outstretched and hands pressing on each of their chests.

Dustin joined the circus, his eyes wide in disbelief. "Jesus Christ! Where did that come from, Albert?"

"Are you okay?" Daisy asked Bunker, her hands grabbing at his vest and backpack.

"I'm good."

She turned to Albert. "And you. Explain yourself."

Albert flared an eyebrow, his face looking smug. "Just answering a question."

"What question?"

Albert ignored Daisy, keeping his eyes on Bunker. "Are we good?"

Bunker sent a nod of respect to Albert.

"So that's it?" she asked, her gaze alternating between Bunker and Albert.

"That's it," Bunker said in his most solemn tone. "Time for me to get moving."

She held for a moment, then huffed before stomping her way to the guard station.

Albert slid around Bunker to change places, now facing the end of Old Mill Road, his eyes peering at Daisy's position behind Bunker.

He put a hand into his pocket and pulled out a plastic bag filled with red crystals, dangling it from his fingertips. "I'm thinking you might need this."

Bunker recognized the infamous red crystals—Clearwater Red, the purest form of meth ever to have hit the streets. "For what?"

Albert lowered his voice. "To bribe your way past a checkpoint. It's my finest blend, but I'm sure you already know that."

Bunker took the gift and tested its weight with a bounce of his hand. It was roughly a pound, he figured, having held the same quantity on a number of occasions when he rode with The Kindred.

"Trust me," Albert said in a confident tone. "That will get you wherever you need to go."

Bunker knew Albert was right, but didn't want to openly admit it, even though the history books were filled with countless examples of military drug use. Most of it heavy. All of it dangerous. Especially during wartime or occupation. He'd seen it firsthand during his tour of duty, despite the public zero-tolerance policy of the Pentagon.

Drugs put a warrior's life in danger from either fatigue, over-stimulation, or euphoria. But it didn't end there. A grunt's comrades were also affected, relying on the addict to cover their six.

At this point, there was no reason to think the Russian troops would be immune to the epidemic of drugs. They were human, like everyone else, regardless of their reputation as ruthless, unfeeling, and ready to kill.

It would come down to pride and honor versus fear and anxiety, both sets of terms representing the primal instincts of a warrior and the root emotions of an addict. A fine line, indeed.

Some of the troops would need an escape from the stressors of constant threat. Others would be looking for temporary relief from the hours of endless boredom between duty shifts. Either way, these crystals would come in handy, if Bunker chose to use them.

Despite the clear advantage of supplying the insurgents with a powerful mind-altering substance, he knew the results would be difficult to control. More than that, it would be dangerous to seek out those troops in need. If he made contact with the wrong soldier first, it would not end well. He'd need to choose his initial target well.

Even if he could manage the outcome, fostering the use of Clearwater Red was something he preferred to avoid. Not because of potential law enforcement issues. But rather, because it would be a constant reminder of why he left The Kindred—drugs and children. Two things that should never mix.

Anytime drugs are accessible, even by accident, the potential for underage abuse is a clear and present danger. A danger he would be responsible for if he kept this gift from Tin Man.

After careful consideration, Bunker decided to hang onto the drugs. Leaving them in Albert's hands would be a mistake. Bunker needed to get the meth out of camp before one of the kids got their hands on it.

If, later on, the crystals just so happened to come in handy with the Russians, then so be it. A bonus, he decided. But his first objective must be securing the drugs, then stowing them somewhere safe.

Bunker slid his pack off and stuffed the baggie inside the upper pouch, keeping his body between the pack and Daisy. She'd only just started to trust him again after learning his secrets. If she caught a glimpse of the drug exchange, it would tear down the foundation he'd rebuilt.

"Is there more?" Bunker asked Albert in a whisper.

"No. That's it. But I can cook up another batch if we need it."

"That won't be necessary."

"I wouldn't be so sure. Once those soldiers get a taste, they're gonna want more. Just need someone to escort me back to my lab."

"Like I said, we're good."

"Suit yourself," Albert said, pausing. He glanced at Daisy, then back at Bunker. "Does the smoking-hot deputy know?"

"About what?"

"Your past."

Bunker nodded, holding back his distaste for Albert's sexual description of Daisy. "Most of it. But she's the only one."

Albert's mouth flopped open. "You told her?"

"Didn't have a choice after we ran into one of my old friends, Grinder."

"No, I guess not," Albert answered, his eyes indicating he was deep in thought. "Then I trust she doesn't know of mine?"

"Not that I'm aware."

"Good, then I hope we can keep it that way."

"I'm sure that can be arranged. But I'm going to need something in return."

"Name it," Dustin said, breaking his silence.

Bunker gave three sheets of folded paper to Albert. He'd found the paper in the drawer of the entrance table by Martha Rainey's front door. On the parchment, he'd written a long list of items and detailed instructions. "If you're as good as you say you are, then I'll need you use those chemistry skills to mix up some special ingredients that Tuttle has on hand. Something exotic, if you know what I mean."

"And deliberate, I'm guessing. Russian deliberate," Albert said after a head nod, his eyes tracking down the list. "Toads, really?"

"Can you handle it or not?"

"Sure. For Bulldog, anything." Albert folded the documents until they were the size of a smart phone, then stuffed them into his pocket. "Anything else?"

"That's it for now. Just have it ready when I get back. Ask Daisy if you need help. She knows where a lot of that stuff is."

"I'm sure I can handle it."

Bunker glanced at Daisy, then brought his attention back to Dustin and Albert. "I need to go have a chat with her. She looks a little stressed."

"Good luck with that," Albert said. "She's a unique bundle."

"That's an understatement," Bunker answered after a roll of his eyes.

He turned and headed to Daisy, needing to smooth things over before he went on his recon mission. If she had any questions, he needed to answer them to eliminate any fear or suspicion that might be building. If he didn't calm her down, she might turn to someone else—someone like the Sheriff—and fill him in on a number of things Bunker wanted to keep secret.

* * *

Dustin turned to Albert after Bunker was halfway to Daisy's position. He lowered his voice. "I can't believe you gave our entire supply to Bunker."

"Wasn't doing us any good, now was it?"

"What about our deal with Burt?"

"That's over with. Even he knows it. That's why we haven't spoken about it since we got here. He's moved on to something bigger and better. I can sense it in his eyes. Just watch him when he thinks nobody is looking. It's pretty obvious."

"The welding projects? I thought that was only for the rifle."

"And why do you think he wants it?"

"Not sure."

"To make a name for himself. Slinging ice for us is the last thing on his mind. I'll bet my last dollar he thinks that kind of firepower will allow him to rule Clearwater County, or some crazy shit like that. But first, he'll need to take out anyone who stands in his way."

"Like the Russians," Dustin answered in a likeminded tone.

"And anyone else who might be in a position to stop his plans."

"You're talking about the Sheriff, aren't you?"

"He's one."

"Daisy, too?"

"That would be my guess."

"What about Bunker?"

"Yep. And the Mayor."

"Seriously? How do you know all this?"

"It's simple. You just have to think like a narcissistic sociopath who is never satisfied with anything. There's no such thing as enough."

Dustin took a second to consider what Albert was saying. "You're right. He doesn't need us anymore."

"Exactly, which is why we step out of the way and stay off that hit list," Albert said, his eyes still on Bunker. "No, I'm afraid the Burt experiment has come to a close. Permanently."

"Still doesn't explain why you gave the batch to Bunker."

"He's the new Burt, whether he knows it or not."

Dustin didn't understand the connection. "I'm sorry, what?"

"He'll do what Burt could never do—get those crystals into the proper hands. Then we'll have some major demand."

"The Russians?"

Albert nodded.

"That's why you told him to use the drugs to get past the checkpoint."

A sly grin grew on Albert's lips. "Imagine the power we'll have if the entire Russian Army gets addicted to our blend! And I'm not just talking about here, in Clearwater County."

"You think it'll spread to other camps?"

"Count on it," Albert said. "We'll be able to name our price. And not just in terms of money, either."

Visions of women, cars, food, and guns raged in Dustin's mind. The scene changed a moment later, showing him sitting on a throne, receiving his weekly homage from the thankful peasants. "I see your point."

"Bunker is perfect for this. He's tougher and smarter than Burt. Plus, he's gonna do all the work."

"And take the heat."

Albert laughed. "Without a cut, no less. All we have to do is prime the pump, then stand back and let it happen."

"It *is* perfect," Dustin said, appreciating the guile of his partner. "No cut means a hundred percent profit."

"You catch on quick, my friend."

Dustin flashed a smile, but it quickly faded when a new idea filled his brain. "But what if he decides to get rid of the meth and not distribute it?"

"Then we're right back where we started. No harm. No foul. Plus, we look like the good guys since we tried to help."

"So basically, there's no downside."

"Bingo. Zero risk and potentially endless profits. All for letting a former biker take a bag of Clearwater Red with him."

* * *

"You okay?" Bunker asked Daisy when he arrived at her location.

She pointed at Albert. "What the hell was that?"

"A little history that needed to be sorted out."

"New history or old?"

"A little of both."

"Does he know about your past?"

"Yes, but only part of it."

"How?"

"That's not important."

She flared her eyes. "Everything is important, Jack. We're all depending on each other."

"I get that, but—"

"Look, I don't like working in the dark with all these secrets floating around."

"No, that's understandable. I don't like it either."

"I think you know by now that honesty is important to me. I don't think that's unreasonable to expect from you. Not after all we've been through."

Bunker paused, running it through his mind. She had a right to know, but he didn't want to lose Tin Man's help by betraying his confidence. Bunker needed to find middle ground to keep everyone happy. "All I can tell you for now is that Albert has certain skills we're going to need, if we have any hope of keeping everyone safe."

"What does that mean, exactly?"

"It means . . . I need you to trust me on this. I have a couple of things to verify on my way to town, then I'll fill you in on my plan when I get back."

"And the Sheriff?"

"Him, too. But first I need to be absolutely sure of something. And to do that, I need you to be patient and let me do what I need to do."

She didn't answer.

"Please. Everyone's life is at stake and this is the way it has to be . . . for now anyway."

Daisy put her rifle down on the butt of its stock, leaning the barrel against the edge of the wooden barricade.

She took his free hand in hers, rubbing his fingers gently. "I hope you know I do trust you. More than you know. But you can't keep putting me in these difficult positions. It's making me question everything I am as a law enforcement officer, and as a woman. Sometimes I just want to throw up."

"You're right. This is not how it should be."

"No, it's not. I'm your friend and I believe in you. But I'm also a deputy sheriff. That means I'm going to need a certain amount of confidence that I'm doing the right thing, Jack. For everyone. It can't just be about you and me."

"I completely understand. But I do have a plan."

Silence filled the air for the better part of a minute, her eyes fixed on his. He could feel her soul reaching out to his, trying to find some level of comfort. Faith is never easy, especially when you're staring down the promise of death.

Daisy squeezed his hand before she spoke again. "Okay. I'll go along for now, but when you get back, everyone comes clean. No more secrets. It's the way it's gotta be."

Bunker wasn't sure Albert would agree, but he decided to accept to her deal. Otherwise, she'd turn against him and that was something he couldn't let happen. Not with the lives of children at risk.

In the end, he saw it as a binary choice. Either his plan was sound and they would defeat the threat, or everyone died. At that point, regardless of the outcome, nobody would care about his checkered past. Or Albert's. More so if his plan failed, because the dead never complain.

He shook her hand loose, then pulled his pack around and set it on the ground. It took a minute of digging to find the set of long-range handheld radios he'd stuffed inside. He gave one to her.

"What's this for?" she asked, inspecting both sides of the device with her eyes.

"To get hold of me while I'm in the field."

"I thought we were keeping these for emergency use only."

"We were, but I think it's wise for the two of us to stay in touch. You know, just in case."

"Okay. If that's what you want. But shouldn't the Sheriff have this?"

"That was my original plan, but he'll have his hands full now that Victor went missing. Your name is next on the list."

She nodded. "What about the batteries?"

"They're fully charged."

"Not what I meant."

"Oh, you mean how long?"

"Yeah, like in hours or days."

"Ten hours at least, depending on talk time," Bunker answered, thinking about how well Tuttle had been prepared. The man even had a spare charger in the metal file cabinet where these radios were stored.

"What if you're gone longer than that?"

"That's why we're only going to turn them on for five minutes at the top of every hour. If you need me, that's when I'll be listening."

"All right, but what if you need me?"

"Same thing. Turn the unit on at the top of the hour and wait. If I need you, you'll know. Don't call out to me. The Russians will most likely be monitoring signals. If we're too active, they'll get a lock on us."

"Aren't these encrypted?"

"Our voices, yes. But not the signal. They can still triangulate if we broadcast too long. That's why we keep communications short, if at all."

She nodded.

"Ideally, if would be better if these civilian models had frequency hopping built in. But since they don't, we'll need to use them even more sparingly."

"Okay."

"I've already set the frequency and keyed in the encryption sequence."

"Cool. What is it?"

"314159265358979."

She laughed. "You don't really expect me to remember that, do you?"

"It's the first fifteen digits of pi."

She tilted her head, sending him a smirk.

He thought it was simple enough, but understood her doubt. "It's stored in the flash memory so you shouldn't need to remember it."

"But what if I do?"

Bunker thought about it, then the answer came to him. "Albert can help you out. I'm sure he knows it."

"Or I could write it down."

"Fine, just don't keep it on you."

"Is this how you did it in the field?"

He shook his head. "Not exactly. Our tech was far superior, plus we changed the code daily."

"That must have been a huge hassle."

"Not really. It was all done by computer so there were no codes to input. A central laptop would dump the new daily encryption keys to a small block device, then we'd plug the block into each radio and update the day's code. It was pretty slick, as long as everyone remembered to have their radio updated each morning."

She tapped an index finger on her naked wrist. "Aren't we missing something?"

"Oh shit. Almost forgot," he said. His hand went back into the pack and pulled out a pair of Luminox Colormark watches. He put one on his wrist and she did the same. "I've already synchronized the time."

She winked. "Good, then I'll know if you're late."

CHAPTER 23

Bunker ignored the reins in Rusty's hands as he walked past Tango inside the corral behind Tuttle's place. He took a seat next to Megan on the end of the feeder station. The homemade box felt solid under his backside even though the set of 6x6 posts framing the wooden platform looked weathered. At least the galvanized timber spikes holding them together didn't show any sign of wear.

The front side of the box spilled into an open trough filled with oats. Wait, check that, half-filled, now that Tango had enjoyed his late afternoon dinner, no doubt with Megan overseeing the feeding process. Next to the box was a tub of water. It, too, was less than full.

"Are you okay?" Bunker asked the ebony child, who was adjusting her knee brace. He knew she was in both emotional and physical pain, but he still had to ask.

The girl pulled her hands from the brace, then looked at Bunker with those innocent, almond-shaped eyes of hers, tears welling inside. "I miss my papa."

Megan's confession wasn't a surprise, not with the layers of anguish he knew were smothering her heart. "We all do, sweetheart. He was a really good friend to all of us."

She dropped her head and sniffed a few times, her tiny hands fiddling with each other. Her fingers looked lost, like her, unsure of what to do.

Bunker wrapped an arm around Megan, then took a finger and put it under her chin. He applied a light upward pressure, bringing her eyes up to his. "Your father was a very special man who loved his little girl very much. I hope you know that, right?"

She nodded, then sucked in a short breath and sniffed again, never taking her gaze from his. "Uh-huh. But I'm still scared."

"I know you are, but there's no reason to be scared. You have a lot of people around here who care about you. Like Rusty and the Sheriff. They won't let anything happen. I promise."

"What about you?"

"Me too. And Daisy."

"But I don't want *you* to leave, Jack. Bad things happen when you leave."

The pressure around his heart intensified, her words cutting into him. "I have to go, Megan."

"But why?"

"To find Star, for one. Plus, I need to check on Daisy's cat and see if I can find Dallas' mom and sisters. They're all missing and scared, Megan. Don't you want me to help find them? Bring them home?"

"I do, but the bad men are out there."

She was correct, but he didn't want to reinforce her fears with acknowledgment of the danger. "I'll be careful. Nothing's gonna happen to me."

"Promise?"

Bunker nodded, never taking his eyes from her. "Promise. But I need you to be strong and take care of yourself until I get back. Can you do that for me?"

She nodded.

Bunker pulled his arm away from the mini-hug, then took out a chocolate-covered energy bar from one of the pockets on his vest. "I brought you a present."

A beaming smile took over her face, her misty eyes locking onto the treat like a heat-seeking missile.

Bunker shook the bar like a finger wave.

She snatched it in a second.

"You need to eat more, to keep your strength up. Otherwise, your leg won't get better."

"I will. I promise," she said, tugging at the wrapper. It wouldn't open. She tried again, this time clenching her teeth as she struggled. Still no luck.

Bunker took the bar and ripped an edge free, pulling the paper down along one side. He gave it to her, feeling like a father tending to a helpless child. Sure, this wasn't his kid and the girl was far from helpless, but that didn't change the fact that she was in need.

Megan took a bite and began to chew, looking as though he'd taken away some of her pain, if only for a few seconds.

Somewhere along the way, they'd formed a connection that had grown by the hour. He knew he could never fill the role of Franklin, but taking care of her still felt like the right thing to do. Someone had to take the lead and his heart was telling him that it was his job to do so. One he planned to undertake after this crisis was over. For now, everyone had to chip in and keep her safe.

Bunker waited until she finished enjoying the treat before he spoke again. "It's getting dark, Megan. You need to get inside where it's safe."

"Are you leaving now?"

He gulped and nodded, not wanting to answer.

She spun and wrapped her arms around his neck, squeezing hard enough to choke off some of his air.

The instant Megan let go, she got to her feet and hobbled on her crutches to Tango. She gave the horse a goodbye hug across his snout, then continued on, never looking back.

* * *

Stan Fielding flinched, dropping the fork in his hand when a loud thud rang out near his home. It took a second to realize where the noise had come from— the front door of his modest three-bedroom home on Lake View Drive.

He flew out of the kitchen chair and grabbed his twin girls when a second thump slammed into his house. He corralled Beth and Barb into the corner beyond the dinette table and spun around with his hands behind his legs to keep the girls in one spot.

A third, more powerful bang hit the door. This time it was followed by a powerful crack, then the sound of wood splintering.

Footsteps grew in intensity as they pounded across the tile floor of his living room, carrying with them the clatter of metal. Glass broke and voices were heard—Russian voices.

Barb screamed as four men scrambled into the kitchen. They quickly fanned out side by side, with their rifles aimed at Stan's face. Three of the men were several inches taller than Stan, including the one with a red goatee.

Stan put his hands in front of his chest. "Please! Don't shoot! Please!"

The shortest of the four approached in silence, his calloused, clean-shaven face buried behind the mini-scope on his rifle.

"What do you want?" Stan asked him, his eyes focused on the man's trigger finger.

The other three circled around in a flanking maneuver. The man with red goatee spun to open the pantry room door, his rifle in a shooting position.

"*Vse chisto*," the solider said in a commanding voice, closing the door behind him.

A spread of hollow thuds raced across the floorboards above. Stan couldn't be sure, but it sounded like three men were searching the second floor and possibly the tiny attic space on the third floor. Doors squeaked open and then closed with force. More glass breaking.

"Daddy?" Beth asked in a frightened tone before Stan shushed her.

"Where is she?" the short Russian asked Stan with a heavy accent, the English barely recognizable.

Stan shook his head, his heart pounding in his chest like a sledgehammer. "Who?"

"Where is she?" the soldier asked again, a dollop of spittle flying from his lips in anger.

"I don't know who you're talking about. It's just us. There's nobody else here."

The short man waved at the two soldiers on his right, both sporting a shadow of stubble across their chins. The camo-covered men sprang into action, slinging their rifles before grabbing Stan by the arms. He tried to resist, but they were too strong, dragging him to the center of the kitchen.

"Stop hurting my daddy!" Barb screeched before her tears took over.

Beth held her sister close, both girls crying uncontrollably.

The short man dropped a hand from his rifle and sucker punched Stan in the gut. The force of the impact doubled him over, sending him to his knees in a search for air. A foot came at him next, barely missing his face, but catching his shoulder. He flopped sideways and landed on his back.

Stan fought through the pain as he turned over and pushed himself to all fours. It was difficult to steady himself with his chest heaving in gasping thrusts.

When he brought his eyes up in search of his daughters, he found them in the corner, holding each other in a cradle of fear, their adorable faces drowning in tears.

Stan continued to fight for oxygen as more footsteps found his ears. They were outside the kitchen. The stairs, he figured, based on the creaks and groans of the wooden steps.

Seconds later, a fifth soldier entered the kitchen with a bloody uniform in his hand. He said something in Russian to the short man before delivering the clothing.

Short man brought his rifle down and let it hang on the sling across his chest to accept the garments. His hands turned red from the transfer of blood as he separated the blouse from the pants. The shirt had a tear across the front, looking as though someone sliced it open with a knife.

Short man's eyes grew wild with fire. He turned to Stan and held the uniform in front of his face. "This was in the attic."

"I don't know how that got there. I've never seen it before in my life."

"Where is she? What did you do to her?"

"I don't know who you're talking about! We didn't do anything. You have to believe me. Please. Just let us go. Please."

Short man looked at goatee man and sent him a signal with his eyes.

A moment later, the boots of goatee man tore across the kitchen floor in a straight line toward the girls. Stan put out an arm to stop the marauder's advance, but another punch from the short man reached him first. The blow penetrated his cheekbone with a crack, slamming him to the floor on his chest.

Stan's mind blinked out for a second, then found its traction as an army of specks filled his vision. The pain was relentless too, shooting across his body.

He could hear the twins pleading with the Russians to stop, their high-pitched shrieks amplified by desperation. He needed to get up and protect his children.

After he opened his eyes, he told his body to move, but it refused. He tried again, but his limbs didn't respond. They were limp, devoid of energy, hanging on his body.

All that remained were the waves of dizziness, pounding at his skull with the force of an ocean current. Then the room started to spin, slowly at first, before it went wild, whirling with ever-increasing speed.

Stan slammed his eyes shut, trying to keep a lock on reality. His mind latched onto the most powerful emotion remaining in his thoughts—his love for his daughters. He prayed it would be enough to keep him in the here and now. But it wasn't.

The darkness came a heartbeat later, taking his consciousness away.

CHAPTER 24

Two hours later . . .

Allison Rainey plopped into the chair by the kitchen table, her leg and back muscles aching. Her mom was in the seat across from her, her hands locked together like she'd been praying. "Misty's finally asleep, thank God."

Martha seemed pleased. "That poor woman's been through a lot today. I don't know how she keeps it together."

Allison's mind flashed a scene of the men digging up Angus' naked body, his skin covered in dirt and bugs. The imagery tugged at her insides, making her want to throw up. "Me either. Finding out that you've lost your father and your fiancé on the same day is more than I could ever deal with."

"I doubt that. You're a lot tougher than you think."

"Thanks, Mom. But I'm really not. I just pretend to be. For Victor's sake." She shrugged after a quick exhale. "Not that it's done any good."

Martha put a hand on Allison's forearm, squeezing it gently. "He'll be all right, sweetheart. The Sheriff will find him."

"I hope so, but it's been two hours. It's getting chilly out there."

"He's a strong boy. You just gotta have faith the Good Lord will protect him."

Allison shook her head, wondering what she'd done wrong. God was obviously punishing her for something. "I wish I knew why he took off like that."

"It wasn't anything you did, if that's what you're thinking. I'm sure it's just the stress of everything that's happening right now. It's a lot for a young man to handle."

"You're probably right, Mom, but I never know with him. I swear, he's moodier than his father."

"We all have that trait, honey. It's just human nature."

Allison nodded, feeling a trickle of comfort ease into her soul. Mom always seemed to know exactly what words to say.

Martha rubbed her arm again, using those tender, side-to-side thumb strokes that only moms know how to do. "You need to get some sleep, too. If the Sheriff comes back, I'll wake you up."

"Okay," Allison said, realizing that she had a tendency to take her mom for granted. Her arms came up on their own and wrapped around Martha in a firm embrace. "I know I've been difficult over the years, but I want you to know how much I appreciate you always supporting me. No matter what."

"No need to thank me, darling. It's what a mother does. Just like you do for Victor. Just gotta give it time. He'll come around. He's a good boy."

Allison let go of the hug and stood up with newfound energy in her legs. "I'm just glad the Sheriff is out there looking for him. Victor's gotta be scared to death in those woods."

"Gus is a good man. He won't stop until he finds him," Martha said, her tone genuine. "You need to go and get some sleep. I'll keep an eye on things down here."

Allison nodded, then turned for the door that led into the living room. The stairs to the second floor were waiting beyond the table, assuming her legs had sufficient strength to ferry her up the fourteen steps.

Just one more time, she thought.

If her legs failed her request, she might have to stretch out on the dining room table and call it a night. It wouldn't do her back any good, but at this point, she really didn't care.

Exhaustion has a habit of changing your way of thinking, even if it leads to a crippling wake-up in the morning.

* * *

Rusty ran through the front door of Martha Rainey's place, his lungs feeling the strain from the sprint down Old Mill Road. The news he carried had supercharged his muscles, allowing him to run faster than ever before.

A blur of movement caught his eye from the left. It was Allison Rainey with her hand on the guardrail, heading up the stairs, her feet on the fourth step from the bottom.

Allison stopped her ascent and locked eyes with him, but didn't say anything.

"They're back!" Rusty told her.

"The Sheriff and Dicky?"

"Yeah, just now. Coming up the road."

"My son?"

Rusty couldn't wait to tell her. "He's with them."

"Is he okay?"

Rusty waved at her. "You gotta see this!"

She turned and flew down the stairs, her feet pounding at the steps like a woodpecker.

Rusty held the door open as the woman zipped past him in a breeze of air. For an old lady, she could run, probably feeling an adrenaline rush like him.

They tore across the front yard in seconds, then turned left onto the dirt road. About fifty feet ahead were three males and seven horses, all of them on a path to the Rainey homestead.

The Sheriff and Dicky were to the left, sitting proudly on their mounts with backs straight and heads high.

Victor was to the right, his face covered in a wide grin as he worked the reins with his left hand.

"Oh my God, Victor!" Allison screamed, somehow accelerating her pace.

Rusty pushed his legs even harder to keep up as the Sheriff waved a hello at him. Rusty sent a signal back with his arm, timing it between his widening strides so he wouldn't lose speed, or his balance.

Victor's upper body had a slight twist to it, one hand trailing behind. Rusty could see a rope in the kid's grasp, linking together four saddled horses in single file formation.

The last animal in the procession had something strapped to its saddle. It was a bicycle—his racing bike—in two pieces—the front wheel strapped to the left side. The rest of his ride was on the opposite side, lashed down and bobbing in concert with the stride of the horse.

When Allison arrived, Victor swung his leg over the saddle and hopped to the ground.

Rusty took position next to the Sheriff's horse, about ten feet from the mother-son reunion.

"I thought I was never going to see you again!" Allison cried as she wrapped him in a powerful two-armed embrace. She picked him up from the ground and swung him around with his feet dangling. The hug continued for another twenty seconds before she put him on the ground and let go.

She grabbed his cheeks in her hands. "Why did you take off like that? We were all worried sick."

"We needed horses, Mom. So I took responsibility like the Sheriff told me to do."

She turned to Apollo and sent him a penetrating stare. "This was your idea?"

"No. It wasn't like that. Not at all," the Sheriff stammered, climbing off his horse in a plop of feet. "He misunderstood what I told him. I was talking about taking responsibility for his actions. I never said to go find the horses."

She paused for a second, then looked at Victor. "Where did you go?"

"Franklin's stables. I knew the horses were around there somewhere, so I went to get them. I thought if I could find Megan's horse, it might cheer her up."

"By yourself? Do you know how dangerous that was?"

"Yeah, but I knew a secret way there. It was easy, Mom. Until it got dark."

"We found him two miles out. I think he'd been wandering around in circles," the Sheriff said, his tone somber and to the point.

Allison hugged Victor again, this time lingering for a good minute.

Martha appeared on Rusty's left, her face covered with delight. She brought her hands up like a preacher, leaned back to the heavens, and said, "Praise the Lord Almighty."

Allison turned to her mom with tears streaming down her cheeks. "He's back, Mom. Safe and sound. Just like you said."

"I told you not to worry," she said, sending a smile to the Sheriff. "Thank you, Gus, for bringing my grandson home. You too, Dicky."

"My pleasure," the Sheriff said, looking proud.

"Just doing our job, ma'am," Dicky said, still seated in the saddle.

Apollo gave Dicky the lead to his horse, nodding for him to continue down the road. Dicky did as he was told, escorting the Sheriff's horse toward Tuttle's place.

"Allison?" Martha said, hesitating until Allison looked her way. "Aren't you forgetting something?"

Allison pinched her nose, but didn't respond. She looked confused.

Martha leaned her head in the direction of the Sheriff.

"Oh, right," Allison snapped, her face blushing red. She sauntered to the Sheriff with a huge smile leading the way. "I'm sorry. I got so excited when I saw my son that I almost forgot to thank you."

When she brought her arms up for an embrace, Apollo stopped her with his hands. "That's really not necessary, Allison."

"The hell it isn't," she answered with attitude, pushing his hands away. "You risked your life to save my son. I'm giving you a hug, whether you like it or not."

Her arms found his shoulders a second later, leaving him looking mortified, his arms hanging down at his side.

Rusty held back a chuckle. It was obvious the Sheriff wasn't comfortable with her sudden affection.

Rusty didn't understand why. It was just a hug, after all. The man had earned it.

Right on cue, as if Apollo had been reading Rusty's thoughts, he brought his hands up and put them on her back. He wasn't giving her a hug, exactly. It was more of an awkward double pat on the back, but at least he responded.

Rusty was close enough to feel the heat from their bodies pressing together. It felt weird to be standing so close. He took a step back to give them room. You never knew when a thankful mom might pick up a hefty Sheriff and swing him around.

A few seconds later, she leaned back from the hug and stared into his eyes, her lower half still pressed into his.

Apollo must not have expected it, pulling his hands free from her back. He held them in mid-air, about six inches away.

Rusty figured the hug was just about over.

Then, out of nowhere, Allison closed her eyes and tilted her head, kissing him full on the lips. It wasn't a quick peck, either. It was an open mouth, vise-like smooch.

Apollo brought his hands up and wrapped them around her back, as if he had given in to all of his most secret desires.

It looked like one of those kissing scenes from the movies—their lips, hands, and bodies reacting to each other like some kind of choreographed play bursting with moans.

Rusty looked at Martha to see what she thought of the kiss.

The old woman's eyes were a mile wide, with a smile showing all of her teeth.

CHAPTER 25

Early the next morning . . .

Bunker pulled back on the reins to slow Tango to a stop, then unfolded the area map. The sun had just cracked the eastern horizon, showering his back with elongated rays of mostly yellow light. He turned sideways to give his eyes a better view of the path outlined in red marker ink.

So far, it appeared Apollo and Burt's waypoints had been spot-on, taking him exactly where he needed to go. He hadn't seen any sign of the Russians, or anyone else for that matter. Only the occasional critter lurking in the bush.

Tuttle's night vision goggles had been a godsend, lessening his fear of relying on Tango's ability to see in the dark. In retrospect, he probably could've saved the batteries since the amazing creature seemed to know exactly what to avoid and where to step to keep its rider safe.

Bunker checked his location on the map to confirm what he already suspected—Patterson's Meadow was only minutes away. All that remained was a hundred-foot climb over the rise ahead.

After an extended yawn and an arm stretch, he tucked the map away, wishing he'd gotten more shuteye. The problem wasn't the campsite he'd chosen on the ridge overlooking a stream. Nor was it the time he'd spent inside the lightweight sleeping bag.

It was the endless deep-throated croaks and ribbits from the frogs. There must have been a thousand of them within thirty yards of his makeshift camp. They were everywhere, never stopping their vocal calls once the sun went down. He finally fell asleep sometime around midnight, but then Tango's unexpected whinny at 4 AM put an end to his slumber.

Yet, despite the final interruption, he wasn't upset with the beast. In fact, he was thankful. If Tango hadn't decided to be a twelve-hundred-pound alarm clock, he might still be asleep and behind schedule.

Then again, he wouldn't have complained if he was able to enjoy another hour or two in dreamland, where curvy women and cold beer were served in abundant supply.

There's something soothing about the constant trickle of water over rock. It pampers one's senses, keeping your mind from dwelling on the shit you forgot to do the previous day. Or in his case, thoughts of all the crap he had to accomplish the following day, including scouting the town of Clearwater.

Bunker continued on, conquering the hill ahead thanks to Tango's steady feet and boundless energy. Each stride of the four-legged taxi sent a rocking motion into Bunker's hips, gently stressing the muscles in his back. At least the saddle wasn't as painful as it had been, meaning his skills as a rider were improving.

Daisy would be proud, he thought to himself after an image of her beautiful face flashed in his mind. Stephanie might have been put together better in the figure department, but Daisy oozed her own brand of sex appeal.

He smirked, thinking about the differences between the two women. They were polar opposites in almost every respect, but he knew deep down that either of them would make a weekend in Vegas memorable. The kind of memorable that would reinforce the adage: *What Happens in Vegas, Stays in Vegas.*

The old Bunker would have entertained the idea of a three-way, taking both of them to bed together. Sure, it would have been an easy solution to the dilemma ahead, but it wasn't who he was anymore.

Stephanie was more about the here and now, while Daisy invested in the long game. He figured either of them could tame a wild man with nothing more than look, or a stroke of their hand.

He'd sensed a growing connection with both of them, but he'd purposely avoided anything romantic. Not because of their history of torrid love triangles. It was more about his own sanity. He was still a work in progress—a reclamation project— trying to figure out who he was and what kind of man he wanted to be.

The last thing he needed was to worry about the emotional needs of another person. Plus, he still hadn't come completely clean with either of them, keeping the darkest of details hidden from those who cared about him.

Chances were, once they learned of his culpability in the Kandahar Incident, they'd want nothing more to do with him. That day in his past was the single most important reason why he needed to keep his distance from everyone, and not get attached. Otherwise, it would make their impending hatred for him just that much harder, once his dark secret sent him packing.

Bunker tugged the reins to have Tango bypass a thicket of scorched trees and protruding rock, all of it covered in the black of carbon. Lightning, he figured, searing off vertical streaks of bark, killing a good portion of the limbs.

He craned his neck to the southern sky and noticed a massive thunderhead forming in the distance. The billowing cumulonimbus cloud rose to the heavens and flattened out like a mushroom of white, towering over the mountain peaks below it.

Daisy would be pleased if the drought came to an end, as would the other residents in the area. Assuming, of course, anyone still occupied their homestead after the Russians marched across the county. He shook his head, realizing that he might be the only person dumb enough to be wandering through the area alone. With minimal supplies and firepower, no less.

He took Tango thirty degrees to the left, guiding him down a natural path that led to an impressive string of mature pine trees bordering the clearing. Based on the straight-line nature of their position along the edge of the meadow, Bunker knew this clearing was manmade. Nature didn't feature straight lines or many right-angled corners, both of which were present in the pasture before him.

The thick trunks of the pines matched their soaring heights; lofty enough to reach the middle of the pasture, he calculated, if someone were to drop them accurately with a chainsaw from either side. That chore had Dicky's name written all over it.

Pine trees were perfect for what he had in mind—narrow and tall, making them easy to rig after a climb. He nodded, storing the information in his memory, with the names of Rusty and Dallas attached.

He hoped Albert was busy working through the items on the list he'd given him, with speed and efficiency. There wouldn't be a lot of time to catch up once he returned from this scout.

Bunker brought Tuttle's high-end binoculars to his eyes to study the sightlines from his position. The scan started at one end of the clearing and finished with the other, carefully checking the tree line that stood beyond.

No threats detected. Time to advance.

The grass in the pasture rose up in a streaky mix of green and brown, its tips reaching above Tango's knee joints. The horse stepped gingerly after a nudge of Bunker's heels, taking them forward to the center of the expanse.

All four corners of this rectangular-shaped meadow were now in view, as were the soaring mountains and endless trees swarming its exterior. He took out the map and studied it again, making sure the printed topography matched what his eyes were reporting.

"Only one way in or out," he mumbled in affirmation, noting the landscape and elevations on all sides. He took another minute to run through several tactical scenarios in his mind, deciding what would go where, and who would be assigned to the various stations.

He smiled as the blueprint came together, visualizing himself running with socks in his hands, each covered in axle grease. "Just might work. But they'll have to over-commit."

Bunker spun Tango around before sending him into a trot toward the closed end of the clearing. He swung his leg over the saddle and dropped to the ground once they arrived.

"Stay here, boy. I'll be back in a flash."

Tango flicked his head and snorted, then resumed his tail-flapping, fly-swatting duties with his head buried in the grass. Tango would soon need water to wash down the feast he'd just started. With any luck, the waterholes on the map hadn't dried up, or else the rest of today's trip might be shorter than anticipated.

Bunker paced the width of the clearing from one edge to the other, counting the strides required. The final tally was more than he expected, leading him to wonder if his crew could complete the critical task he had in mind.

The lack of rain in recent weeks meant the ground was harder than normal, and would slow the process. However, if the rising storm over the mountaintop did its job, then they'd have a chance to complete what he needed in time.

A chance was all they needed. Something that would galvanize hope and lead them to victory. Yet it would take everyone, including Burt and his mechanical magic. Even the little ones would have to pitch in.

It was obvious the strategy evolving in his brain needed a bit of luck to succeed, but that was all he had at the moment. Well, luck and a few friends who believed in him. Some of those same friends had a deep connection to God, or so they claimed.

He smirked, realizing their faith had started to rub off on him and affect his decisions. God or luck, they were the same thing, he decided. After all, if God wanted to step in and lend a hand with a downpour, who was he to complain? He'd take it and any other help that came his way. Divine or not, he wasn't picky.

He went back to Tango and climbed into the saddle. "You ready, boy? It's time to take care of a few errands, then head into the lion's den."

Bunker leaned forward to rub Tango's neck, sending the four hooves under him into a prance, almost as if a veterinarian had just shot a dose of adrenaline into Tango's body.

He tapped his hand twice before leaning back in the saddle with a squeak of leather. "Oh yeah. You're ready. So am I. Let's ride!"

CHAPTER 26

Dustin put a stack of boxes containing steel wool onto a portable table he'd just set up outside of Tuttle's barn. Albert placed a dozen glass jars on its surface and Rusty delivered a few other household items they'd scavenged from Tuttle's inventory.

"Why can't we do this inside, out of the sun?" Dustin asked, wiping a bead of sweat from his brow. "It's frickin' hot out here."

"We could, but this reaction will create toxic gas that I'm betting your lungs will hate. We'll need proper ventilation."

"Okay, that makes sense. Good safety tip."

Albert gave him a handful of magnets he'd acquired from Martha Rainey's fridge. "Put the steel wool into the jars, then secure it to the bottom with these."

"On the outside, right?"

"Yeah. They'll keep the steel wool from floating once we add the chems."

Dustin dropped the first piece of steel wool into the container, then lifted the jar to gain access to the bottom. He put the magnet to the underside of the glass, then set the assembly back on the table. He completed the same process with the other jars. "Now what?"

"Pour in enough vinegar to cover the steel wool completely. But don't go crazy."

Dustin took off the twist cap from a bottle of white vinegar and poured in enough liquid to soak the steel wool and cover it. "Like that?"

"Perfect. Now the others."

Dustin filled the remaining jars with vinegar, then put the bottle down and secured its cap.

"Now the bleach."

Dustin grabbed the plastic container of bleach. He removed the cap and held it near the opening of the first jar. "How much?"

Albert pointed at the glass, aiming at a point about two inches above the steel wool. "Fill it to here, but hold your breath. The gas will start almost immediately."

Dustin took a deep breath before pouring the bleach, using a thin stream for control. He stopped when the level inside the jar reached the height

Albert had indicated. He backed away, took another breath, then went back in to fill the rest of the jars. Once done, he put the bleach down, closed its container and stood next to Albert.

He exhaled, using an exaggerated lip pucker for effect. "How long will this take?"

"Couple of hours. Then we drain, filter, and repeat until we have the supply Bunker asked for in his notes."

"That's all there is to it?" Dustin asked, watching the chemical reaction turn the steel wool a red color.

"Yeah, simple, if you know what you're doing."

"Huh. I never knew you could make rust this way. I suppose we could've used some old nails, too."

"They'd work, but this method is faster. Steel wool has much more surface area, accelerating the process a thousand-fold."

"I take it you've done this before?"

Albert didn't answer, turning his focus to the Mayor's grandson. "Let's get the aluminum ready."

Rusty nodded, opening a cardboard box that he'd hauled from Martha Rainey's house. He unfolded its flaps and pulled out a black-colored device about the size of a lunch thermos.

Dustin recognized it. "A coffee grinder?"

"I hope she doesn't mind," Albert said, taking the lid off the machine.

"You didn't ask her?"

"Nah. This was too important to waste time on politeness. Though we could've melted down a bunch of Tuttle's empty beer cans and put them on a spindle for the lathe, to create the shavings. But then we'd also need to make a ball mill to grind them into powder."

"That's a lot more work," Dustin said after visualizing Albert's alternative.

"Absolutely. The coffee grinder is a lot faster," Albert said, turning to Rusty. "Just need the foil."

Rusty took out a box of aluminum foil. "How much?"

"Tear off a couple of six-foot pieces. One for both of you."

Rusty drew out two runs of foil and tore them from the roll, giving one to Dustin.

"Now we need strips, gentlemen. Lots of them," Albert said.

"How small?" Dustin asked.

"As small as you can make them."

The two men started building a pile of foil strips, while Albert grabbed two handfuls and stuffed them into the coffee grinder.

He put the lid on and secured it, then plugged the unit into an exterior electrical outlet near the barn's entrance. The power light illuminated, thanks to Tuttle's backup power.

"First we grind them with the coarse setting." Albert pressed the power switch and held the lid as the aluminum foil was ground into tiny flecks by the whirling blades inside. The high-pitched squeal of the motor was annoying, but it appeared the device could handle the process easily.

Albert turned the unit off and opened the lid to add more strips. He repeated the process until all of the foil strips had been processed with the coarse setting.

"Now, we run it all through on fine." He flipped the setting, sending the flakes whirling a second time.

Albert turned off the motor after another ten minutes of grinding. "Time for the moment of truth."

He removed the lid from the container, his eyes darting about the area. "Where's that strainer?"

Rusty went back into the box and pulled out an extra fine strainer they'd found in Martha's baking cabinet.

Albert held the wire mesh over the worktable and poured the aluminum shavings through it. The smaller fragments slipped through and landed on the table. When he was done, almost eighty percent of the powder he'd made with the grinder had passed the size test.

"Is that enough?" Dustin asked, his eyes locked onto the modest pile of aluminum powder.

"Not even close. We'll need several more batches of everything. Once that steel wool is done cooking, we'll filter it as well, then we're good to go."

"That's it? Just mix them together and we're done?" Rusty asked.

"Basically, though the mixture has to be in the proper proportions, depending on who you ask."

"What does that mean?" Dustin asked.

"It means there is more than one answer to the mixture question. It depends on the purity of the components and some other goodies that we could add to the recipe."

"Like what?"

"Plaster, for one. Bunker didn't ask for any, so I'm assuming he's planning to make some kind grenade with TH3, based on the components on his list."

Rusty took out four coffee cans, the eight-ounce variety. Each of them carried labels that said *Folgers* on the side. "I'm guessing that's what these are for?"

Albert nodded, his eyes tight with focus. "We just need to be careful once it's mixed."

Daisy showed up after Dicky relieved her at the roadblock. "What are you guys doing?"

"Making thermite charges," Albert said, sounding as though he was trying to impress her.

"For Bunker," Dustin added.

Albert shot him a glare while Daisy's head was turned.

Daisy bent forward and studied the jars on the table. "What's in there?"

"Steel wool," Dustin answered.

"We're making iron oxide," Albert added. "One of the core components."

Dustin pointed at the mound of gray powder on the table. "That used to be aluminum foil."

"Bunker asked you to make this?" she asked, her tone hesitant.

Albert held up the list of items. "Among other things."

"Are you sure?"

"Positive. Just need to get it done before he gets back."

Daisy seemed to accept Albert's statement.

Albert continued. "But there is one problem. Unless we find a supply of magnesium tape around here, we'll need to figure out a way to light it. Something that will burn with a sufficient temperature."

Her eyes went round. "What about the pocket torch Dallas found?"

"Good idea," Albert responded in a flash. "But we still need sulfur and some barium nitrate to complete the TH3."

Daisy cleared her throat, looking proud of herself. "I know where the sulfur is, gentlemen."

Albert sent a suspicious look her way, but didn't speak.

She didn't seem to care. "It's under the chicken coop. Bunker and I found a bunch of explosives and chemicals down there."

Albert's expression remained unchanged.

Daisy shot Albert a sidelong glance, her eyes scanning his midsection. "But you'll never fit down the hatch."

"Yeah, well, being a gopher really isn't my thing."

"I'll go," Dustin said.

"Me too," Rusty added.

Daisy continued, with one eyebrow raised, "I think there's aluminum power, too. And maybe the barium nitrate."

Albert's face scrunched like he'd just sucked on a lemon.

Daisy let out a short chuckle. "Tuttle has all kinds of chemicals and explosives down there."

"What about iron oxide?" Albert asked, his tone indicating he didn't want to know the answer.

"Is it a red powder?"

"Yep."

"Saw that, too."

Albert's tone turned harsh. "You've got to be kidding me."

She shrugged. "Like I was trying to tell you before, I don't think you guys had to make all this stuff from scratch."

Albert exhaled, shaking his head. He looked at Dustin. "Why didn't Bunker tell us?"

Dustin paused, sifting through his memory of the conversation with Bunker about the list. Then it hit him. "Well, technically he did. He said to ask Daisy if we needed help finding anything."

"I guess I missed that part," Albert said, sounding defeated.

She put her hand out, palm up. "Maybe I should take a look at that list."

Albert gave her the paper.

She scanned it for a short minute and then nodded as if she had reached a conclusion. "Follow me, boys."

CHAPTER 27

Bunker crawled forward on the hilltop rise outside of town, keeping his profile low to avoid detection. He'd left Tango behind after tying him to a tree two hundred yards to the rear.

The storm clouds had doubled in size, painting a section of the distant horizon black. He wasn't sure if the build-up meant the storm was heading his way, or only building in size. Either way, the inclement weather might come into play soon.

Storms look closer than they truly are when you're in an elevated area with sparkling clean air and tremendous visibility. The rain might arrive in minutes, or hours, or not at all. There was no way to be sure, not without active radar.

He brought the binoculars up and began his surveillance. To the right was the main road leading into Clearwater. It was the same swatch of pavement he'd used to lead the kids into town after their rescue from the bus accident.

A Russian checkpoint sat on the pavement, blocking access to town.

It featured all the usual trimmings: Russian flags, razor wire security fence, sawhorse-style barricades with white and black stripes, sandbags protecting a machine gunner's nest, single-man guard shack, squad of heavily armed soldiers milling about, two armored vehicles sitting at intersecting angles behind the barricades, and a red and white colored pedestal sign that he assumed said STOP.

There were also guards walking a pair of German Shepherds on a leash.

He watched a convoy depart in a slow crawl after approaching the checkpoint from somewhere in town. The two lead vehicles were military issue: all-terrain Russian GAZ Tigrs. As were the pair of chase vehicles holding up the rear.

Three American-made flatbed trucks were sandwiched between the infantry carriers, ferrying a load of civilians wearing bright orange coveralls. He could see the grille on the lead truck—its emblem said GMC and it appeared to be an older model.

Wooden boards surrounded the truck beds, reminding Bunker of three-rail cattle fencing. Each civilian had their wrist attached to the plank closest to them. All looked to be adults, their heads hanging and bobbing with the movement of the transport.

A few minutes after they drove off, another convoy came into view—this one arriving at the checkpoint. Like the first, it featured two lead vehicles and two chase vehicles. However, this procession only carried a single truck of civilians. They, too, had their wrists secured to the rails.

When the middle truck stopped, he was able to get a better view of the prisoners. Their coveralls were dirty, noticeably so, the orange color covered in black splotches and not as bright.

Some of the captives looked young and fit, mid-twenties if he had to guess. Both male and female. Others were heavyset with gray hair, looking as though they should have been enjoying retirement in an assisted living facility somewhere.

"Slave labor for the mine. Or the fields. Maybe both," Bunker said in a mumble, working through the facts as the vehicles drove inside and disappeared. The Russians weren't concerned about age, but at least he didn't see any children.

Bunker brought the glasses down and let his eyes take in a view of the city below. He figured razor wire had been installed around the access points of the perimeter. It also seemed likely that other checkpoints had been erected, somewhere beyond his vision.

He was even more confident that the insurgents were watching everything with the helium-filled Aerostat balloon floating fifteen hundred feet above the center of town. He'd seen that type of surveillance blimp in Afghanistan many times. In fact, almost every base he visited back then had one deployed.

The tethered, 117-foot dirigible resembled a giant all-white fish, except this floater came complete with infrared and high definition cameras. During his tour in Afghanistan, they were part of the Pentagon's Persistent Threat Detection System, though it looked like the Russians had adopted a similar program.

The locals hated them, but the commanders loved them. So did the bean counters in Washington—saving the cost of multi-million dollar drones flying overhead 24x7.

Bunker still remembered his shock when a maintenance team brought one of the blimps down to repair the bullet holes in its skin. He counted twenty-two, but there may have been more. Apparently, the Aerostats were almost impervious to target practice, able to withstand several hundred hits before they could no longer fly. They were also safe against incendiary rounds since Helium is a noble gas and noncombustible.

Weather was usually the flight technician's biggest headache. Most notably, the frequent sand storms. Climate concerns weren't the only drawback. Blind spots were also an issue, depending on how the cameras were mounted and deployed.

Bunker brought the binoculars back into position when a black Land Rover approached the roadblock from his right. He couldn't get a count of its occupants, not with its windows tinted dark.

The truck slowed to a stop about twenty feet from the barricades as the guards spread out to cover it with their rifles held high.

He imagined one of the guards yelling something along the lines of "Halt and be recognized."

The driver's door swung open. A man stepped out with his hands up. He was dressed in dark-colored attire, including long pants, long-sleeved shirt, and shoes.

"The men in black," Bunker muttered, remembering his painful encounters with the Pokémon men in the miner's camp.

The driver pulled up his shirt and spun around, showing the guards he had nothing strapped to his torso. Nothing that might go boom.

Three additional men slid out of the vehicle in a controlled manner, one from behind the driver and two on the passenger side—all of them with their hands over their heads.

They too, completed the bomb vest security spin before three guards escorted them to the driver's position, herding the group together like cattle.

Finally, the fourth soldier checked the inside of the Land Rover, starting with the open door on the driver's side. His rifle went in, then his head, looking for threats.

A few moments later, he swung around to the other side of the truck and completed the same maneuver through the rear passenger door. As Bunker expected, he climbed out and signaled for the canine units to approach.

The dogs began to sniff the exterior, following the finger pointing commands of their handlers.

The search for weapons and explosives was a slow and dangerous process, for both man and beast, but these units showed little fear.

Once the outside of the truck was secure, the handlers led their dogs inside with a tug on the leash. One handler cleared the front seat, while the other focused on the back.

When the search was over, one of the guards retrieved two duffle bags, one suitcase, and a black backpack from the vehicle. He stood them together, leaning their weight into each other like a rudimentary teepee.

A tall, slender man appeared in the doorway of the guard shack, then made his way to the SUV with a clipboard in hand. He looked to be unarmed, though his beltline did feature some kind of device attached to the leather. The tall man stood in front of the driver, checking the paperwork with a flip of his hand.

Russians love their lists, Bunker thought to himself.

The tall man took a step back and brought the device up from his belt. He aimed it at the man's crotch for a ten-count before motioning to the driver to step forward.

The driver did as he was told, bringing his arms down in the process. Tall man turned his attention to the second visitor and went through the same scenario with the clipboard and scanner, before moving onto detainee number three.

Right then, a new idea hatched in Bunker's thoughts. He dug into his pocket and pulled out the Pokémon card Jeffrey had given him, holding it in front of his eyes.

"Holy shit. That's what these are for," he said in a whisper, more facts lining up in his brain. "A covert ID."

The men in black didn't carry identification, so the Russians would need a reliable method to clear them for entry.

He knew from experience that checkpoint verification was a common problem at most military bases, given the sheer number of troops under command. Especially when you're under standing orders not to wear insignias, nametags, or ID badges in a red zone, where snipers are a constant threat.

The same would be true for those who went out on patrol. Or in this case, hauling civilians outside the wire for some kind of work duty.

Usually the guard at the gate would need to know one or more of the troops leaving the compound. Otherwise, they could never be sure if a returning squad was a threat or not.

In this case, though, these were unknown operatives joining their base, and probably doing so for the first time. They'd need a method to identify covert personnel.

He smirked. It was brilliant. The cards would look harmless to the uninformed.

Bunker took a minute to run through the Russians' check-in protocols in his mind. He realized the visitors must have supplied a codename to the clipboard guard first, which was then confirmed with a scan of the hidden card. He nodded, appreciating the simplicity of their double-verification system.

If his theory were correct, it would also explain something else. Something that had been nagging at him ever since he first set foot in the miner's camp. The men in black spoke perfect English. Not a hint of Russian.

"Wouldn't need to speak Russian," he muttered, thinking about the reasons behind a double-verification entry system. Especially while in-country and welcoming unknown operatives who may have only spoken English.

Bunker held the card up to the sunlight like Jeffrey had done the day before. That was when he noticed it—a tiny dark spot in the corner—something embedded between the layers of paper. He guessed it was metallic, with micro-encoded circuits. Something a scanner could read.

"Clever boy," he said, thinking about Jeffrey. The inquisitive youngster wasn't fooled, not for a second, noticing the difference immediately.

After more consideration, Bunker decided the men in black must have been either Russian sleeper agents who'd just been activated, or Americans conspiring with the enemy. Nothing else fit what he'd learned thus far.

"Guess this is useless," he said, putting the card in his pocket. If he had the codename, he could have used it to gain entry to Clearwater and gather valuable onsite intel regarding troop placement and strength.

Part of him was tempted to tear the paper apart to expose the technology, but he'd made a promise to keep the card safe. The tech was useless anyway, so no need to break a kid's heart.

Bunker opened his rucksack and fished out the baggie of red crystals. "I guess this is all that's left." He sifted through a number of approach scenarios, trying to find one that wouldn't get him shot before he could deliver the drugs to a corruptible addict.

Albert's idea had merit, but he decided it was too dangerous. The plan would work better if he were traveling with a non-threatening visitor. Someone distracting in all ways. Someone like Stephanie. Her curves would be far more effective than a missing codename. Assuming, of course, she was wearing the proper outfit.

He flushed the idea, chastising himself in the process. She'd never go for it. She had Jeffrey to think about, not to mention her own wellbeing. If he put her in that situation and she got hurt, how could he live with himself?

No. If he was going inside, it needed to be his risk and his alone. Codename or not.

Out of nowhere, an image of the demon-looking squirrel creature on the Pokémon card danced in his mind. The vision called to him, begging him to refocus and dissect. He yanked the card out of his pocket and stared at it.

Jeffrey's voice rose up from his memories in an echo. "His name is Charmeleon."

Bunker's jaw dropped open, thinking about the other odd but unique names the kid had mentioned: Metapod, Arcanine, and Parasect.

"Could it be that simple?"

His logic dug through the cloud of clutter surrounding the cards and their origin, the facts lining up one at a time.

Each card a different character.

Each card sewn inside the pants.

Each card scanned for verification.

Just then, the data points coalesced like the perfect storm, leading him to a new conclusion: each undercover operative carried a unique Pokémon card and knew the name of the character.

"That has to be it," he stated. "Simple and efficient."

Bunker dug into his pack, pulling the microscope out first. He gently put it aside, standing it upright on its base. When he found it in Albert's house, it was bigger than he expected but located exactly where Albert had indicated.

A red-colored pet collar came out next. Unfortunately, Daisy's cat was a stiff lump of fur when he'd arrived at her trailer. He buried the lifeless feline near Daisy's withering flower garden out back, but kept the collar as a memento. He wasn't looking forward to delivering the news to her when he got back to camp.

He found his civilian clothes near the bottom and began to change his attire, his mind churning with more theories.

Jeffrey had told him there were over eight hundred characters in the Pokémon world. Bunker wasn't sure if they all had their own card or not, but it seemed likely. The organization behind the game never would have invented all those characters if they weren't going to take advantage with trading cards and other collectibles.

Regardless of the count, he figured it was more than enough to cover a few dozen operatives. Possibly a lot more. In fact, the higher the number, the better his chances of getting past the checkpoint unscathed.

The Russians had their choice of codes and could have chosen anything. Hell, old baseball cards would have worked. Yet they went with Pokémon. He figured it was due to the sheer number of characters and their unique names. They needed both.

It saved them from having to devise a system of codenames and do so on a large scale. Especially if the number needed was in the hundreds, as he suspected. Plus, the cards were available everywhere in society and easy to obtain. Both in the US and elsewhere.

Sure, he was guessing at this point, but the odds favored his conclusions. Even more so if the Russian invasion had been launched in a rush, like his gut was telling him. He couldn't explain why, but the feeling of Russian urgency was clear and consistent, ever since he'd witnessed the Area 51 jet crash site.

If he was correct about the high number of cards needed, it also meant the soldiers on guard duty had their hands full. Operators would arrive at all hours and in different modes of transportation. Some might even be walking, if their rides broke down.

"Or crashed," he mumbled, looking at the bandage around his left arm. Then he remembered the scars on his neck.

A new idea came unbidden to his mind—one that might increase his chance of success. He couldn't do much about his missing all-black attire, or the fact that he was arriving alone. However, if he could distract the guards long enough to get close, he might be able to provide the codename and be scanned.

Bunker took out his knife and drew it across the palm of his hand. The blade opened a gash about a half-inch long. He held the wound over the bandage, letting the blood drip onto the cloth and down his arm. A quick smear of the blood hastened the process, then he painted his neck and shirt collar red, making it appear he'd been injured in a car wreck. His forehead and cheeks were next, taking only seconds to help conceal his face from any cameras that might be active at the checkpoint.

The final item needed was a limp—something that would be noticeable from a distance. The guards would be curious and let him approach for inspection, where the blood prep would take over to complete the backstory.

The problem with a fake limp is remembering it when you're under duress. Consistency is critical; otherwise, you'll find yourself under arrest, or worse.

The best way to sell a limp is to actually give yourself one. Pain is an effective reminder.

A pebble with jagged edges caught his eye in the dirt. It was the perfect size and shape. He put it into his pocket, planning to stuff it into his sock and walk on it as he advanced on the checkpoint.

CHAPTER 28

Allison took a deep breath and let it out, hoping to rid her body of its anxiety as she continued her trek down the hallway in Tuttle's place. For a moment, she thought about turning around to avoid the encounter, but Misty needed her to deliver a message to the man Allison knew was in the master bedroom.

She found Sheriff Apollo sitting on the foot of the bed, his head tilted back at an angle and facing a wall covered in newspapers. He looked lost in the visuals before him, his eyes pinched and scanning the articles.

"Excuse me, Sheriff. Do you have a minute? Misty would like to talk to you."

Apollo nodded, never looking her way. "Sure, just send her in."

"Not here, Gus. She won't leave Martha's bedroom."

He brought his eyes around and let out a gentle smile. "Okay. I'll head over as soon as I finish up here."

His sudden gaze brought a tidal wave of pressure to her heart. It felt like a bulldozer had just smashed into her chest, making her want to run for the exit. Yet somehow, she found the courage to hold her position, even though she wasn't prepared for any of the newfound feelings.

He scooted over on the bed in a single lift and shift of his rear end, obviously making room for her to sit down.

Allison gulped, standing there like a mute statue. She needed to move or say something, but her body wasn't reacting to commands. All she could do was blink at him like a zombie. It was embarrassing.

"Please. Sit. I have something I want to show you," Apollo said in a gentle tone. He tapped the bed next to him, then nodded as if he'd just issued a direct order to one of his deputies.

Her feet finally responded. She sat down, with her breath growing shorter by the second, keeping several inches of space between them. "Is something wrong?"

"No, it's not that," he said, pointing at the newspapers hanging on the wall. "Tell me, what do you see?"

She peered at the newsprint, seeing headlines highlighted in yellow. Other articles had sections outlined in black ink. Next to them were handwritten phrases in the margins. Most of the notes were messy and unreadable.

Allison shrugged, wanting to answer intelligently, but her thoughts flickered in disarray. "I see a bunch of crazy."

"I thought that at first, too. Then I got to thinking. Why would a high-strung recluse like Tuttle mark up the maps the way he did? It was almost as if he knew exactly what we were going to need and left them for us."

She peered at the newspapers again, this time pushing aside the emotional thoughts bubbling inside. The Sheriff needed her to understand the point of this exercise and she wanted to oblige. "He must have known something was coming."

"That's exactly what I thought after I sat down and took a long, hard look at this little project of his."

She took a look around the room, hoping her intellect would rise to the top. It was time to contribute to the conversation. Otherwise, she'd continue to come across as a blithering idiot. Or more accurately, a middle-aged woman caught in an emotional snare, all because of a single unexpected kiss.

The newspapers were everywhere, covering most of the walls in front of her and behind. Some were on the adjacent walls, near the door and around the window. "He must have been at this a while."

"Trying to put the pieces together."

She pointed at the folded papers, stacked up on the floor. "Looks like he wasn't done yet, either."

Apollo stood and walked to the left. He pointed at a headline that read, *Uranium One Purchases 20% of US Reserves.*

"Okay, so?"

"Wait, just read them all and let it soak in like I did."

She nodded as his finger moved from headline to headline, her eyes taking them in one at a time:

Russia / China Purchase More US Debt

China on Massive Gold Buying Spree

The Holy Grail of High-Pressure Physics

New Super Fuel on the Horizon

Miracle Material Disappears from Lab

Discovery of Miracle Element Debunked

Secret Russian Land Grab Inside USA

China Buying US Stocks by the Truckload

Canadian Firm Sells Out for Billions

Cash Flows into Foundations after Approval

Uranium Production Falls to Record Lows

Defense Cuts Leaves USA Vulnerable

Border Crossings Surge

Record Debt Cripples States

Law Enforcement Cutbacks Planned

Jade Helm 15 Rollout Commences

Washington Ignores Cyberthreat Study

Power Grid Upgrades Stall in Senate

Apollo continued with the headlines for another minute or so before resuming his seat on the bed. "What do you think?"

"I know you're trying to make a point, I'm just not sure what I looking at here."

His tone turned serious and deliberate. "It's the greatest conspiracy of all time, Allison. This is all about our government's systematic sale of assets, technology, and territory to foreign countries, just to save its own ass."

She looked at the articles again, her mind in stutter mode. "You got all that from this?"

He nodded. "It took me a while to connect the dots, but it's all here. Tuttle must have figured it out.

That's why he went off the grid and built the underground bunkers."

"So he wasn't crazy?"

"Crazy like a fox. But nobody would listen to him, including me. That's why he spent his wife's inheritance to stock up on everything. He knew this was coming."

Her throat ran dry in an instant. It took a full minute to find her voice again. "If what you say is true, we need to tell somebody."

"Who would we tell? They're all in on it."

She couldn't believe what she just heard. "No, that can't be. It just can't."

"You need to open your mind," he said, aiming his hand at the papers around the room. "The proof is all right here. You just gotta be willing to see it."

She didn't respond. There were no words.

He continued, pointing to headlines as he spoke, "Here, let me walk you through it . . . It all starts with our country being buried up to its eyeballs in debt, with more piling on every minute of every day. We're talking about an imminent, massive bankruptcy, the likes of which the world has never seen."

"Yeah, I've seen the numbers before. Everybody has."

"Then you also know there's no chance in hell that we'll ever pay any of it back."

She smirked. "Not with the way our government spends."

"Yet our enemies are lining up to buy our toxic debt at record levels, even though they know we can barely afford the interest as it is."

"Which gets a lot worse if interest rates rise."

"Exactly. Investors don't pour trillions into something they know will fail, not unless there's another way to profit."

"I see your point."

"This all centers around Cowie's new super element," Apollo said, looking sure of himself. "Something that will change the energy industry forever, but then it suddenly disappears from a lab. Unfortunately, nobody cares or pays much attention because the scientific community comes out and claims that it never existed in the first place."

"I remember something about that on the news."

"It's all just a little too convenient, wouldn't you say? First, we have Metallic Hydrogen being discovered. Something that will get us off fossil fuels forever and make trillions in profits for whoever controls it. Then it just disappears and nobody seems to care because some scientist says it never existed in the first place."

"Okay, I get that. Oil companies made it go away. Not the first time, right?"

"Actually, I don't think Big Oil was involved this time. It looks like Washington sold the discovery to the Russians for a huge payday. Or a ransom, if you believe what Misty said about the stolen formula."

She nodded, the theory coming together as he explained it. "A ransom payment is a sellout, depending on how you look at it."

"True, and it's not the first time our leaders have done it, either. Remember in January 2016 when the State Department paid Iran four hundred million dollars in return for those hostages?"

"Yeah, vaguely."

"That's how it starts. Once they know you can be manipulated like that, our adversaries will never stop. They'll hold a gun to your head for all kinds of reasons, like foreclosing on all your debt."

"Those bastards."

"But there's more. In recent years, foreign investment in our country has exploded, with trillions of dollars pouring in to buy stocks, land, and businesses all across our country. And it doesn't stop there. A huge chunk of our uranium deposits were sold to Russia, without anyone blinking an eye. Think about that for a minute. Uranium, the stuff nuclear bombs are made from, sold to our biggest enemy. And you wanna know why?"

She flared her eyes but didn't respond.

"Because politicians on all sides were paid off in the hundreds of millions to look the other way. And I'm talking Republicans, Democrats, and Independents. All that money funneled through backdoor projects and charitable donations, then paid out as needed to keep the swamp creatures happy. It's unbelievable, Allison. It's all here, on these walls, in black and white."

"Unreal," she said, unable to utter anything more intelligent.

"Now here's where it all starts to come together. First, US production of uranium falls unexpectedly, which I assume is to make room for Russian dominance in the marketplace. And again, nobody gives a crap. Then we see border crossings surge to get their troops and operatives in place while nobody is looking. Defense spending is slashed to the bone, leaving us weak and vulnerable. Debt spirals out of control across all fifty states, leading to local law enforcement cutbacks," he said, pausing. "There's a pattern forming here."

"Like chess pieces being positioned."

"For the kill. But what really sticks out is Jade Helm 15—an unprecedented military readiness exercise that's conducted inside our own borders."

"To move equipment into place," she added.

"Yep. Right under our noses," Apollo said. "And the media never bats an eye."

"God, how could we have been so stupid?"

"Because we've all been brainwashed by the news media and the Deep State who control them. We're supposed to believe everything they tell us, like good little slaves who are too stupid to think for themselves."

"You're right. Nobody pays attention anymore. We're all too busy trying to keep food on the table."

"Or trying not to kill each other."

She nodded. "It seems like every other day, another riot breaks out and the news goes nuts over it."

"That's all by design."

"To keep us divided."

"And distracted. If we're too busy fighting with each other, we don't have time to notice how we're being sold down the river."

"Unbelievable."

"But it gets worse. Despite all the research studies and the dire warnings, our leaders decide to leave our computer networks wide open to cyberattack and never upgrade our power grid. Does that make any sense to you?"

"No. Why would they do that?"

"Because the decision makers were paid to look the other way. They knew the attack was coming and agreed to let it happen."

"My God."

"Let's face it, when there's no way out, those in power will sell their souls to the devil if that means saving themselves. Especially if that devil is holding all the cards."

"You're talking about blackmail, right?"

"You're damn right I am. Russia and China must have gotten together and threatened to foreclose on all our debt," Apollo answered. "That's why there's been no resistance. Our enemies held a financial gun to our head. We either surrender to their demands, or they destroy us by flatlining our economy. We're talking about massive bank failures, starvation, and social anarchy. That's why we turned over technology, leaving ourselves ripe for takeover. This has all been planned from the start. Step by step."

She shook her head, not wanting to believe what he was saying.

He threw up his hands. "They just let them march right in and take over. It was easy once all the equipment was positioned a few years ago as part of that huge military exercise."

Her heart ached, for her country and her son. "Okay, let's assume what you say is true. It would mean Tuttle knew they'd invade Clearwater County, specifically."

"There's no doubt. Just look around."

"That's why he created those maps—" she said.

Apollo continued her thought before she could finish. "—to show where the roadblocks would be and to mark possible escape routes. He knew this was coming."

"But how exactly?"

He shook his head, looking tired. "I haven't figured that part out yet, but the clues must be here somewhere. All I know for sure is that this was meant to be kept quiet until it was too late."

"How do you figure that?"

"It's why we haven't seen any Russian jets or helicopters. They'd be too noticeable in our skies. A secret ground invasion could be kept quiet, especially in the backcountry, as long as communications and transportation are taken out first."

"By the EMP."

"Once the Russians got everything into place, it would be too late for anyone to do anything about it."

"So . . . what you're saying is that the EMP and cyberattack were done to cover it all up."

"Bingo. Nobody would ever expect that our own government was in on it from the start. Not after the EMP and computer hacks took everything down. It's the perfect excuse, Allison. Think about it. Our guilty leaders can claim the attacks caught them off guard. They can use them as the reason why the Russians were able to waltz right in. They can say they tried to stop it, but weren't able to. In fact, it wouldn't surprise me if the EMP and cyberattacks were done by us, not Russia, to make sure it all went as planned. Who else would know exactly what to do and where?"

"To save their own asses."

"And get rich in the process."

"Do you think the President is in on it?"

"I don't think so. The Deep State doesn't need the President to pull off any of this. We all know that presidents come and go. So does his staff. They only exist to give the citizens the illusion that this is a democracy, and that we have some say in what happens. But it's all a lie, Allison. The Deep State runs the show. Always has. Always will. They are always there, decade after decade, lurking in the background with their fingers into everything. They have the real power. Not the elected officials."

"It's always about the money and power," she said.

"It's just like with the UFO conspiracy," Apollo said, pointing across the room. "There's an article over there that talks about how Bill Clinton and his CIA director tried to dig into the truth about Roswell and Area 51. But they were stonewalled by those who are really in power. Nothing was ever revealed to the President of the United States, if you can believe that nonsense, because the Deep State knows he'll be gone in a few years. All they have to do is stall long enough and it goes away on its own, without having to answer a single question."

"You're right. He's just a figurehead to keep us in line."

"Tuttle highlighted another article that proves Marilyn Monroe didn't commit suicide, either. She was murdered by the Deep State because she was getting ready to go public and tell all. Remember, she was sleeping with both of the Kennedy brothers in the White House, and we all know what happened to them. Men in power like to brag when they're in those types of situations with a sexy woman. Imagine the secrets she learned."

"Okay, I get all that, but why invade now? Why this week?"

He shrugged. "Something must have triggered it."

"What about that Area 51 jet? The one Bunker and Stephanie saw crash. Could that have been the reason?"

"Sure, anything's possible. Word might have leaked out about the sellout of our country, and someone on our side decided to take action with some kind of new tech to stop it. That could be why the Russians launched their plan now, before Area 51 got everything in place."

"Or someone on that plane was headed to NORAD to spill the beans."

"That, too. I'm afraid we'll never know. This might have been scheduled to happen this week, or it was a last-second thing."

Allison paused to search her memory. "Misty did mention she had a meeting planned with an old friend in NORAD. Maybe that's how word leaked out?"

"Or at least raised the question in someone's mind. The truth has a habit of working itself free, no matter how much money has been used to bury it."

"You know, something just occurred to me. Back when Angus spent that first summer here when he met Misty, Angus and Tuttle might have started talking about conspiracy theories. What if that's when Tuttle got the idea about the sellout?"

"Sure, that's as good a starting place as any. Something had to trigger all this research."

Allison pointed at the article with China in the headline. "What about China? Why haven't we seen anything from them yet? They're part of this, right?"

"I was thinking about that very thing before you walked in. Assuming this is happening elsewhere, then some of the other cities might be under Chinese control. Not Russian."

"It's like they're carving up a pie."

He sucked in a lip and nodded. "A red, white, and blue pie, and we're the cream filling."

TO BE CONTINUED IN BOOK 5
Bunker: Zero Hour

Did you enjoy this book?

If you could, please provide feedback to the author by posting star rating (5-stars being the highest) and include a short comment about what you liked this book. It only takes a few seconds to do and your comment doesn't have to be anything fancy—a few words or a single sentence is sufficient.

Every rating/review helps spread the word about this series and lets other readers know this book and author are worth reading. Ratings/reviews are critical for independent authors like Mr. Falconer. Your feedback also helps the author focus his efforts and publish the best stories possible.

Thank you for reading and for your feedback!

Want a FREE Jack Bunker Book?

All you need to do is sign-up for the author's VIP Newsletter on his website at www.JayFalconer.com and you'll receive a free copy of the prequel *Bunker: Origins of Honor.*

Find out what happened in the days just before Bunker got on the train. There's plenty of action in this exclusive story, so be sure to visit www.JayFalconer.com and join the author's VIP Newsletter while this free book is still available.

BOOKS BY JAY J. FALCONER

Frozen World Series
Silo: Summer's End
Silo: Hope's Return
Silo: Nomad's Revenge

American Prepper Series
Lethal Rain Book 1
Lethal Rain Book 2
Lethal Rain Book 3 (Coming Soon)
(previously published as *REDFALL*)

Mission Critical Series
Bunker: Born to Fight

Bunker: Dogs of War
Bunker: Code of Honor
Bunker: Lock and Load
Bunker: Zero Hour

Narrows of Time Series
Linkage
Incursion
Reversion

Time Jumper Series
Shadow Games
Shadow Prey
Shadow Justice
(previously published as *GLASSFORD GIRL*)

CONTACT THE AUTHOR

Jay J. Falconer makes his on-line home at the following address:

www.JayFalconer.com

If the mood strikes you, please use the Contact the Author form on his website to connect with him. Mr. Falconer would love to hear from you. He personally reads and responds to all inquiries.

You may also connect with him at the following addresses:

www.facebook.com/NarrowsOfTime

Twitter: *@JayJFalconer*

Email: *books@jayfalconer.com*

ABOUT THE AUTHOR

Jay J. Falconer is an award-winning screenwriter and USA Today Bestselling author whose books have hit #1 on Amazon in Action & Adventure, Military Sci-Fi, Post-Apocalyptic, Dystopian, Terrorism Thrillers, Technothrillers, Military Thrillers, Young Adult, and Men's Adventure fiction. He lives in the high mountains of northern Arizona where the brisk, clean air and stunning views inspire his day.

When he's not busy working on his next project, he's out training, shooting, hunting, or preparing for whatever comes next.

You can find more information about this author and his books at www.JayFalconer.com.

Awards and Accolades:
2020 USA Today Bestselling Book: Origins of Honor
2018 Winner: Best Sci-Fi Screenplay, Los Angeles Film Awards
2018 Winner: Best Feature Screenplay, New York Film Awards
2018 Winner: Best Screenplay, Skyline Indie Film

Festival

2018 Winner: Best Feature Screenplay, Top Indie Film Awards

2018 Winner: Best Feature Screenplay, Festigious International Film Festival - Los Angeles

2018 Winner: Best Sci-Fi Screenplay, Filmmatic Screenplay Awards

2018 Finalist: Best Screenplay, Action on Film Awards in Las Vegas

2018 Third Place: First Time Screenwriters Competition, Barcelona International Film Festival

2019 Bronze Medal: Best Feature Script, Global Independent Film Awards

2017 Gold Medalist: Best YA Action Book, Readers' Favorite International Book Awards

2016 Gold Medalist: Best Dystopia Book, Readers' Favorite International Book Awards

Amazon Kindle Scout Winning Author

Made in the USA
Monee, IL
20 September 2024

66134793R00233